THE VALKYRIE GENESIS

FACES OF INVASION

DAVID PAUW

First published by Ultimate World Publishing 2021

ISBN

Paperback: 978-1-922597-69-4
Ebook: 978-1-922597-70-0

Cover design: Ultimate World Publishing
Layout and typesetting: Ultimate World Publishing
Editor: Isabelle Russell
Front cover photo license: Artur Tomskiy-Shutterstock.com
Spine photo license: Vadim Sadovski-Shutterstock.com

Ultimate World Publishing
Diamond Creek,
Victoria Australia 3089
www.writeabook.com.au

The Valkyrie Chronicles Series is dedicated to Anne-Marie Pauw, a hugely valuable resource and great encouragement throughout the process of writing, regardless of fruition.
This, being the first of many books, is dedicated to a most dear friend, strong woman and valued mother, who encouraged and believed in me all the way.

Books in the Series

Valkyrie Chronicles

Valkyries Genesis

Faces of Invasion

Faces of Survival

Faces of Hope

Faces of Royalty

Faces of Reinforcements

Faces of War

Faces of Ascension

Valkyrie Dawn

Rise of the Valkyries

Valkyrie Paradise

Valkyrie Campaign

Valkyrie Eminence

Valkyrie Ascension

Valkyrie Overwatch

WAR IS HISTORY WRITTEN IN BLOOD

When new technology is found on a planet undergoing colonisation, it triggers a conflict that engulfs the human colonies.

The Consortium, along with every faction that held themselves outside of the central political rule, sought the new technology for themselves. Pirates, smugglers and warlords all rose to claim the power that it offered and the ability to expand further into the reaches of space.

A bitter war ensues and the source of the technology is lost, hidden behind the fog of war.

The victors make use of their new discoveries, retaliating swiftly on the rim worlds that stood up against them, pushing the warring factions beyond the edge of known space, deep into an unexplored nebula, vanishing into obscurity and legend.

Law and order reigned once again under the Consortium.

After a generation of peace, unrest breaks out when the rim worlds are attacked. Each engagement comes swiftly and out of nowhere, as the the raiders vanish back into obscurity.

The Consortium sends out their fleets into a bloody and costly war that probes into the fringes skirting the nebula of Sigma Prime.

As the war heightens, six more fleets are sent into the far reaches of the nebula to quell the enemy forces, only to be lost forever.

Hostilities ceased and the surviving fleet returned to friendly space.

Heralding a victory, the Consortium brought its heroes back to uplift its reign of order in the face of unrest among the systems.

Thus stands the birth of the Galactic Terran Space Command (GTSC), the new military political order to protect the people of the central rule within the systems.

When the threat from Sigma Prime rises once again, the neutral rim worlds on the far reaches of Galactic Terran Space rise up against the GTSC, forming an alliance with the foreign warriors, plunging deep into GTSC held territory, only to find that the fleets were mobilised and ready for launch.

A savage retaliation took place as the GTSC started pushing back, capturing many new worlds in a reign of fire, expanding its influence across territories over the ten-year conflict of the War of Ascension, carving through enemy forces right up to the fringes of Sigma Prime in a pincer move that cut off a significant portion of the enemy troops that were subsequently captured and drafted into the ranks of the GTSC.

The facade of peace was short-lived as the General of the Condor legion began a march from the fringe worlds towards the central system to take supreme power over the GTSC.

Thus began a decade of the War of the Republic.

Lieutenant Jessica Wind-Hawk
On board the GTSC *Yucatan*, Heavy Cruiser
Two days, three weeks before Operation *Trident*

Jessica glanced up and down the corridor; it looked stark and alien to her now. The GTSC *Yucatan*, a Heavy Cruiser in the Alliance Navy, had once felt like home, but now it was hostile and cold as she faced the door of the Captain's quarters, preparing to have a strip torn off her.

Looking down at her uniform, Jessica pulled at the hem of her jacket to straighten out the invisible creases before knocking. She took a deep breath. Nerves churned her stomach into a swirling storm and her breath caught in her throat.

She steeled herself against the impending future and raised her hand to knock on the solid metal door before her. The overhead lights caught the glinting gold of her signet ring and flashed in the stone. It was a rare gem, dark blue in hue with a cosmos quality, its inky blue strains of intense blackish purple twinkled deep red at its core.

Her father, the Captain, had passed it down to her on her eighth birthday as his father had on his eighth birthday. It was a tradition started by her great grandfather who had fashioned the ring from the jewel that he had found as a young fighter pilot during the Archean war. She remembered that birthday well. It had been the last time her father was home before being ordered to take his squadron of ships to join the Kar'Gon campaign where he had been killed in a monumental battle that had formed the turning point in the War of Ascension.

Growing up without her father had been an unpleasant and painful reality, but the ring had become the symbol that strengthened her resolve to join the Navy despite her mother's discouragement.

Seeing the gem gleaming up at her now gave her a sense of both comfort and failure. Her father, a hero of the Alliance, had been an example of all that the Navy stood for, as her instructors had constantly reminded her during her training, and now, she was about to face the greatest telling-off of her short career. Something in the pit of her stomach told her that it was different this time, that she was going to face the music, if not a court-martial. She wrapped her knuckles on the solid metal door.

"Enter!" the gruff, raw voice barked from behind the door. It was the voice of the Captain, a man who was used to getting his own way and very particular about what he wanted and when.

Brushing a hand over her uniform one last time, Jessica took another deep breath before letting it out as she opened the door, stepping in over the combing into the familiar dim setting of the Captain's quarters. This was not the first time she had been in trouble with the Captain, but it felt like this time would be her last.

Although lights were on around the cabin, it seemed to be enveloped in perpetual darkness. She wondered if the Captain had always naturally existed in the dark.

Making her way further in, she headed for his abandoned desk where light pooled on a file that lay open, the paper seemingly the only bright spot in the vicinity. The Captain always insisted on crew members saluting in front of his desk, regardless of where he stood in the cabin.

Her salute was textbook as she stood to attention; anything else would only inflame the situation more. The Captain stood off to her right by a corner bookshelf, opening a cigar, his positioning deliberate, in control of the room, the air of intimidation dominating the quarters, his presence feeding her unease, yet he remained detached so as to hide in a game of 'cat and mouse' until he was ready to destroy her, just like she had witnessed him do to others.

Looking down at the desk in an attempt to break her inner tension, Jessica could read the file where it lay open, the upside-down text stark against the white pages:

"Lieutenant Wind-Hawk, Jessica, 170453277428 attached to the 264th fighter wing as a member of the 23rd reapers squadron, having been posted from the 453rd lancers…"

It was her file.

Ignoring Jessica's salute, the Captain left her standing at attention while he took out the thick cigar. Taking a deep breath, he snipped the ends, clearing the cutter with three sharp movements, savouring this moment. It was a day he was going to remember for a long while. He disliked this young lieutenant immensely and he was finally going to get rid of her from his ship. She had overstepped the mark several times, but now, this one was clean cut — he was going to destroy her career once and for all.

Lighting the end, he warmed the cigar until it held a deep glow at the tip. He exhaled through his nose, twin plumes of smoke streaming from his nostrils as if he were a beast awakening from slumber. He savoured the moment a while longer; revenge was a long time coming. Glancing at an officer's portrait photo on the wall-stand, he smiled, cruelty curling his lip. Victory!

Jessica partially read her file while the Captain took his time with his cigar. She knew it was his way of showing someone that they were beneath him. She had seen him do it to other officers even on the bridge, including senior ranking officers.

The Captain finally puffed out a cloud of bluish smoke from his nose and withdrew the cigar in his right hand, as Jessica straightened her already ramrod pose anticipating his turn.

Since joining the fleet air-arm, she had tried to do her best with the tight regulations and the 'Navy way', but the truth was, she had never really taken to the strict rules. She performed her role with her own personality, even though it was not always in the 'accepted' manner.

Unbeknownst to her, she was a lot more like her father than she was aware of, his temperament reflected in her beyond any memory she had of him. When he had been home on 'shore leave', he had run his family like he had run his ships — with discussion and respect. He had taught her many things, but the man she knew had been overshadowed by his reputation in the Navy, the flight school had presented to her a very different figure. His hero status had outweighed her family connection, and his final actions were heralded as the pinnacle of heroism, but what they left out was that he had been nothing of the model officer for the majority of his career, advancing mainly because of his tactical success and the casualties of those around him.

But Jessica knew none of this, nor the fact that her actions were being measured by a past that was similarly unknown to her. The truth was that the Captain had served with her father and resented his promotions, deeply jealous of his advancement. Her father had risked everything and snatched victory from the jaws of defeat while Captain Russ Allers had already sounded the retreat, the fate of his career sealed in that moment.

Captain Russ Allers turned, heading for his desk. Jessica remained at attention, her salute as rigid as before, but the Captain ignored it. Sitting at his desk, he started reading through the open file before him.

"Lieutenant: Athena…" the Captain read aloud as he finally looked up, a disapproving scowl on his lips, the daughter of his dead rival at his mercy. "Goddess of war and strategy," he continued, waiting for Jessica to react, but she remained silent. He seemed put out by her silence, "Your record alone should have given the Navy enough reason to kick you out. The clerk who passed you onto my command must have been as incompetent as you have proven to be." Closing the file, the Captain avoided the pages recommending Jessica for the commendations she had been put forward for but that he had roadblocked.

"I won't tolerate to have an officer like you disgracing the uniform and dishonouring *my* ship any longer." His voice dropped to a cold rasp as he continued, "You will be charged with misconduct and stripped of your rank. I will see to it personally that you are dishonourably discharged and removed from this ship as soon as we enter orbit! You shall be court-martialled once you reach the naval base at Polinaro! Your days of freeloading off the Navy are over!" The Captain's voice suddenly rose until he was practically yelling, her calm silence having broken his savoured victory, as his temper flared in an uncontrollable outburst.

It was all Jessica could do to keep from sagging inwardly. There was time enough to be dismayed later, but she would not crumble in front of the Captain, of that she was determined.

He sat there, as if waiting for her to beg for another chance, but when she would not, he reached for another file on his desk. "Dismissed," he hissed, his voice low as though it was an afterthought. Jessica saluted, perfectly controlled. The Captain waved his hand dismissively without looking up. She turned and headed for the door. "Nothing can save you this time." Jessica didn't turn. The venom in the Captain's voice was unmistakable.

The door slid shut behind her once she was out in the corridor. The hiss of the air seemed to mock her, an extension of the Captain's disapproval.

The long walk back to her cabin was made even longer by the surreal, dream-like quality that plagued her every step. It was as though she was on the ship for the first time, lost in the maze of corridors, yet she knew exactly where she was going. A veteran of these halls, it was a strange experience of *jamais vu*. Everyone who looked at her felt estranged as though they already knew, that it was some cruel joke — and she was the last to find out.

Avoiding eye contact with everyone, Jessica finally reached her cabin. The door slid open and she entered without thinking, simply standing there in the doorway of the small anteroom, an enclave that fed into her main cabin. She looked around the room that had been hers for just over a year but would be hers no longer once they reached orbit.

She heard the door hiss as it slid shut behind her. The light from the corridor vanished, plunging the room into semi darkness, her eyes adjusting to the dim glow of the security lights that never left the room in full darkness.

Silence — the silence of a tomb. She shuddered with a tingle down her spine as though with premonition. Normal shipboard noises could not be heard. She put her face in her hands and sank to the floor, sliding down the metal door. *How could it have come to this?* To be here, a dishonourable discharge facing a court-martial, she had failed the memory of her father so dreadfully. Dropping to her knees, she spread her arms out wide and screamed; all the frustration coming out in that moment. Tears ran down her cheeks, her fists clenched so tight that her ring dug in, blood running between her fingers and down her forearm.

Her screams turned to sobs as she slowly sank to her hands on the floor.

Time had little meaning right now. Jessica went from the single-room living area into the ensuite to wash the blood off her hand and arm. In shock, she saw just how much there was; the ring had torn into her skin quite badly. As she examined the wound, she noticed the stone twinkling, the deep red within drawn out by the crimson staining her hand and etched into the carvings on the ring. As she examined it, she could see deeper into its depths than she could ever remember. She stood there for a while, engrossed in its hidden mysteries, a strange tingling running up her arm, before washing her hands and the ring free of her blood. On it, she could see different shapes and colours previously hidden from her view. The water washed away her blood, as crimson and scarlet tendrils twisted in the flow before the cloudy whirlpool spiralled down the plughole. That was a resemblance of home, the artificial gravity suggesting false similarities.

Taking her uniform jacket off and hanging it on the hook in the main room, she pulled her black t-shirt up over her head, throwing it in a heap on the floor of the washroom. She was going to have a shower to try and feel more human again in the hope it would help her to think clearly once more.

Turning the water on, she let it fall onto her open palm. She loved the sound of the water falling; it was a favourite memory of her childhood, camping with her family and listening to the rain on the tent and the wind through the leaves.

She pulled her trousers off, the belt buckle jangling as it swung, removing her bra and kicking off her black undies onto the same pile as her t-shirt and trousers, as she stepped into the shower. The water running over her body was sensational, and her skin prickled with goosebumps as she ducked her head under the flow.

Ordinarily, she would go for the sonic shower as it was much faster — no need to dry herself before getting dressed made getting ready for combat patrols much quicker, but when she had the time, she enjoyed the peace and relaxation of a hydro shower.

Running her hands over her face, she brushed her hair back over her head.

Today, however, she did not care. She had only two days left to enjoy the life of a fighter pilot on board one of the most powerful Heavy Cruisers in the GTSC, and then she was going to leave this life with the same integrity as she had started, just as her father had taught her.

"Icca, you here?"

Jessica heard Melissa's voice call from the main cabin.

They had been roommates when they first arrived at the flight training Academy, both quiet and shy at first. However, the two of them had become as close as sisters over the course of their training, and fortune smiled on them both as they had been posted to the same squadron together before getting deployed to the *Yucatan*, now to be separated. Shutting off the warm, refreshing water, she stepped out and grabbed her towel. Wiping her face dry, she looked in the foggy mirror. The blurred image of herself was exactly how she felt: lost, the future indistinct. She wiped it away, angry at herself for allowing herself to think like that.

Rubbing herself dry, she thought about the last couple years in the Navy, then she hung the towel over the side of the shower and grabbed a new t-shirt, black again, only this one bore the insignia of her flight Academy. She wore it whenever she felt low, as somehow it brought the good days of flight training nearer. Donning the t-shirt, she pulled her damp hair from under the material, shaking the wavy lengths free. She found a fresh pair of black underwear before turning on the extractor fans to clear the room. She loved the thickness of the air from the humidity, but every drop of water mattered on a combat patrol that couldn't readily access more fresh water supplies.

***

Melissa stood in the darkened room, looking about her surroundings. She had come as soon as Viktor, one of their flight mechanics, had told her of the news about Jessica while they were on the flight deck.

She left the fighter inspection immediately so that she could try find her friend after a quick apology to the engineer.

Taking a guess that Jessica would have gone to her cabin, she headed straight there, but found the place empty at first glance — but the sound of running water indicated that Jessica was already there.

She looked around the room. It was much like hers: slightly rectangular, the cabin door behind her in the enclave, with no windows but security light strips that lined the corners from ceiling to floor, a writing desk recessed along the wall adjacent to the corridor and a bed fixed to the wall opposite. The ensuite was behind the wall at the far end of the room beyond the foot of the bed. It was not a big space, but it was private, somewhere to hide away when necessary. Thankfully, pilots and officers rated their own quarters — the room size depended on their rank, but it was still better than the rank and file who had to share sleeping space in a cabin lined with bunks.

There had definitely been times when privacy was necessary, as Melissa recalled the first time she had killed someone on a patrol. They had been on their way to rendezvous with another cruiser to search for reported hostiles that had attacked a supply convoy.

Despite her training, she had needed a secluded place to come to terms with the act of taking a life. The adrenaline of the chase had carried her all the way home, but once it was all done, in the quiet of her cabin, that was where everything came crashing in.

Melissa took off her jacket and draped it over the foot of Jessica's bed. As she stretched out, she felt a pinching of her forearm. Twisting her arm around, she saw a deep scratch that traced almost the full length of her forearm. She was just rubbing it when the ensuite door slid open.

Jessica came out of the shower room, rubbing her damp hair with the towel.

"You've heard!?"

"Yes."

Jessica nodded and turned back to the bathroom.

"What are you going to do?"

"Captain's seeing to a dishonourable discharge, *personally*. There's nothing I can do," her voice becoming venomous with the realisation of defeat.

"How long?" A short question, with so much meaning.

"Two days." A friendship that had built to become so strong was now going to end in a little over fifty hours. The two of them looked at each other as Jessica came out of the shower again. "There's still time. We haven't docked yet."

Jessica shot her a look that cut Melissa off. She had battled so hard to get here, only to be shot down now. "Don't you ever give up? It would take something pretty monumental to stop the Captain this time. He's got the Group Captain's father to think about. After all there's no better promotion than that from a grateful Admiral," her voice dripping in sarcasm. "Not even Squadron Leader Jacox has been able to divert the Captain this time."

Melissa moved from the archway pillar she had been leaning on by the enclave door to the bed and sat down, while Jessica walked to her desk and swung the chair around. Sitting down, she crossed her long bare legs, her t-shirt dragging across her damp skin. She pulled the front of it away to free herself and sat back, sliding open a drawer in the desk, reaching into it, she brought out a bottle, the golden amber liquid catching the light with a reddish black twinkle.

"K2?"

Melissa nodded and Jessica lifted out the two tumblers they had acquired when on leave in the *Dan'Zar* system after basic training before they started their combat training.

"One last time?"

"This can't be it. You're too good a pilot to be discharged."

"Tell that to the Captain."

"What if we went to Admiral Fraser?"

"And what? Ask him to overrule one of his Captains' decisions in order to keep an untested pilot with a black record, however unfairly blackened?" Jessica snapped back.

She put the two tumblers on the desk, poured out a generous dash for them both and handed one to her friend. Melissa took it and nodded, there wasn't much else she could say or do that would change anything.

Neither one of them ever drank much, but they had made it a tradition that any time either of them had something to celebrate, or counsel was needed, it would be done over a glass of something strong, just like that first time early on in basic flight, that trip to the bar still fresh in her memory.

They clinked glasses in salutation and sat down to talk. Jessica returned to her pose, crossing her long bare legs again and rested her arm that held her glass on her thigh.

"Remind me again how you got this bottle of K2?" Melissa asked.

"I won it on the Klava station, a whole case in fact."

"That's right, you were playing *Red Loca* and the guy was cheating but you still beat him."

"And then he tried to start a fight…"

"And you pulled your gun on him. He backed off pretty quickly after that."

"Until the next day, when he and his goons tried to corner me at the docks. I had to get away quickly and the only choice that presented itself was their light corvette."

"I remember watching that depart." Melissa's face cleared with realisation. "It got so many violations, I'm still surprised that the patrols didn't try to shoot it down. How did you escape again?"

"I locked myself in the cockpit, guided it out into open space and set the computer to jump. They figured out what I was doing and tried to stop the jump by disabling the core reactor."

"But how did you know there was a secret passage from the cockpit to the hangar?"

"I spent some time on that class of ship as a kid with my parents... So, I stole a fighter and launched before the ship jumped."

"Didn't their core go critical?"

"Just as I hit the afterburners and got out of there." Jessica nodded once.

Melissa shook her head. She loved hearing this story.

"It just so happened that there were a couple cases of loot in the fighters' cargo bay."

"You nearly got kicked out for that. How many times have you 'nearly' got kicked out?"

"One too many now."

"Hmmm…" Melissa took a sip of her drink, as she continued, "how the hell did you get this on board though? I thought everything in the fighter was checked."

"Well, not all of it made it to my cabin."

Melissa laughed, her eyebrows raising, as she asked, "Who?"

"The Chief."

Melissa held up her glass and Jessica clinked it again, a big smile lit up her face. She leaned back in her chair, raising one foot onto the seat, resting her elbow on her bent knee.

"We made a great team."

"Yeah, I can't believe that I had to join the Navy to find the sister I always wanted."

"At least you'll still be in the service. I will probably have to sell my soul to some greasy, little cargo merchant to keep flying."

"It's not going to come to that. There's still time, something will happen."

"You're so sure of that?" Jessica's question was more of a statement.

"No more than you were on the moon of Ka'raz."

"That was different."

"How? Only because the fighter could have exploded as we went orbital. You could have been killed."

"I knew I wouldn't be."

"You had no idea that your modifications on the engines would not cause a critical core temperature."

"Well, it worked, didn't it?"

"That's what I mean, something will happen, you'll see."

Jessica smiled. She poured herself another dash of K2. "You want some more?" Melissa held up her glass.

Their conversation drifted into other topics. They had done a lot together over the last few years since the beginning of basic training.

If these were going to be the last two days before Jessica was discharged, they were going to spend them together.

***

Melissa came out of the bathroom and looked at the bed. They had been talking for the whole night and now Jessica lay asleep face down on her black sheets, head turned away towards the wall. She was still dressed as before in her black t-shirt, the training squadron insignia emblazoned between the two wings across her shoulders. Her legs were sprawled across the one side of the bed, the black sheet up to her waist leaving one leg exposed from the knee down, her skin pale against the darker material.

Melissa moved her uniform jacket from the bed and hung it over the chair. It simply could not be the end of their friendship. Jessica had saved her life during combat training. Without her, Melissa was certain that her flight suit had been damaged enough that she would have vented atmosphere before the rescue ship would have reached her.

Instead, Jessica had ignored every rule and order and came into land next to her damaged fighter.

Without Jessica, she would not be here today, that was the simple truth of it.

Moving to the bed, Melissa sat down and stretched. The tiredness was getting to her now.

Jessica shifted, rolling over; her dark, walnut hair fanning out across the pillow. It blended into the glossy blackness of the pillowcase in the deep twilight gloom of the cabin.

Rubbing her hand through her own hair, Melissa wondered about her friend. Jessica had always worn her hair longer than regulation, but until coming to this ship, she had gotten away with it.

Stretching, Melissa was about to lay down next to Jessica. She pulled her shirt down around her mid-section and lifted her legs up onto the bed. She considered taking her uniform trousers off but couldn't be bothered. Her head hit the pillow and her eyes closed.

***

Jessica sat bolt upright, her dream still fresh as she threw back the sheets, jumping over Melissa's prostrate body.

In the two steps it took her to cross the room, alarms rang out filling the room with noise and the flashing security lights. Melissa was galvanised into action as Jessica was pulling on her trousers.

"ALL HANDS TO DEFENCE STATIONS. PREP FOR SLIPSPACE JUMP!"

Melissa lifted herself upright. She had not slept nearly enough and had no idea what time it was.

Jessica pulled on her boots as Melissa found hers where she had tucked them under the bed.

"What do you think this is?"

Jessica looked up from lacing her boots. "I have no idea. Let's go to the hangar and find out."

The two of them ran out of the cabin without further ado, both in their black t-shirts, neither one following the dress code for an officer.

A general air of efficiency had been injected into the ship since they had gone to Jessica's cabin. Everyone was hurrying in all directions. Jessica ran down the corridor, Melissa close behind her, heading for the hangar on the port side.

They ducked into the quick access point and slid down the ladders to the flight deck.

All the pilots and mechanics were gathering around the Wing Commander who stood atop one of the short, havoc fighters. As the crowd grew, the Wing Commander began,

"LISTEN UP! Command has just ordered us to join Admiral Fraser's new task force. This time tomorrow, we are on our way to the war in earnest. Those with shore leave can forget it for the time being…" There was a loud groan from the group, as he continued, "I know it has been a long patrol with little excitement, but if the Intel is right about this one, we will be the spear head to invasion." The Wing Commander looked around the group. "I don't need to tell you what is expected of you. Those with families have first priority on comms. After we make the next jump, it will be radio silence from then on. DISMISSED!"

The group broke up into individual conversation, the Wing Commander climbing down to the flight deck. Jessica wove through the crowd towards him.

"Sir, can I have a moment?"

"What is it, Athena?"

"Has the Captain spoken to you about me?"

"I know of his decision, if that's what you mean."

Jessica tried to find the right words to form the next question, but the Wing Commander beat her to it.

"But it looks like Mars is smiling on you today. Transfer will take too long, and the shuttle won't get back in time for us to jump. We won't be entering orbit this time. So, you're along for the ride. It will be up to Admiral Fraser to decide what happens to you next."

The Wing Commander put one hand on Jessica's shoulder, locking eyes with her. "I won't lie to you, Lieutenant, your record isn't great, but neither was your father's. If I'm right about this, I'm going to need all of my best pilots, and you're very much like your father was as a junior officer. I have seen your record, Lieutenant. It's got more black marks than most, but you're one of the best cadets I've ever seen. You have natural skill and the willingness to risk your life for your comrades, I'm going to need that in combat in the coming days…" His tone softened a fraction, "… who knows, you may even save my life one day, breaking more rules than have been written, no doubt."

"Yes, sir. Thank you, sir." her voice trailed off, not knowing if that was actually a compliment.

"You fly until either you die, or the Captain finds something else to court-martial you for." He leaned in a bit closer, "I think even he will be glad to have you aboard by the time this finishes, no matter how much he'll hate to admit it."

Jessica saluted as the Wing Commander turned away, his attention on the next task.

Everyone was jostling around her in the clamour of excitement with the prospect of real action, one bumping into her as he jumped up and down right by her, his shoulder catching her in one of her breasts, pain shot through her and she shoved him away and turned back towards Melissa.

"You lucky she-devil, Icca. I told you things could change."

"Yeah, saved by the war." They both laughed. "Are you sure you didn't send a false signal to High Command for me?"

"I wish I had thought of that."

"I'm going to tidy up, we're about to go to war, and I don't even have a bra on."

"You know what we should do to memorialise this?"

"What?" Jessica shook her head.

"Get a tattoo together."

Jessica stopped and looked at her friend.

"Since when did you get so crazy?"

"I don't know. I met this crazy pilot who's like a sister. She taught me to really live."

"So, what shall we get?"

"What did Jethro call us at the Academy?"

"The 'Valkyrie Sisters'."

"So, how about some Valkyrie wings?"

"Sisters to the end, huh?"

"You bet."

They headed off, leaving the noise and excitement behind them as they made for the lower decks.

***

Jessica looked at her reflection in the mirror on the wall of her bathroom. The new tattoo was stark and alien on her skin. She liked the intricacy of the design emblazoned on her back. Twisting, she examined the detail in the wings that spread across her shoulder blades, the tips of the feathers just curling around her deltoids, flames reaching up from the base of the wings.

The whole way from the hangar deck they had been talking about what they should get and had decided on something small like wings on the back of the neck, but with their own personal touch, however when they had arrived at the lower decks, the room that held the black market tattooing parlour was laid out with a multitude of designs from previous tattoos. Their ideas changed and grew from the simple to the personal as they explored the realms of possibilities.

One of the deckhands had met them. He was going to be their artist and had helped them design their insignia, each holding the same base design of wings spreading wide with three helmets facing outwards arranged at the base. One was Athena's Spartan helmet three-quarter profile in the centre, flanked by Jessica's and Melissa's individual combat helmets. Flames branched upwards, engulfing the back of the helmets, extending through the centre; a bare woman partially hidden in the flames, rising from the depths between the helmets, hair wavy, blended with the flames closest to her, her face up turned, one hand reaching for the heavens, with the Excalibur behind her, handle above her head, as its gleaming blade extended below the pedestal of helmets.

She was the Valkyrie herself, rising from the fires of war.

Hidden inside the feathers of the outspread wings on Jessica's tattoo were the names of her mother and father, discernible only to those who knew they were there. She also had added a sparrow that sat on the hilt of the sword.

By the time they had finished, Melissa was quiet with nervous anticipation, almost expecting Jessica to abandon the idea, but instead, her friend was tensed up with excitement; Jessica took a deep breath in, letting it out on the impulse of agreeing to it.

Accompanying Jessica into the room, Melissa sat on the small chair in the corner while her friend stripped off her shirt and lay down on her front, throwing the shirt to Melissa, who put it on the chair and left. The artist arranged the machine that would etch the image into her back, discussing last minute details about size and placement.

While it was working, the artist had taken Melissa to finish her design with her personalisation.

The fierce burning sensation came to a stop as the tattoo was complete. The artist entered with a tumbler of K2 and poured it over the newly finished design. It burned as the alcohol washed over the raw area, the already-red skin inflamed with the liquid. Jessica bit her lip and barely a wince of pain escaped her lips.

Melissa handed Jessica's t-shirt back to her and she had sat up, covering herself as the artist talked.

"The finest whiskey. The alcohol will give the tattoo a unique element: it will glow blue in ultra-violet or plasma light," he explained, as he rubbed a balm over the whole area. The balm held some properties that would trap in the hidden blue glow, letting the skin heal with it.

Moving was a little painful, but Jessica pulled her t-shirt over her head before getting up so that her friend could have her turn.

Melissa looked apprehensively at her Jessica.

"It's her time now." Jessica nodded towards where Melissa stood.

"I don't know," Melissa said. "I was going for something smaller, as we discussed."

"So was I," Jessica replied, "Valkyries to the end." She held up her hand, fist clenched.

Melissa's deep breath could be heard as she inhaled, "OK." She met Jessica's fist end on with her own as she made her way to the bench asking the artist to adjust the wings length to fit within her shoulder width instead of extending around her deltoids. Sitting down, she pulled her shirt up over her head, holding it to her front as she lay down, pulling it out from under her and chucking it to Jessica who caught it as Melissa waited.

***

Jessica pulled her black shirt on over her head, the dark image still foreign on her skin and it burned like deep plasma burns, with every movement, each brush of her clothing still made her clench her jaw tightly. She hadn't worn a bra since she got it done. The straps rubbed against her skin like sandpaper over an open wound.

Pulling her hair out from under the shirt, she grabbed her uniform jacket and pulled it on as she headed for the door, her wince becoming a grimace.

Another few hours passed before they emerged from slip-space and she had arranged with Melissa to watch their arrival together; to see the new system and the fleet they were going to join.

For Jessica, it was a rendezvous with destiny.

Their first stop after receiving orders had been for barely an hour, but to join a fleet and make all the arrangements before departing for invasion would take days. Plenty of time for her to be transferred off the ship. This could still be the end of the line for her.

There was no such assurance as there had been for their first rally-point. Her Squadron Leader had personally assured her at that time that the new squadron they were going to form up with was already waiting. There had been zero chance she could be transferred off the ship — but not this time. This time their new flotilla, comprised of the *Yucatan's* own two destroyers and two frigates, and the additional two cruisers and four destroyers, would be falling under the command of Admiral Fraser.

Jessica remembered the sight of the six ships awaiting their arrival at the first stop; the grand salute that had been presented, just the way Captain Allers insisted on, in proper recognition of his rank.

Jessica had seen plenty of fleet deployments in her father's days of command and knew how long things could take. Her transfer could still be impending, especially if they were going to remain in orbit for some time.

Approaching the double doors to the observation deck, Jessica walked quickly with nerves of uncertainty. The doors slid open, revealing the open plan deck that had windows surrounding the entire area, the darkened room lit only by the revolving world of slip-space. It was an elongated dome on the upper surface of the Heavy Cruiser that backed into the superstructure. Designed during the time of peace, the observation deck had been intended for the officers to be able to watch parades and regattas; a place where officers and their ladies could watch in comfort, their uniforms gleaming in splendour, their chests emblazoned with medals and ribbons, their ladies in colourful dresses adorned with jewellery as they sipped champagne, laughed and chatted.

As Jessica entered, security lights illuminated the interior — just enough so danger had no shadows in which to lurk, yet not so bright as to distract from the view out of the window.

Making her way to the front, she leaned against the railings, pushing herself up on her hands, like a schoolgirl at a parade. How many times had she done that at her father's regattas?

She felt a strange comfort, as though he was standing right behind her; it was the closest she had felt to him in many years, yet unknown to her at that moment, this would be one of her last times of sweet innocence in her life, the future hidden behind the impenetrable revolving colours of slip-space.

Lost in thought, she only partially heard the doors open behind her, but it was not until Melissa spoke that she finally snapped back to the present, Melissa's voice loud in the silence.

"Just like at the Academy, first on the parade ground." Melissa came across to where Jessica stood. "How are you adjusting to the tattoo?"

"I still can't believe we went through with it."

"I especially can't believe that *I* was the one to suggest it." The two friends smiled at each other.

"What will my mother say?"

"I know, right? We're fully trained fighter pilots, and yet we're still scared of what our mothers will think," Jessica smiled.

"That'll probably never change."

Turning back to stare out the window, Jessica couldn't hold back her nerves for long. The future was crowding in with uncertainty, their peace a veil like the slip-space panorama beyond the armoured bay windows.

The tannoy blared, interrupting their thoughts.

"All hands, stand by to exit slip-space."

The soft thrumming whistle of the hyper cores came to an end, the revolving world of spinning lights started peeling back from the pinnacle of their trajectory.

Planets, stars, and the awaiting array of warships jumped into sharp relief as the Heavy Cruiser decelerated.

The fleet amassed before them showed that someone in High Command was taking the intel to indicate a very credible threat.

Jessica noticed that the fleet stood too far out to hold geostationary orbit. They were ready for departure without delay. Maybe, just maybe, she was safe, as a small seed of hope began to grow within her.

The grand constellation class battleship, the GTSC *Pegasus*, dominated the centre of the fleet, towering over those ships closest to it.

There were evident gaps in the awaiting lines indicating where the new arrivals had been allotted their positions. It was customary for squadrons to be kept together when joining a fleet so that each unit would work together more effectively as they would know the characteristics and behaviours of each ship in the squadron.

Admiral Fraser must have had a good reason for splitting the ships up throughout the fleet. Captain Allers no doubt would contest it as soon as he had an audience with the Admiral, as he was not one to let even a temporary increase in power slip from his grasp.

Jessica watched as the impressive sight angled across the curved windows of the viewing deck, their squadron splitting formation as each ship headed for their respective location in the grand procession in accordance with their firepower.

Melissa, however, watched the rest of the fleet as the squadron split up to take their places in the columns of ships, taking note of the size difference between the individual ships and wondered what kind of firepower was possessed by the fleet. From what she had gleaned from the briefings, this invasion was an impromptu affair as the forlorn hope that it would test the strength of an unknown force.

It was evident that their squadron was the last to arrive at the staging ground for war, the next time they jumped would be the last for many of them.

Engine cores glowed blue, indicating the fleet's readiness for departure. This was the final preparation before the command would be given.

Their squadron had received orders to report what stores and munitions replenishment they required while en route — the reason now evident. Supply ships and containers were waiting off to one side of the fleet, waiting, no doubt, for their arrival.

As the squadron took up position a message came over the tannoy for Lieutenant Wind-Hawk to report to the bridge. The two friends looked at each other, glancing up at the bulkhead where the message was coming from as it finished; was this to be the moment of truth? Jessica swallowed nervously which belied the façade of calm she had been maintaining since their last jump.

The GTSC *Pegasus* was larger than the Heavy Cruiser, its shape dominating the view and held both friends' attention as the *Yucatan* slid into position. They had gone from being the most powerful ship in the squadron to being the ugly duckling, the beautiful lines of the battleship were undeniable, however the GTSC *Yucatan* conspicuously flanked the *Pegasus* in the place of honour. Jessica could well imagine both the pride of the Captain having the second most important position in the parade, and yet the tension of having all eyes watching each and every manoeuvre that his ship made, a lot would be expected from the second highest ranking Captain in the fleet.

Captain Allers would undoubtedly be overseeing everything, ensuring perfection in the execution as the coxswain conned the Heavy Cruiser into position. To have an Admiral of Fraser's skill and reputation watching the second grandest jewel of his fleet completing a peacetime manoeuvre would definitely put the pressure on.

"Better go see what that's about," Jessica said as she started for the door, but Melissa caught her arm.

"It's going to be OK. You wouldn't have gotten this far only to be court-martialled now. Look at the level of preparation! The fleet is ready to depart!"

"Let's go see, shall we?"

Melissa took her up on the offer and followed Jessica out.

On the bridge was a scene of controlled chaos. At one of the most crucial times for a ship to perform and show off, the Captain was absent.

Looking around the open bridge, Jessica took stock of the efficient nature of the officers at work.

"Lieutenant!" the XO called from where he stood next to the navigation command across the bridge. Jessica weaved through the command terminals.

The XO stood with his back to the approaching fighter pilots, his close-cut hair style and white hair made him look almost bald.

He looked over his shoulder to see how close they were.

Swallowing, Jessica offered up a silent prayer for the future.

Captain Allers only kept those officers around him who sang to his tune; however, the XO had never been overly hostile towards her, not more than required by the Captain's favour.

"Lieutenant, you have been ordered to report on board the *Pegasus*." He held up one hand to stifle any protest or questions.

"The Admiral has requested you to be ferried over as soon as we dock."

As they spoke a shuttle arced away from the side of the *Yucatan*, its engine trails clear against the background.

"The Captain is already on his way," finished the XO, turning away and back to running a powerful warship in the absence of the Captain.

***

They had reached orbit three hours ago. The final preparations were being finished, the stores had been loaded and the munitions were nearly all on board. They had taken on extra stores and munitions, packing the hull full, every compartment overflowing with ammunition. Not long now until they would detach from the last of the supply containers.

Down on the hangar deck, Melissa had been helping the Chief with stores, packing spare aircraft parts in every available storeroom and ammunition in each locker until they overflowed.

She had been there since Jessica had climbed into the transport shuttle bound for the flagship.

Waiting for news was torture, not knowing if it had all been for nothing.

Neither Melissa nor Jessica had been on board a major warship preparing for a campaign before. There was an atmosphere that she had never felt before.

About an hour ago a shuttle had pulled into the hangar and Melissa had allowed excitement to rise, but then the Captain had disembarked. He had swept the activity on the deck with a cold glare until his gaze settled on Melissa, an ally of Jessica.

Anger flared in his eyes before he ignored her completely, turning his head away and walking past her.

What had happened to Jessica?

***

Jessica sat alone in the shuttle; her thoughts and fears were her only companions. Looking forward to where the pilot sat, she could see out the front window and the lines of warships ahead.

What had happened on board the flagship? The Captain's shuttle had left nearly an hour before hers. It was a long trip out across the open expanse between the towering leviathans waiting patiently to be unleashed in war.

Based on their telemetry, Jessica knew that none of the GTSC *Yucatan's* shuttles would be able to make it to the planet surface and back in time before launch. A one-way trip would take a quarter of a day, but she was not so naïve as to not realise that the munition storage and shuttles could be used to hold her for transport long after the fleet had departed. It made the flight seem all the more empty, as a hollowness in the pit of her stomach grew with every passing second.

The *Pegasus* seemed larger than any other ship she had witnessed. She could still remember the nervous wonder she had felt when their transport had drawn close to the *Yucatan* for the first time a year ago, but that had been shortly after their first operational tour and Melissa and a few others had occupied the cabin with her, the air had been one of excitement rather than silence that now seemed to mock her worries.

Staring out the window, Jessica had seen the impressive armament that adorned the sides of the battleship. Her mind flicked to imagining herself flying down the length of the ship in her fighter, all the guns hammering in a powerful display of might.

Blinking away the vision and the momentary sense of being alive again, she focused on the docking procedure, trying to control her emotions as the shuttle landed. It was important for her not to look nervous when the door opened.

Watching the hangar opening slide past, Jessica observed the inside of a vast hangar that made the *Yucatan* seem like a relic from the previous war.

It was an interesting experience watching the difference in the new ship.

As the shuttle spun on its axis, Jessica saw two officers standing by the side of the flight line, watching as it settled down.

Jessica checked her uniform before the door opened, once again immaculate.

She threw up a textbook salute to the Officer on Watch as she stepped from the cabin onto the wing, but it was the two officers that held her attention. They too were saluting her, but there was something about them that puzzled her.

As she stepped down, the newcomers intercepted the OOW, one talking to him rapidly before he turned away and left.

Jessica faced the two as they approached.

"You're the daughter of the hero of Cal'Mar Gar?"

Jessica nodded; a flicker of confusion and surprise showed in her eyes for a brief moment only. She had never expected to hear that as a question. *Who are these two?* she wondered.

"I'm Jacqueline, and this is Gideon," the woman indicated to the silent younger guy next to her. Neither one seemed hostile, but it was definitely no accident they were here.

Both of them wore pilot's uniforms and Jacqueline had the pilot's wings that indicated that she was a Special Operations pilot.

Jessica couldn't quite make out what their friendship would be, but Jacqueline had an easy way about her. She was someone who seemed to live in every moment of life, while Gideon was unreadable, quiet, like a hunter. They both had ribbons and citations showing that they had fought in the Gregorian campaign, amongst many others.

"We will take you to the Admiral's quarters," Jacqueline answered Jessica's unspoken question.

Stretching forth her hand, Jessica shook Jacqueline's offered token of friendship.

"I'm Jessica," she said to Jacqueline's knowing smile. "But my friends call me Icca."

There was a flicker of some emotion in Gideon's eyes, but he never smiled.

Heading out of the hangar, Jacqueline continued the introductions, "I understand you're known as Athena?"

"Yes, an instructor in the Academy called me that in the first week, it stuck ever since."

Jacqueline nodded, "I'm Zatara. Gideon is known as Malakh. We've been aboard the *Pegasus* for only a few months, ever since it came back for repairs in dry dock."

Jessica still had no idea why these two officers had come to meet her on, potentially, the eve of her banishment from the Navy.

"You must be very proud of your father? His exploits have literally transcended the textbooks; up here he is a legend, not just a hero."

Following the pair, Jessica felt as if she was learning about someone else's past, never before had she heard of this side of her father's life.

The instructors at the Academy had made mention of his selfless exploits, always insinuating that she should be much more than she was with a father like that. Except for a few, who treated her with a respect that showed their reverence to her father, although they had never met him, almost treating her as a celebrity simply because she was his daughter.

But this was a whole new level of history that she felt as though everyone else had known her father far better than she ever had.

To her, he had only been the man in uniform that she had loved as a father, the daring fighter pilot who had showed her how life could be lived!

"It is a great honour to go to war with you. I look forward to seeing you in action. If you're anything like your father, you'll need to promise to leave some for the rest of us."

They talked as they walked down the corridors and up the lifts and access ways to the Admiral's quarters.

"What's the Admiral like?"

"He's fair. Unlike a lot of officers, he knows when to give credit and when to discipline." Jacqueline looked over her shoulder as they walked. "We know the reason why you're here. I also don't think you have anything to worry about." Jacqueline had a knowing smile on her lips when they reached the cabin door to the outer office of the Admiral's abode. With a twinkle in her eye, she faced Jessica. "You're in for an education," She remarked, and with that, she knocked on the cabin door before Jessica could say anything further.

The Admiral was nothing like she had imagined. From his reputation she had thought that he would be taller, more heroic, but when Jessica entered the Admiral's quarters she was met with an older officer who was a little shorter than she was, gun metal grey hair, and a lined face that still seemed to hold a youthful energy that was likely the reason he had risen through the ranks with a record ascension. He had very keen blue eyes that could also turn icy when he wanted them to.

Crimson red blazed on his chest against all of the other medals and ribbons on his uniform. She saluted him, trying to make it as perfect as possible — Admiral Fraser held an eminent position in the GTN.

Returning her salute, the Admiral came across to shake her hand.

"I received a report from Captain Allers with a personal request from him." He paused, watching her, watching her every move, the pulse in her neck, the movement of her eyelashes, the way her eyes assessed her surroundings, seeing not just the pretty face and dark blue eyes, but into her so she had no place to hide, unlike with Captain Allers.

"There are those in the service who will do anything to carry favour with a superior officer." Again, he paused and watched her as though waiting for her to respond, but she said nothing. Something flashed in his eyes as though he had reached a private decision about her, but she couldn't make out what it was.

"I knew your father; we served together as pilots and I watched his rising career." He paused as if deciding whether to say more, "I know it was several years ago, but I am sorry for your loss. He was a great man **and** a great friend. It is a pleasure to finally meet you after all this time."

"Thank you, sir."

"Your father used to talk about you all the time when we were on assignment. I was always rather jealous of his family and you, his pride and joy."

Jessica nodded, it had been many years since this subject had brought her to tears, but it was not far away now; her love for a father that had not been around while she grew up, not having her father to share the special moments of her life with, now magnified a thousand times by the uncertainty of her future, the vivid memories of the Admiral, and her own feelings of being alone. She bit back the sob that plagued the back of her throat and caused her eyes to glisten.

"I sometimes miss having your father around, especially when I have to make a hard decision. He would always think outside of the box, but there's time enough for stories later."

The Admiral turned, gesturing for Jessica to enter and take a seat.

"I asked you to come so that I can clear up this matter of your discharge." Admiral Fraser moved to the drinks cabinet and started pouring what looked like golden amber into two tumblers.

As he spoke, his presence filled the room along with his baritone hum. It was easy to see why he held the reputation that he did, and she could well imagine him as the leader in battle, the calm figure amongst the hell breaking loose around him and yet personable as well, his conversation flitting between subjects as he changed tasks.

"How is your mother? I haven't seen her since the funeral."

"She's OK, I guess. I haven't seen her much since joining the Academy."

"I'm sorry to hear that."

"We drifted apart after my father's death. She didn't want me to have anything to do with the Navy."

Admiral Fraser nodded, "I guess that's understandable, given everything that happened." His eyes went distant for a moment.

"From her point of view," Jessica nodded.

The admiral placed the decanter back on the desk, turning back to her.

"I have received a report from Captain Allers laying out your crimes against the GTN and the GTSC *Yucatan* particularly." He held up a hand to cut off whatever Jessica might have been about to say. "I am also aware of the little fiasco of that display for the new 'unbeatable' manoeuvre designed by Group Captain Walter Burke." He took one of the two tumblers and handed it to Jessica, cradling the other in his hand. She accepted it with a nod. Admiral Fraser's eyes flicked to the signet ring on her finger as she accepted the tumbler, something flashed in his eyes, but he turned away before she could be sure.

"I have seen this kind of report before," he cleared his throat. "Only that time it was filed against one of the captains in my squadron," he said as he stood next to his desk.

He looked down at the dark liquid in his glass, swirling it around once while he was deep in thought for a few seconds.

"Captain Allers didn't like your father either."

"They knew each other?"

"Why do you think you had such stellar performance until you reached the *Yucatan*?"

Jessica looked at the Admiral where he stood. He was lost in a past that was vivid before his eyes.

"I will not allow the daughter of my friend, a hero of the Alliance, to be kicked out of the Navy because of the petty jealousy of one of my captains, no matter how important he thinks he is."

Jessica was a little shocked by the sudden outburst from the Admiral and wondered what to do next.

"You're along for the ride, and if you're anything like your father, we'll need a fighter pilot like you before this is over. That was certainly true of your father as both a pilot and a captain."

Jessica was not sure if she should stand up and salute or just thank the Admiral for his comments.

He saved her from having to make a decision with his next comment, "We don't have much time, the fleet is almost ready to set off. I just wanted to let you know that the charges against you are dropped and will be removed from your record. You will serve the remainder of your tour with the GTSC *Yucatan* and then I will see to it personally that you are transferred to another command."

"I have a friend in my squadron; we have been together since the start of flight school …"

"So much like your father." the Admiral cut in, "I will see to it. Now, you had better return to your ship, it is nearly time."

Jessica stood, finished off her drink and gave the glass back on the Admiral.

"Good hunting, Lieutenant."

"You too, sir."

The Admiral turned and walked with Jessica to the door, shaking her hand before she left, neither one spoke, Jessica understanding more of her father's past now. There was a deep history that connected them together and would be revealed in due course.

***

Back on board the *Yucatan*, Jessica and Melissa were once again standing on the unlit observation deck watching the glow of engine cores shimmer bright blue against the planet backdrop that darkened as the shadow of night fell across its surface. Four more ships had jumped in to join the fleet while she had been on the shuttle returning to the *Yucatan*. Four more powerful destroyers, their lines showing their speed and inciting the feeling of confidence.

She thought of her mother then, the slender tall woman who had raised her until she was nine and had declared her resolve to join the Navy like her father had. There had been a lot of shouting that weekend, and to a great degree, her mother had checked out. Their relationship changed that day, their communication consisting mainly of arguments hence forth.

She could picture her mother's face, bright eyes, small mouth and prominent cheekbones, her short cut, trendy hairstyle made her look much younger than she was. By the time Jessica had joined the Academy, their inability to see each others' point of view had driven them so far apart, hate had subsided into indifference.

The last time she had spoken to her mother was a week before the graduation ceremony.

"Here." She had thrown the invitation onto the table from where she stood by the door. "I'm graduating, if you care at all."

"So much like your father; always putting the service first. He never had time for this family either."

She had cried most of the way home that day, only Melissa had been able to cheer her up in her quiet way she approached any melancholy situation.

Her mother's face faded into the void of space, leaving the fleet before her, all thirty-three ships ready for war.

Jessica watched as the glow from the engine cores brightened and the fleet began to move out of orbit heading for the coordinates of their next jump.

Seeing the four columns laid out before them, Jessica felt the first welling of deep excitement within her. The words of the Admiral, the lost connection with her father, the renewed belief of her father's reputation and skill. The renewed belief in herself.

She watched through the curved bay window on the viewing deck. Having never served as part of a fleet before, the closest being Captain Allers' squadron, Jessica drank in this moment.

This was the greatest concentration of warships Jessica had seen since she was a young girl. Her father had taken her and her mother to witness a regatta that was held to celebrate a victory in one of the campaigns. It was also the launch of a new battleship that was joining the fleet her father was a part of. A new battleship that had barely lasted a year, destroyed in the same battle that had taken her father's life.

Inexplicably, the sight filled Jessica with an excitement that was hard to contain. She knew the new venture was an extremely serious one that held the ultimate consequence for many, if not all, in the fleet. However, the thrill of the adventure, outweighed the dangers along the way. She was so close to living the life she had imagined her father had done during the War of Ascension. All of his stories crowded her memory, made closer by the surrealness of the pseudo-regatta before her eyes. She could hear his voice recounting the details of his adventures, missions and dogfights. She could feel his presence, reassuring her that there was no longer any chance of her being dishonourably discharged after they launched to the new theatre of war, and her record would be stamped in such a way that **no one** could touch her.

Jessica turned to look at her friend, standing a few feet to her left, watching the procession.

Melissa looked distracted. Her expression was deep in thought, but her stare extended beyond the ships.

"Are you OK?"

Melissa didn't reply so Jessica reached out and touched her hand where it rested on the railing. It was eerily ice cold and when Melissa spoke, her voice was quite toneless. "We're going to walk through the fires of hell and see the face of Azarel himself. Neither the victors nor the vanquished shall be left from torment. We are not coming back as we are."

It was as though the voice of the ages had spoken through her.

Jessica withdrew her hand, a cold shiver running down her spine. Her friend had shocked her a little.

"Are you OK?" Jessica asked again.

"Yeah, why?"

"Your hand was cold," she said, avoiding what Melissa had just uttered.

"No, I'm fine. See?" Melissa touched Jessica's hand. Her skin was warm and soft, perfectly normal again.

Jessica watched her friend with a side long glance. Melissa smiled, "What?"

"Nothing," Jessica shook her head and looked out the window again but could not shake the feeling her friend had left her with earlier.

She watched as the fleet drew near the coordinates to jump and could hear the engines spooling up as great spindles of colour began circling before them, lighting their path as each ship accelerated towards their jump.

In a matter of one week, they would reach the target system, the final jumping-off point.

Expanding beyond the veil of
slip-space was the great unknown.

Turning away, Jessica leaned against the railing and looked at Melissa, saying, "Let's go to the simulators, get as much practice as we can before we get there. This is everything we have been trained for since joining the Academy."

Melissa paused before nodding, she took a deep breath, Icca was right, they were going to a very different scale of war, one that they had not seen before. Practice was definitely a good idea, but her friend's training regime was going to prepare her in a way that would keep her breathing long after others had ceased. "You're right. It shouldn't be any different from chasing those enemy scouts on our patrols when we joined the conflict on Thermopylae prime, but every bit helps."

***

One Week Later

The deck rocked underfoot from another impact as Jessica sprinted down the corridor towards the hangar, Melissa's footsteps pounding close behind her.

It was a surreal experience to feel the solid metal of the deck heave beneath them. The whole ship shook as yet another booming echo resounded throughout the hull.

Twice she had nearly fallen, steadying herself on the sides of the passageway, stumbling on, pressed against the wall as the floor lurched beneath her.

This was their first taste of real war. Out of the whole year that she and Melissa had been on board the Heavy Cruiser, they had experienced multiple patrols and often a short dog fight, but never an actual battle, never something of this scale where the GTSC *Yucatan* was perilously exposed to uncertainty.

Another blast shook the ship, jerking the floor from under Jessica's feet like a rug. She fell, catching herself on the archway leading into the hangar, bracing herself with both hands. Melissa slammed into the wall, sliding to the floor as the ship righted itself. Jessica watched as she scrambled to her feet, the ship still shaking with more explosions against its hull. She reached out her hand to help Melissa who stretched out to grab hold. Their fingers touched before Melissa was thrown against the other wall with the force of another impact. Catching a handle, Jessica watched as Melissa hauled herself up, placing a booted foot on the wall as the deck dropped underneath her and launched herself through the hangar door. Jessica leaned back to allow her friend to pass and then followed close behind.

As they ran down the gangway offering access to each fighter bay, Melissa drew ahead, racing towards the fighter bay just past the one Jessica was aiming for.

As Jessica ran, she became aware of a thrum underfoot. It seemed like the whole ship was vibrating at high frequency.

With a jolt, she realised that the entire superstructure was pulsing from the main plasma beam cannon being fired. It was the first time she had ever experienced it being used. She pushed it from her mind as she sprinted for her fighter.

But before she could reach it, she was sent sprawling across the deck as the whole ship bucked under another explosion.

In that moment as she lay prone, she saw the chaos in the hangar as pilots and deckhands alike measured themselves along the unyielding deck.

Two mechanics were finalising the last of their preparations for her launch. The ordinance was ready: the fighter looked like a bird of prey waiting to be released.

Pushing herself up like a prize fighter about to deal the knockout blow, Jessica accelerated into a sprint, covering the remaining distance in three strides, launching off one foot into a leap, her next step pushing off the fighter's wing, hurdling the side into the cockpit. She landed with one foot on the seat and slid into position at its controls with a natural ease.

Thumbing the system switch, she brought the fighter online, the flight instruments coming alive around her as though a warrior had awoken.

She snapped her harness in place as the fighter ran through its own diagnostics.

One of Jessica's erks materialised on the wing, snapping life support systems into place. She looked up at him as he lifted her helmet over her head, helping to seal it in place, checking the vitals on screen.

Giving her the thumbs up, he slid off the wing again, casting one last glance under the fighter to check that all ordinances were secured correctly. He stood up seeing Jessica's head turn away, acknowledging his imperceptible nod. The fighter lifted in the bay behind him and glided out into the flight lane.

He gave her another thumbs up and saw her nod back at him as the canopy slid closed.

It gave him a thrill to see Jessica handling the aircraft with such precision despite the situation. It roared to life, the fighter an extension of herself – a wild beast let loose from a cage, ready for the hunt.

Jessica manoeuvred the fighter out of the bay with the ease of someone who had done this their whole life. It slid into the open area between the flight lane and the fighter bay. Her eyes took stock of the scene around her; there was already signs of the war here in the hangar. Two fighters were unceremoniously being pushed to one side. Various new scratches showed in the flight deck and charring blackened one stanchion from a plasma fire.

The reality of war came rushing in, her systems checked out and pre-take-off checks completed, the board was green, cleared for take-off from central command.

Looking across to Melissa, where her fighter was easing out of her bay. Their eyes met for an instant.

Jessica came to a conclusion in that moment.

As if her private thoughts had been transmitted to the fighter, the great bird of prey lifted higher, entering the flight lane and accelerating even before straightening up. Without looking, she knew that her friend was watching her go, making the same calculation she had.

Ordinarily, the Squadron Leader preferred all of his pilots to wait for his lead and then depart together, with him at the head of the formation, despite several of his pilots being heavily reprimanded by the Captain for being ready and not lifting off when the squadron had been scrambled and yet, the Squadron's Leader was one of those who carried the Captain's favour.

Jessica had no intention of waiting. Her mission was to fly and protect the GTSC *Yucatan*; the best way to provide that defence: attack.

Deliver such punishment to the enemy force that they withdrew their attention from the Heavy Cruiser, or at least destroy as many as she could.

From the corner of her eye, Jessica could see Melissa starting up and lifting off the deck. She would not be far behind.

Engaging the thrusters, Jessica began to accelerate towards the light blue shimmering plasma field covering the hangar opening. She lifted the fighter higher into the flight lane between the side of the hull and the metal stanchions that bracketed the inner wall, isolating all the fighter bays into individual pens.

Jessica dropped the throttle, engaging boosters and accelerated down the length of the hangar, the sound of the engine hammering against the walls, reverberating against the hull and down the gangway and each corridor that connected to the hangar. The sweet tang from the high bypass plasma core engines filled her wake; a fine cloud of plasma carbon settling in blue, black clouds that wafted over everything.

Accelerating hard, Athena chewed up the length of the hangar within a matter of heartbeats, controlling her pace perfectly so as to observe the maximum departure speed, as it was the limitation for passing through the plasma shield across the hangar entrance. If she went too fast, the viscosity of the plasma would react the same as if her fighter was a projectile of high velocity ordinance, such as a missile or a phosphorous or plasma round. Her fighter would disintegrate against it just as though she had flown it into the armoured hull instead.

Reaching the far end of the hangar, Jessica gritted her teeth. She knew the theoretical maximum speed for passing through the plasma shield, but she had never done it before, nor had she known anyone else who had tried. Unconsciously, she eased a fraction back on the throttle as the shimmering blue closed in on her. A guttural cry escaped her lips as her fighter reached the shield. She felt the fighter shudder as her shields crisped with the speed that she punched through. It was the same as taking a full broadside in a dogfight.

Her cry turned into a savage laugh as space opened up around her, the Heavy Cruiser diminishing behind her.

Turning sharply, Athena boosted power and sped away from the hangar. She could see fighters like fireflies all over the sky ahead of her. In the intense, savage dogfights laser fire scattered like sparks against the dark.

The GTSC *Yucatan* had remained on the outskirts of the battle, the faster ships being the ones to dart into the melee.

Power output was maximum with afterburners on full blast. Behind her she heard Melissa's voice on the radio.

"Athena, on your six, closing."

Athena eased the speed just a little allowing Melissa to catch up to her. Together they flew at maximum power with full boost towards the closest dogfight.

Off to the one side, Jessica could see one of the capital ships firing upon the *Yucatan*, the heavy rounds and beam cannons targeting the grand Heavy Cruiser.

Radio chatter filled her helmet like the night calls of a swarm of birds.

Reports and warnings were coming in thick and fast; it was hard to distinguish individual conversations, even harder not to let the threatening panic take over and rule her within, but she pushed it deep down, she was her father's daughter, after all!

Estimating that she was nearly two thirds of the way to the closest dogfight, she checked her radar. More transponders indicating 'friend' or 'foe' cluttered the screen; one cluster behind her was the rest of her squadron showing they had launched.

"Athena! Mila! Get your asses back into formation. *Now!*" Squadron Leader Rex Barnwell roared, but Athena looked ahead, seeing another explosion, while a friendly fighter disappeared from the screen. She ignored him.

As she looked back down at the instruments, sixteen jump signatures appeared on the radar angled between their two fighters and the rest of their squadron.

"Mila, form up!"

Athena banked the fighter steeply back towards the attacking fighters, six of which had broken off from the main section to attack the two lone fighters before they were re-enforced by the rest of their squadron.

Melissa was close behind her, quartering on her wing as they headed straight into the swarm of fighters.

Jessica rolled out of the way of the first volley that tore past her cockpit, plunging the two of them into the first major dogfight of their war.

The six fighters streaked past Jessica's left side, passing between the two of them.

Ahead, Jessica could see the rest of the enemy squadron engaging with her compatriots, the enemy force being outnumbered by four. As she turned back towards the six that had attacked the two of them, she couldn't help but think that the deadly scene of fighters darting around the sky, their engine cores creating coloured arcs that curved like the tips of scimitars, as if dancing a macabre ballet at the threshold of Valhalla.

Six rounds slammed into her fighter's shields, triggering warnings across her instruments. Turning into the attack, Jessica thumbed the override to give the shields a boost in energy.

Two enemy fighters flashed past, so close Athena felt as if she could reach out and touch their wings. Without even thinking, she reversed course so hard that the g-forces pressed her into her seat hard enough that it felt as though she was becoming part of the fighter itself.

Melissa entered the turn to follow, arcing wide as she couldn't stick the manoeuvre.

"Mila, break formation, join two six." Jessica could hardly believe that she could talk at such a time as this, her voice strained with the effort of holding the fighter in the wild manoeuvre.

The two fighters weaved through aerobatic manoeuvres to throw her off, but Jessica stuck to their tails as though her life depended on it.

Firing short bursts, Athena closed with the second fighter, her turning circle was tighter than what the other pilot could sustain. The two went vertical as Athena fired high; she raked the fighter from nose to tail. It exploded, bright blue and orange flames bursting outwards with a shower of sparks and hailstorm of shrapnel. In that moment, the balance of war and life seemed to become clearer to Jessica as never before, like the first light of sunrise on the horizon in the dawn of a new era. At that precise moment, she felt closer to her father than she had ever done hitherto.

Without missing a heartbeat, Jessica pursued, turning onto the tail of the other fighter, but this time it was with a new vigour, an understanding that transcended the war, with her mind and thoughts clearer now than she had ever experienced. An awakening had begun within her; one that she was not aware of, nor would perceive until the transformation was long underway.

Jessica followed the upward curve, leading the target as the fighter climbed desperately to escape. It never did. The fighter blew up as it climbed over the top.

Melissa completed her turn ending up far out from Jessica's chase. The other four fighters that had attacked them closed in on her tail. Three of them shot at Melissa as they flashed past, her shields taking a savage beating. Alarms rang in her cockpit as she dodged and weaved to get out of the clutches of her pursuers.

"Lead them in a high arc, I'll be there."

Melissa turned, her objective now not solely survival. Locating Jessica's fighter, she worked towards her friend.

Athena continued the loop after killing the two fighters, she saw the four attackers on Melissa's tail.

Rolling into an attacking position, she dived on the four fighters, latching onto the tail of the last one. She immediately opened fire, tearing through its shields before it had time to take evasive action.

She moved from one to the other, quickly accounting for the first two. She had to break off from Melissa's chase when the third one spiralled off from the dogfight. Jessica followed, twisting and turning in close pursuit as she doggedly hung onto the enemy fighter's tail.

Shouts of victory erupted from her radio; Melissa had managed to put down the fighter that had been chasing her. She put it out of her thoughts as she zeroed in on the last of the six fighters.

As the fighter exploded, it sent fragments and debris into the path of Athena's fighter: she heard the pieces impacting on the hull of her fighter as she ploughed through. Ahead of her, the sky was lit up with multiple slip-space ruptures as yet another squadron jumped in.

Engaging boosters, Jessica continued her trajectory heading straight into the path of the new force. She had no idea what was happening to her squadron, all that mattered was the enemy signatures identified on her radar.

Melissa's voice rang somewhere in Jessica's fighter, "Icca, are you going to take on the whole squadron by yourself?"

Jessica didn't trust her voice for a reply. Adrenaline flooded her system as she flew into the teeth of the oncoming attack.

Ten fighters were closing in fast. Selecting her target, Athena weaved through the torrent of fire that poured forth like a wall from the oncoming squadron. Opening up when she was in effective range, Athena tore hell for leather straight at one single fighter in the midst of the formation, knowing that she was not going to be the one to break.

Her shields were taking a hammering, and as she drew closer, the concentration of enemy fire becoming more accurate with every shot. She maximised the forward quadrant, draining the rest of her shields. Jessica's chosen fighter lost its nerve and pulled up, Athena raked it from nose to tail, chewing through its shields, her shots hitting home into the underbelly of the fighter with devastating results. The fighter exploded right in the midst of his comrades.

Jessica was counting on the psychology of a squadron having lost a friend in the safest place of their formation.

Pulling away as hard as she could, Athena rolled inverted as another fighter flashed beneath her. Reversing her trajectory, Jessica began the chase of another fighter, reverting her shields to cover equally. The remaining fighters scattered, momentarily lost by the savage attack that had just taken the heart out of their formation.

Jessica made good use of that time, accounting for two more before the squadron managed to get reorganised.

Three came at her from the side, leading her latest attack with devastating accuracy. Her fighter screamed warnings at her as her shields took another severe beating. She could see her quarry in close range streaming smoke, its engines flickering as the pilot over boosted the damaged cores in an attempt to escape.

Slogging impacts tore into the side of her fighter and she pulled away. She thought she understood the art of war, but there was a lot she was learning about herself and the finer points of aerial warfare. Turning into the attack, Jessica knew to do that much instinctively. Rolling onto her back, she pushed her nose up, letting the three fighters pass underneath her canopy before pulling through a half loop to follow.

As she pulled out on their six, Jessica had to bank hard as yet another fighter came straight for her, guns blazing. She let it pass before turning into another fighter that was passing her in hot pursuit of someone else. Athena nudged the fighter around, bringing the guns to bare, deluging the cockpit in fire. The pilot never had time to pull up; it exploded before Athena had chance to consider the possibility of a collision.

As her fighter rocked from the explosion, she heard a triumphant shout on the radio. Melissa's voice was ecstatic as she knocked out another fighter.

Pulling around, Athena assessed the situation. Mila was close on another fighter's tail while three more tried to close in on hers.

Athena dived, adding power while she positioned the aircraft so that she could catch the fighters from behind. Adding afterburners, Jessica closed the distance, shouting, "Mila, three on your six, break left!"

Melissa's quarry blew up and she banked hard left, the three on her tail following in close formation. Athena opened up, the stream of fire cutting across the nose of the trailing fighter. It must have been enough to spook him as the fighter pulled away leaving the other two to their fates.

Their dogfights had taken them deep into the midst of the battle, the larger warships slugging it out using maximum firepower all around them.

By now, nearly every fighter and bomber in the fleet must have been launched in an aerial combat of such epic proportions, the likes of which hadn't been seen since the closing battle of her father's war: she imagined it was like the battles of old which they had learned about in the Academy.

Most of the ships had also been carrying a full complement of ground troops which had been launched within the first moments of the battle.

Dodging between shell bursts and debris from destroyed aircraft, Jessica amazed herself by wondering if any of the transports had made it to the planet surface.

More shots slammed into her shields and she pulled away, scanning the battle for her attacker.

The fighter was coming right at her, guns hammering. All of a sudden, the background lit up as a frigate behind erupted into white and orange, its engine cores going critical, shrapnel and debris scattering across the battlefield like a claymore detonating.

One larger section crashing into the side of a nearby destroyer that also began to lose steerage.

How many was that now? Numbers were beginning to thin on both sides.

She spun her fighter as she fired, pulling away at the last minute and felt the enemy fighter explode close by.

Turning her fighter again, Athena caught sight of three bombers weaving their way through the bracketing fire from medium and short-range weapons that deluged the no-mans-land between the larger ships with a deadly display of firepower. Closing on them, her erratic flight path keeping her from being targeted, Athena opened up, catching them by surprise. The first fell quickly to her guns, the other two took evasive action, but Jessica chased them down and finished the job before they could launch their ordinance.

A strange looking fighter flashed past her, his guns lighting the dark space. She turned to follow, but not quick enough — two GTSC fighters faltered under his relentless and deadly attack.

Determined that no more would fall victim, Athena gave chase. The pilot, however, was skilled beyond anything she had seen up to this point.

Following his every twist and turn, Athena knew that her own fighter was inferior in performance, but she hung onto his tail with every ounce of skill she possessed.

Not for the first time Jessica wondered about Melissa, they had gotten separated in the chaos of the battle. It was as though her mind had transcended the war, as if she shared two existences simultaneously.

She followed into a private duel between her and the strange fighter, as though the backdrop of the war, even the intense danger of simply flying between the warships, had dropped away, the campaign's significance lost to them both, their roles reversing unremittingly in a vicious dance that spanned the length of the battle.

Every time the fighter would faint and change the chase from being the hunted to the hunter, Athena would put her fighter through the most stringent display of aerobatics she could imagine, but she knew that she could not keep it up forever; she had to break free.

Having lost count of how many times they had changed roles, she could feel her energy fading. The dogfight seemed interminable, the longest she had ever experienced with a single opponent. Her whole body felt drained from the constant fighting, hard turns, evasive manoeuvres and crushing g-forces.

The unrelenting combat in the hours since she and Melissa had launched had left her weapon's cores depleted and her missiles had long dried up, but she was not letting her opponent go if she could help it.

All around them the battle raged, its intensity only building. She had not heard of a battle lasting this long since the one that had claimed her father.

Gritting her teeth, she pressed on, hitting the afterburners again, closing the distance and letting lose with another volley that hit the fighter square on.

The sky was lit up as one of the enemy destroyers was hit by three heavy beam cannons broadside. They burst right through, the internal damage escaping at various places as the hull split open, but miraculously the destroyer held together, drifting out of formation.

A nearby frigate that had taken refuge just behind it got caught in the blast, its engines failing all together and it swung end-on.

Athena was aware of it all, yet didn't let it distract her from her pursuit.

The fighter went vertical, heading out and away from the fight.

Athena followed.

It had now become just the two of them, their skill and aircraft pitted against each other in single combat, a duel of the ultimate consequence, but neither could gain an advantage; each hunting and being hunted alike.

Jessica did not know how long she could go on for, and if she depleted her weapon cores, she would be a sitting duck, with nothing but her flying skill to keep her alive.

As she pursued, the fighter closed with one of the GTSC capital ships, with a slight surprise, Athena saw that it was the *Yucatan*.

The grand ship had taken a beating, having worked its way closer, along with the grand battleship, GTSC *Pegasus*.

The two warships were under massive bombardment with such ferocity it was amazing that neither one had been destroyed.

As the two fighters swept low across the *Yucatan's* side, Jessica was in close pursuit, call it a renewed vigour, as she pressed home her attack with a newfound determination.

A warhead streaked out of nowhere and struck the side of the *Yucatan*, the blast knocking Athena off course and she fought to regain control, but her opponent was drifting in the blast, systems functioning, but the pilot seemed incapacitated.

Jessica had a sudden idea, calling for a refit, she waited the few long minutes for a supply vessel to arrive while she circled the drifting fighter, examining the strange lines and elegant, sleek design.

A returning supply ship was heading back to the *Yucatan*. It, too, showed signs of having been in combat, even if just on the outskirts as was the standard for refitting. It still carried a few missiles and had a minimal amount of plasma left, but Jessica took the opportunity that it presented. Talking to the pilot, she came to a complete stop for the first time since launching, the strange fighter square in her sights just in case the pilot recovered. She took the opportunity to examine the sate of her fighter. It was badly torn up; great rents adorned her wings from where she had been hit. She wondered what the rest of her fighter looked like, but put it out of her mind as the supply ship drew close.

Manoeuvring into position, the supply ship sealed with the fighter and rearmed Athena. It only held a few missiles and once it had off loaded everything it had into her plasma cores, her system still only registered barely half capacity, but it was considerably more than she had a few moments ago.

"Latch onto that fighter and take it back to hangar four for me."

"Are you sure, Lieutenant?"

"Positive. Tell the Chief that it is a gift from Athena."

"Yes, sir." The pilot didn't sound overly enthusiastic about such an order, but nevertheless he obeyed. Jessica watched just long enough to see the two ships seal together before she boosted power and turned, heading back into the fray.

She took a look around; the ferocious battle still raging with mounting intensity. For the first time since launching, Athena found herself alone. Taking advantage of the precious moment, she surveyed the battlefield. Nine of their Fleet were gone, blasted into fragments except for one that had been so badly damaged it had ditched on the planet's surface. Two wounded destroyers and a frigate had retreated, their damage visible even from this distance. They would have a hard time making it back to friendly lines in that state.

There was a large concentration of fighters and bombers around the GTSC *Pegasus* while it was pitched in a savage match to the death with two enemy battle cruisers and a Heavy Cruiser.

At this point, she was flying automatically, guiding her fighter to the next engagement without conscious thought of where that would be, but her instincts knew.

The hulls of the destroyed ships from both sides drifted in various states of fragmentation. The enemy destroyer that she had witnessed its final moments swung end on as Jessica closed with it, using it as cover, she was aiming to get as close as she could to the crippled frigate hidden in its shadow.

Each of the three holes had burned through multiple layers of decks, twisted metal and burned stanchions that jutted out like blackened bones of a carcass.

It was eerie nosing inside; she had to be careful as the hull of the dead ship drifted, its world ever changing.

Reaching the other side, she slowed to a halt, hiding in the shadows while she assessed the scene. Her position was too far away from the frigate, so she reversed her course and headed back into the superstructure.

"There must be a way through." She searched

'The hangar deck!' realisations dawned upon her.

It lay open to the destruction, its length a direct artery down the length of the ship. Diving in, she flew fast, but watching out as the hangar deck revolved around her.

Bursting out the other end, she could see the rest of the flight deck continuing on the other side of the second blast hole.

This time she was closer to the frigate. Easing to the edge of the destroyer, she exposed herself just enough. Targeting the frigate, she launched a missile at the drifting ship and reversed course back into the dead hulk: locating the hangar deck again, she boosted power, flying the length of the ship until she came to the third blast hole and dived into the attack.

Bursting from the side of the destroyer, Jessica was at full power and maximum boost on the afterburners. Noting that the other fighters were making rapid tracks to where she had fired the missile from, she closed with the crippled frigate as quickly as she could. Selecting her last warhead, she armed it to explode on a timed delay. Gaining as much speed as she could, she executed the tightest turn the aircraft could structurally sustain and fired at the apex of the turn. The combined forces sent the warhead streaking into the side of the frigate with such force that it punched through the damaged armour plating and buried itself deep within the bowels of the ship. Punching the boost again, Athena put as much distance between her and the ship as she could.

Spiralling down, the enemy fighters were quick in seeking their revenge for the surprise attack.

Four of them were on her tail, all shooting when they had a clear line of sight. Three others were closing to protect the frigate from more attacks.

The arena turned white, Athena's fighter heeled over, propelled as if by a huge hand from behind. The firing from her pursuers ceased as the frigate disintegrate. Those close to it were crushed in the blast.

Being the furthest away, Jessica was the first to recover. She righted her fighter and engaged thrusters, heading back in towards the enemy fighters before they could recover, catching them by surprise with the savageness of her attack. Laser fire tearing through their plating, accounting for two of them in the first pass.

Jessica raced for the drifting fragments of the frigate as the remaining two fighters recovered and re-engaged the chase.

Dodging and weaving through the debris to throw off the enemy fighters' aim, Athena's task was made all the more difficult with the flotsam while outrunning her pursuers.

Her fighter was responding well despite having been hit several times in the previous engagements. When and wherever possible, she reversed her turns and attacked the two fighters, driving them around, catching them off guard. One such attack went better than she could have hoped for. Nosing over, she hit the thrusters to flip her over, just as the rearmost fighter fired a missile that latched onto her engine signatures, but as she inverted, it lost tracking and guidance and went for the next target – the enemy fighter closest to Athena.

Letting lose a long stream of laser fire, Jessica watched the twin lines converge on the pursuing fighter and advanced along the armour plating. The missile came headlong into the rear of the fighter and detonated, the warhead decimating the fighter in a vivid flash of fire.

Switching targets to the undamaged fighter, Jessica boosted power in the combat version of chicken. Heading straight for her opponent with guns blazing. Neither one seemed to want to break, but the other pilot lost his nerve and pulled up, Athena raking his fighter from nose to tail before it exploded just above her.

Something clanged against the hull of her fighter, but all systems seemed to be still functioning.

Jessica slowed her fighter for just a moment, the magnitude of the battle sinking in as the pieces of the frigate drifted in blackened fragments around her. The reality of war driving home as she identified the body of a young woman floating in space. Her uniform was torn and charred; her hair loose and floating as if underwater. It was obvious that she had sustained massive internal damage, but she must have been in one of the fragments that had survived the blast.

The young woman wouldn't have been much older than Jessica and suddenly she wondered about the *Yucatan*. The friends she knew on board and those she had witnessed their destruction in combat. She thought about Melissa, losing her and how that would feel. It was no longer a great and deadly game of life and death, but a cold brutality of mankind written in blood through the ages.

Clearing the side of the drifting destroyer, Athena saw the battle laid out before her as if she were a general on a hilltop in the ancient days.

One of the battle cruisers was no more, the other streaming plumes of fire and only half the guns firing while the cruiser was still locked in combat with the flagship of the GTSC.

As she accelerated back in towards the battle, the GTSC *Pegasus* began to fall out of line.

A single broadcast seemed to momentarily silence all others: "THE *PEGASUS* IS DITCHING!" yelled one pilot, his voice a crazed battle-cry.

Alarms screamed at Athena as the radar screen in Jessica's cockpit frantically demanded attention. She saw the incoming missile and broke away, firing chaff. The warning disappeared as Athena continued turning to seek out her attacker. Instead, she saw a mass of slip-space ruptures of an entire fighter wing jumping in. Two lead fighters were closing on her, the fighter's targeting function seeking the closest signature.

Once locked, Jessica boosted power, spiralling in a series of rolls as she fired. The spiral of shots coated the shield in front of the enemy fighter effectively blinding him.

Launching one of the last remaining missiles, she pulled up, heading in a direction neither of the opposition fighters could have expected.

The first didn't even have time to try and follow, the missile impacting his cockpit and exploding. The other pulled hard into the turn, but Athena was ready for him – she had launched a sleeper missile which came alive and started tracking as the enemy fighter shot past.

She didn't have long to try and outrun his guns as the fighter fire-balled behind her.

The rest of the wing didn't seem very happy about the first two of their number being shot down so quickly. Twenty broke off to deal with the lone enemy fighter, the rest heading for the *Yucatan* and other supporting ships.

Just as Athena went into the largest dogfight of her short career, she noticed more slip-space ruptures as an entire group of bombers jumped in. Each squadron had a different configuration, but what made the sight all the worse were the two cruisers following, more fighters streaming from their hangar bays.

Jessica took in the impressive display in front of her and dived, chaff firing like ammunition in a furnace as she spiralled.

She dived and climbed, twisting, and turning, engaging every and any fighter that crossed her path. The good thing about being the only friendly fighter was that she didn't have to worry about who she was shooting at; the downside was that it was a battle as hard as she had ever imagined.

She accounted for three of them, going on the offensive as much as she could; three more streamed smoke from their engines, but her fighter was starting to show signs of combat fatigue. She had been hit multiple times; a large ricochet scar burned across the canopy side window and several holes were visible in the wings. She had one more missile remaining in the racks, her guns were blackened and 'low power' warnings indicated in desperation on her screens. Now, it was a matter of outrunning the fighters that still doggedly clung to her tail.

Her muscles ached with the strain, Athena dared not glance at her clock, the dogfight had been going for a long time: she could feel herself tiring.

Her training with Melissa was paying off. Despite her limbs feelings heavy the remaining adrenaline kept her sharp enough.

Pulling the fighter around, the airframe shuddering under the strain, Jessica was just in time to see the stream of laser fire flash overhead, the fighter close behind and she heard the tearing crash of metal as two fighters collided just above her.

Not pausing to find out the result, Athena was rolling away in yet another defensive manoeuvre. As more hits slogged into her fighter, Athena could feel the sluggishness of her controls, she had been hit – badly!

Another fighter on her tail fired – more impacts. It would not be long now.

Athena went cold, clarity forming in her brain and her body ceased to have all connection to her senses, the tiredness falling away like a physical cloak dropping from her shoulders. It was as though she had already died and now been sent back by Ares, the god of war himself.

She slowed the fighter, feeling more impacts as the trailing fighter got closer, his stream of fire relentless.

Jessica kicked the rudder bar over and forced the fighter headlong into the path of her attacker. She fired the last remaining missile and opened up with her main guns. The enemy pilot tried to evade, but his fighter exploded. The two closest behind her staggered under withering fire from above. Athena almost didn't even register it, simply switching to the next target. She had crossed a line at that point, elevating to a new threshold that she didn't understand, but made her more lethal than she had even been before.

Three friendly fighters dived into the mix, all firing colourful laser flashes that illuminated the battlefield. Athena heard Melissa's voice calling to her, but her mind couldn't form a reply. Instead, she climbed into close formation as Melissa's wingman. The other fighters were just off the starboard quarter, both baring the insignia of *Pegasus'* most elite fighter unit. One had the *Pegasus* emblem behind crossed swords while the other bore the nose art of raised wings and a sword pointing skywards through the centre; a ship's emblem partially hidden in a cosmic starburst behind.

The one with crossed swords also had telltale scorch marks on both wings from where it had been hit by enemy fire, the other, had barely a scratch from even the worst anti-aircraft fire.

These two were legends in the GTN, talked about almost as much as her father had been at the Academy. Their sleek fighters and the precision with which they handled them was like watching a dream.

Athena had never flown with a formation that worked seamlessly before; but now, it was an experience that worked without conscious effort as if they were of one mind.

***

Watching another fighter succumb to her guns, Athena looked up at the large form of the GTSC *Yucatan*. It was an impressive sight, the anti-aircraft guns were firing continuously, the short-range weapons providing a barrage to ward off all attackers, it was a token gesture at best, but in the grand scheme of the battle, it did account for a small percentage of enemy aircraft, but enemy fighters and bombers still swarmed around the Heavy Cruiser like flies attracted to fresh blood.

The *Yucatan* was putting up a fine display, but the friendly fighters on Athena's Head Up Display were vastly outnumbered.

Just then the main battery of the Heavy Cruiser opened up, all heavy weapons following suit, the massive rounds projecting beyond the immediate battle.

That's when Athena realised that the two cruisers were now in range and the ferocity in the battle renewed in intensity.

Jessica and the rest of her impromptu flight dived back into the combat – theirs was not to question the greater actions, but to fly and fight as hard as they could, till death do they part.

Watching another two friendly fighters pull away from the battle, Athena turned hard, following her target. The two fighters were holding formation, but both were trailing smoke and looked badly damaged with laser scarring across their wings and hulls.

As she rolled inverted, the two turned inside of their quarry. The twin streams of laser fire caught their enemy fighter in crossfire; it disintegrated.

Another bandit came down vertically, guns hammering as it caught the two fighters in their brief moment of victory.

The first broke up, exploding, knocking the other off course, ironically saving it from their attacker. Using the brief lull in the battle, the fighter took the opportunity to make a run for the hangar entrance.

Jessica continued her roll, diving onto the enemy fighter, boosting power, Athena ignored the power warnings flashing on her system. She was going to put down her target, that was final.

Chasing the fighter close into the *Yucatan* as it angled for the damaged fighter making for the hangar bay, Jessica got as close as she could and fired, sitting on the trigger as alerts screamed at her.

The enemy fighter staggered under Jessica's guns and exploded, her fighter passing through the cloud of fragments, with more hitting her fighter.

Assessing her situation, Athena rapidly rolled into a dive, approaching the hangar entrance at an extreme angle.

"I'm landing to refit. Keep them busy until I'm back."

"No problem, Athena." Melissa's voice was flat. Who knew what the scene would look like when she returned to the fight.

She barrel-rolled in a manoeuvre that sent her headlong into the hangar plasma shield at high speed. Had Squadron Leader Rex Barnwell seen that, he would've had a fit, but she didn't care, after the battle she had just been in, she didn't care for the traditions of the service at all now.

Throttling back, Athena slowed her fighter as the end of the hangar approached rapidly. The other fighter was settling down in a bay at the end, smoke billowing from the engines, sparks shooting out of the acrid black plume.

***

The Chief watched as the fighter billowed smoke the whole way down the hangar deck, its unsteady flight path indicating massive damage to the control surfaces. Extractor fans pulled the burning black fumes from the enclosed space.

Deckhands swarmed around the fighter, hoses and safety equipment being brought forth to control any outbreak if the pilot was to lose control and plant the machine into the unyielding surroundings.

From behind him came the sound of a fighter punching through the plasma shield at high speed.

Turning, the Chief saw another fighter charging down the flight lane, a thin stream of smoke pluming from one engine and sparks flying from the armoured skin. The hull was battered and bent, with black scorch marks that scarred the fighter as though it had been flayed alive, including one that had burned the canopy in a heavy ricochet.

Its guns were blackened, the insignia hidden under the scorched damage.

As it passed, the Chief thought he even saw blood splattered on the cockpit and smeared over the nose and wings.

The fighter flew remarkably well for the damage it appeared to have sustained. He followed it with his eyes as the fighter settled into Jessica's bay, the Chief indicated other deckhands to assist.

Walking over, he watched as the canopy opened and the pilot detached her helmet and lifted it clear from her head. Her hair was wet, plastered down with sweat from the exertion; her face pale.

Unclipping the harness, Jessica made to lift herself, but she had no strength left in her arms.

"Mic! Tab! Help the Lieutenant. Foster! Jike! Give me a hand to get a bird ready to fly."

Jessica gratefully accepted the help from the two men stood either side of her cockpit as she was lifted from it. As she reached the deck, the Chief spoke up, "It appears you have been given a formal reprieve, Lieutenant. Your accusers are no more."

She looked at him, shocked that through everything that had happened, she knew exactly what the Chief meant, surprised more by the fact that they still cared about her unfair dismissal. She could have been killed, as many others had, but they cared.

Somehow it gave her a strength to continue. She straightened, her tired body stiffening with a formality that felt odd after such a battle.

She saluted, "Thank you, Chief."

The whole group saluted her back.

She made her way slowly out of the hangar, the vibrations from the gunfire still present, but she wasn't sure which made her less stable – the weakness in her legs, or the motion of the Heavy Cruiser.

Passing the flight board, she saw the blank spaces, names once known, now washed away as if they had never existed. There were conspicuous empty spaces near the top, Group Captain Walter Burke, Wing Leader Timothy Jenson, and Wing Leader Julian Cartwright were erased so too was Squadron Leader Rex Barnwell and Squadron Leader Jesse Furlong, their names missing from the order of battle.

She felt no joy nor triumph over seeing her Squadron Leader meet the final curtain, or now, hearing that the Group Captain was bereft of life. They were just two pawns in a much greater game of chess between Olympians and Titans.

She reached the exit and then remembered, turning, one hand holding the doorway for support. "Chief, what happened to that fighter?"

"I wish I had more pilots who brought me souvenirs. I'll play with it later, but the pilot is in custody."

Nodding, Jessica turned and left.

***

Reaching her cabin, Athena peeled off her uniform, chucking it in the wash and went for a hydro shower, she needed to feel revitalised, which a sonic shower couldn't give her.

Once she was finished, she still didn't feel refreshed enough, but much better than before.

Putting on a new compression under layer and flight suit, she was about to grab her jacket when there was a knock at her door.

She opened it to find the medical assistant standing there.

"Is everything OK, Heather?"

"Yes." she held up her bag of tricks. "We've been giving combat boosters to all pilots who come back to refit."

"I see." Athena retreated back into her room, the door shutting behind Heather.

Jessica undid her flight suit and underlayer, peeling them off to her waist, and took off her shirt, turning to chuck it on the bed. She shifted her bra strap off her shoulder to give Heather her shoulder to work on.

"Nice tattoo! It looks fresh."

"Melissa and I got them done just before we jumped."

How ridiculous things seemed. They were in a battle as ferocious as ever, they could all be killed, but here, now, in the normality of the shipboard surroundings, untouched by the war, they were having a casual conversation about her tattoo. Was she going mad with the situation to be able to switch so easily?

Heather pulled out four vials, she connected the first one: "These will take effect in the next ten minutes and slowly release over the next four hours. Based on how long you were out there the first time around, I'm going to back it up with these." She held up two other vials with different coloured liquids in them.

"Surely, having too many of these in such a short timeframe is going to be bad, isn't it?"

"So is being killed, Lieutenant. I hear that that has a greater effect on your life expectancy."

Jessica smiled. "Tomorrow's problems are on the other side of the veil?"

"Just survive, Lieutenant."

Jessica looked at her over her shoulder, Heather glancing up at the movement, their eyes met for an instant before Heather looked back at her work.

"Eat this." Heather handed her a bar of something that Jessica recognised from the endurance training in the Academy. She took it and opened it as Heather cleaned the patch of skin she had worked on. Jessica readjusted her bra strap over her shoulder.

"Reign hell on them, Lieutenant."

Picking up her shirt, Jessica pulled it on; "I will, Doc."

She did up her flight suit and grabbed her jacket. In the space of an hour spent back on board the *Yucatan*, she felt like she had grown up; she felt more confident and could feel the surge of chemicals in her body begin to work. Energy started to fill her, mental clarity and focus returned to her senses and her tiredness faded into a dwindling memory. The battle began to make sense in her head, just like the debriefings after a combat exercise in flight training. She felt as though she was learning through someone else's eyes, understanding things in a new, deeper way.

She knew she would crash physically later from the combat boosters, but that seemed irrelevant at this point – it all depended on there being a 'later' for her at all.

Saluting the medical assistant from the door of her cabin, Jessica left, heading for the hangar, a strange tingling at the roots of her hair while she walked, her thoughts on the battle previous. She was lost in thought to notice the familiarity of the sensation.

Heather let her arm sink to her side; she looked down at the eight empty vials instead of the six she had told Athena that she was going to administer, but the other two would bring a greater mental clarity than Jessica could have imagined. It allowed her brain to repair and learn the lessons that would normally take months, but would now take mere minutes for the synapses to make connections.

"Go get them, Athena," she said to the silence of the empty cabin.

***

Jessica thought back to when she had entered the hangar. Flying the damaged fighter had become normal for her by then, but the sight that met her in the hangar had told a different story. Broken fighters littered various bays, their end trails scattered across the flight deck: scars and dents marred the surface from where the lucky had made it back by the skin of their teeth or blackened patches, the floor and walls burned and buckled where others had not been so lucky.

Two hulks of crashed fighters had been pushed unceremoniously to one side, their fragments piled against the wall to clear the flight deck, the remains forgotten until such a time that someone had a minute to search for spare parts. Blood smeared the deck at one bay where a mechanic had been cut in half by a flying segment of metal that had detached from a fighter that had collided with a stanchion, other crews were fighting to put the searing flames out. Yet three other erks had been crushed behind a crashed fighter when the Heavy Cruiser had heeled over from the impact of another direct hit.

The sight of so many empty fighter bays had been hard to witness, but it had not hit home as hard as when she had returned to the hangar after changing her uniform.

The scene was worse. Another fighter had just belly landed on the flight deck, flames and smoke enveloping the aircraft. The screams of two people somewhere filled the air, their thin cries told of all there was to know about pain and fear.

Mechanics and deckhands frantically fought with hoses, trying to put out the inferno before it could spread.

Jessica could vaguely make out the sight of the pilot slumped over the flight instruments.

When the fire crew finally got control of the blaze, she saw blood splattered on the inside of the pilot's helmet visor.

A lump caught in her throat, "Was it Melissa?"

The medic was there, unclipping the helmet. Jessica breathed out a sigh of relief. She wasn't aware she had been holding her breath when she saw the short cut hair. The young guy had been in a different squadron; she had hardly known him.

"Chief! Is there a bird for me to fly?"

The Chief came over; "You're going to love me."

"You have a magic wand and fixed my fighter enough to fly?"

"No. I have something better." He gestured to the bay at the end. A brand-new fighter was sitting there, the next Mark up from her own fighter, paint gleaming in the lights.

"Just come out of a major check. Rearmed, refuelled and ready to go. You'll be interested to know that I've upgraded the load out and boosted the weapons cores. Call it the trial upgrade that I was going to propose to the Admiral, if only I had more time."

"Chief, you're amazing."

"Knock hell out of them, Lieutenant."

Jessica nodded, climbing up onto the wing of the new fighter. "That's my plan, Sir."

The Chief watched the young officer, now one of the highest-ranking and most experienced pilots left alive in the fleet.

Installing herself into the cockpit, the Chief came across, two erks made sure Jessica was strapped in and all hoses were connected.

"I don't know if we'll even get many parts out of your last one." The Chief had a serious expression, but he cracked a smile. "Look after yourself, Lieutenant. Good hunting." He saluted, a rare event for the Chief.

Jessica saluted back, closing the canopy, and lifting the fighter from where it stood. The undamaged fighter looked foreign and out of place, its fresh exterior and 'new' look was totally at odds to the damage and destruction all around them.

The fighter was virtually the same as her previous one, similar enough that a pilot could jump from one to the next and be able to fly both. However, as Jessica was rapidly finding out, the new aircraft was a lot more of a thorough bread than her other one. It was more powerful and much more manoeuvrable; where she had been fluidly proficient in her fighter, this one moved effortlessly.

The Chief turned from what he was doing, watching the fighter lift and ease into the flight lane, the telltale blue ion trails still catching his attention. After all this time, he still loved the smell of burned ion plasma – there was something rich in the tang that it left behind.

He couldn't help but think about the young officer in the cockpit. Jessica was a pleasant girl, one who should have been enjoying the company of some young guy on the beach, where the days were warm and life was peaceful, maybe starting a family, with a wild story to recount in the years to come. Instead, she was heading back out to a fight to the death with an enemy that seemed to have endless re-enforcements; a continuous stream of fighters dancing in an epic macabre ballet which was beautiful and yet terrible.

Standing for just a moment longer, the Chief watched Jessica's fighter slide through the plasma shield, the engines reflected white as she boosted power. Next a string of shots stitched across the shield, the plasma rippling from each impact.

The Chief saw Jessica's fighter turn and disappear out of sight, the plasma still pulsing with vivid colours before a fighter exploded just outside, the fragments punching into the shield; the wrecked hull falling from sight. Tension built on the flight deck until they saw an enemy fighter flash past the entrance, Jessica's new fighter seconds behind it, guns hammering, the plasma shield once again lit up with cannon fire.

***

Launching out into space again after the refit was a reality that Athena would become very familiar with. She felt the rush of speed as the end of the flight deck approached rapidly, the transparent blue plasma shield shimmering as she punched through it, the soft zing of her shields as they heated from the friction caused by her speed.

Leaving the hangar was bittersweet. It was a headlong catapult into a battle every bit as ferocious as when she had left it. A dance of life and death that so many familiar faces had fallen to, but leaving the sight of so many broken fighters, their crippled remains stowed away in the fighter bays, waiting to be torn apart for spare components, was a welcome reprieve from the truth.

As she punched through, two fighters caught her attention, they were on an attack run, one of them firing at her, the shots fanning harmlessly below. She boosted power and pulled, extending away from the ship in an inverted reversal turn. The fighters passed under her, close to the side of the Heavy Cruiser. Pulling hard through the loop, Jessica dived onto the enemy fighters, calculating the deflection perfectly, depressing the firing button, unleashing a deadly stream of fire with such precision the two fighters never stood a chance. The first exploded, its wreckage ploughing on and almost careening into the entrance. The second continued down, attempting to pull up at the last minute to create room to manoeuvre, but he never made it. Athena's cannon fire tore through its shields and armour plating, deluging the cockpit in fire.

Turning, Jessica headed back into the fray, her fighter disappearing into the pell-mell maelstrom of the battle.

Jessica pushed the toll to the back of her thoughts as she boosted power, joining the fight once more. She had no idea where Melissa was, having lost contact with her when she had dived into the hangar to rearm. Despite her concern for her friend, Athena could feel elation in her spirit, the sensations of the new fighter combined with the combat boosters that Heather had administered made her feel on top performance. Renewed energy coursed through her, the tiredness from before the refit all but forgotten.

It was a long time for a battle of this intensity to last. The majority of battles lasted no more than an hour or two, but as their numbers had thinned out over the hours, the ferocity had intensified, with neither side willing to let the other profit from any setbacks.

Just for the GTSC *Yucatan* alone the battle had been extremely costly: of the original ninety-six bombers that had launched, only seventeen remained, likewise of the one hundred and ninety-two fighters, there were fewer than thirty still flying, their voices falling silent as the macabre ballet raged on. Jessica hoped that the other ships had fared better because it seemed like the enemy forces had an unlimited supply of re-enforcements.

A movement caught her eye and interrupted her thoughts. She turned towards it automatically and would have been amazed at how natural that had become if she had thought about it. Instead, she had become the huntress again, her instincts reading all the information that she could gleam from the situation ahead.

A flicker of light came from the base of the missile as it scored a straight line across the battlefield towards the *Yucatan*. Athena hauled the fighter around in the tightest turn she could manage and boosted power on an intercepting course.

She angled across the missile's path and waited impatiently for the fighter to get within range. Power at maximum, Jessica was pushing the fighter as hard as it would go, willing it into range sooner. She could imagine the Captain ordering everyone to brace for impact as they picked up the radiation signature of the warhead.

Watching the range decrease, Athena opened fire early, purple flashes cut a curved line across the projectile's path as it streaked towards the *Yucatan*. One of them must have touched off the warhead as it exploded passing through the tracer; the shock wave rocked her fighter as if she had passed through a solar wind. They would most probably have felt that back on board the *Yucatan* as well.

Renewed adrenaline flooded Athena's body as some of the time-released boosters kicked in. This was only the beginning – where there was one missile, there would be more. Turning her fighter, Jessica scanned the radar and the void in front of her for her next target. The missile could have been one that missed its original target, or even one that had been fired from extreme range. There was nothing obvious at first. She assessed the battlefield – the absence of the GTSC *Pegasus* was an ominous hole in their lines. Theirs was a race against time. If they stood any chance of gaining a foothold in this system, they had to get the upper hand, but with the balance of power in favour of the enemy forces, it was going to take a miracle.

Twin streams of laser fire tore across her nose, lighting up her shields as the bright reflection danced in her canopy. Athena turned into the attack just in time to see another of the sleek strange fighters flash close overhead. Reversing her turn, she followed it. The new power and performance showed quickly as her fighter was able to keep up with the enemy fighter much easier than the last time.

The pilot streaked at full tilt towards the middle of the battle, seeming to want to hide amongst the chaos.

When she had launched again, Jessica had felt renewed, vindicated, as though she could meet her end knowing that her father's name would no longer be tarnished by her. Maybe it was the combat boosters in her system, but she felt free, for the first time since joining the *Yucatan*, she was free, free to be the fighter pilot she was destined to be.

Without missing a beat, Athena followed the fighter in, sticking to its tail and chewing away at the shields until she closed the range enough and poured a long stream of fire into the fighter, watching it explode.

A welcome, familiar voice caught her attention: "Welcome back." Melissa was still alive.

"If you don't mind, we could do with a hand dealing with these pests." The sarcasm was strong in her voice and Jessica recognised the signs of strain in her friend.

"All yours, Mila. Lead the way."

She latched onto Melissa's wing and followed as she dived into another swarm of fighters.

It looked as though Melissa's fighter had taken a harsh beating. Tell-tale scars lined the wings and one of the engines was out. She had to give it to Melissa, they were a lot more like twin sisters than she had realised.

The ensuing dogfight was savage. Athena stuck to Melissa's wing as long as she could until a head on attack forced them to separate.

Athena made quick work of the three fighters that tried to get on her tail. The third one exploded as the fighter passed by, some fragments clanging against her hull. Athena saw two fighters on Melissa's tail as she chased a third. Knowing what a damaged fighter felt like to fly, Jessica dived down on the string of fighters.

Just as she was about to open fire, a glowing fireball flashed passed. It was one of the GTSC *Protheus'* medium range weapons. The shell struck the second trailing fighter square on as it exploded in a vivid flash – a lucky shot in a million.

Instead of flinching, Athena kept her chase going, working into position to catch Melissa's other pursuer.

Clearing Melissa's tail, the two friends turned together in time to be broadsided by an entire new flight that had just joined the fray.

Jessica went on the offensive immediately, whereas Melissa seemed to be having real difficulty keeping the fighter on an even keel.

In that moment, the game had changed. Melissa was now the target while Athena fought off all the attackers like an angry fury.

"Head for the *Yucatan*! I'll cover you!" Jessica almost shouted the command in her desperate attempt to keep her friend alive.

It took them what seemed a long time to make it back. Slipping into the hailstorm of anti-aircraft fire, Jessica half expected the fighters to leave them be, but rather they pressed on in their attack, determined to catch their prey before Melissa could make it into the safety of the hangar.

Seeing the damage to the fighter, the blood smeared on the canopy, Jessica had fought like a fury who understood the shadowy line between life and death; but after watching Melissa get hit, a recklessness from the newfound freedom had been matched with a cold understanding of the balance they swung on.

As if the voices of the ages whispered in her ear, an utter calm came over Athena, she saw things more clearly, understood mysteries about life and death that she had never even wondered about. And then, watching her friend's fighter slip beyond the protective barrier of the plasma shield, Jessica screamed like a banshee in her cockpit as she turned her fighter towards the squadron who had taken pursuit of Melissa and herself.

The air combat controller in the *Yucatan's* bridge had to pull his headset away from his ears to avoid blowing his eardrums, he turned a white face to the Captain, but no words emerged when he tried to speak.

They watched and saw the impossible happening as Jessica plunged into the depths of an entire group single handed, but her fighter seemed to have a charmed life.

Athena had stopped wondering who would make it back. She was merely existing, lingering in limbo, as the chiffon veil between life and death rippled in the breath of war.

Yet beyond that, everyone on the bridge was transfixed as they watched the GTSC *Niran*, a large destroyer, accelerating out of formation, angling towards the two cruisers, life pods firing from its side like chaff.

Closing the distance, the destroyer was continually accelerating; the Captain of the closest cruiser recognising the danger, took evasive action.

The two ships were drawing closer to the second cruiser. Any impact managed by the destroyer at this point would be superficial at best, but the cruisers had not let up in their merciless bombardment of the destroyer, the close proximity making the damage all the worse.

Swinging the helm over, the *Niran* slammed into the side of the cruiser alongside it; that was when they all watched in horror as the *Niran* jumped away or tried to.

It must have had the jump drive spooled up and ready, but something went wrong. The destroyer disintegrated, as an imploding slip-space rupture tore the side of the cruiser apart before both ships erupted as each of their cores went critical. The second cruiser had no chance, the combined detonation hit it broadside, rolling the great ship on its side, causing the the armoured plating to buckle along its entire length. The cruiser was finished and would be lucky to escape the battle now.

Pulling up in another attack, Athena felt her fighter rock to the explosion of her previous victim, she went straight into the attack of another two fighters that were diving on her. Behind them she saw the backdrop light up with multiple slip-space ruptures as even more enemy aircraft jumped in. There was no end to them, but what was worse, was the larger ruptures behind them: a Heavy Cruiser and her smaller consort. They had jumped in just outside of firing range but were closing quickly. Athena heard the controller on the radio: "All fighters return to base! We're bugging out."

Jessica ignored the order, remaining in the dogfight; she would keep fighting to try help as many of their fighters get home safely as she could, a number of which were closing with the Heavy Cruiser as she watched.

There were various fighters and still a few bombers in the battle, most of which, their parent ships had either retreated or were destroyed, their hulls drifting in varying fragmentation.

Massing around the closest GTN vessel, the skies were clearing of friendlies in readiness for retreat.

Three fighters were making straight for the hangar when the enemy ships opened fire. The massive shots swept aside the three fighters as though they were gnats and struck the *Yucatan* square in one of the engines.

Athena didn't need to hear the announcement from the controller, she knew what that meant. The GTSC *Yucatan* wasn't going anywhere.

Out of the original fleet, four of their number had ditched on the planet, twelve had been destroyed and four had limped away to make the jump back to friendly skies.

Only thirteen remained: the *Yucatan* and one cruiser, the *Protheus*, three fleet destroyers, two heavy frigates, one frigate, a corvette and four gunships.

Outgunned and outnumbered, the remaining GTSC fleet had to make a tactical retreat or face annihilation against the ever-increasing enemy numbers.

Jessica knew that it was only a matter of time.

In an uncharacteristic moment of self-sacrifice, Jessica watched as the *Yucatan* stood its ground while the three smaller vessels accelerated past, giving them chance to retreat to a safe distance.

Those that lived long enough to remember this day would have a hard time forgetting what they had seen.

The remaining fighters massed around the *Yucatan* and three consorts as three more enemy fighter wings closed in, a bomber wing trailing behind.

The GTSC defenders were outnumbered three to one forget about the additional ninety-six bombers joining the enemy forces.

The Heavy Cruisers were pitched in a fierce battle with the *Yucatan*, but the damaged GTSC Heavy Cruiser was the underdog in the fight leaving the enemy consorts to focus on the GTN destroyers.

Rolling in a dive, Jessica switched targets, as three supporting fighters fell to her guns in quick succession. Two of her dwindling squadron were making tracks for a flight of bombers closing in on the *Yucatan*. With the fighters out of the way, there was a clean shot at the approaching danger.

Her view misted over as a series of shots slammed into her shields; turning into the attack, Jessica was in time to see another fighter flash overhead, guns still hammering. She reversed course and latched onto its tail, closing the distance and letting loose with a volley of fire that made short work of its shields. Just as he was pulling up, Jessica launched a rocket, its lack of homing made it impractical for dogfighting, but at this close range, the high explosive projectile didn't miss. Rather, it tore through the engine housing, igniting the fuel cells.

Athena pulled away, the explosion bouncing her fighter with the shockwave. Sparing not even a thought for the luckless fellow, she reverted her attention back to the bombers she had seen. Four of them were still flying – she saw no sign of the others nor of any friendly fighters on their tail. That was a little odd, but just like she had been attacked, perhaps they had split off to engage someone else.

Engaging the afterburners, she closed with the four bombers as quickly as she could. The lead bomber launched its missile, the warhead scoring a perfectly straight line towards the *Yucatan's* armoured side.

Athena was almost within range, her targeting retinal locking onto the nearest bomber, she fired a missile, accompanying it with a long stream of cannon fire. The missile was close to her bomber, switching targets she opened up on the second bomber which was thrown over onto its back as its comrade exploded, the second collided with the third bomber just as Athena's missile struck home, both bombers fire-balled.

Keeping her speed up, Athena closed with the lead bomber, opening up with all of her guns as she raked it from tail to the nose, plastering it with shots, but her main targets were the warheads that were rapidly closing with the Heavy Cruiser.

From the corner of her eye, she saw the fleet destroyer GTSC *Krasev* nosing out of formation, a descending trajectory towards the planet: they had just lost another one.

Soon, if not already, the cruiser and the other destroyer would be using their speed to catch up with the three smaller ships in an attempt to retire far enough that the enemy forces would not give chase.

Athena switched her attention back. The missiles didn't show up on the radar for her to lock onto, instead she would have to be swift and accurate with her shots.

Leaving the bomber to its demise, Jessica opened fire, the twin streams of purple laser fire lit up the scene before her. One warhead exploded, caught quickly in the chase, a vivid flash of colour and the usual shock wave. It was close enough that it set off the second which blew up as well.

The two furthest away were only just coming into range. Athena poured a long stream in a desperate attempt to destroy the next closest warhead. The range to the Heavy Cruiser was decreasing far too rapidly, but eventually Jessica managed to hit it with tracer, the explosion rocked the final missile, but it merely wobbled before regaining its course.

Afterburners still on full blast, Jessica chased the fourth warhead with everything the fighter had to give, guns hammering, but the missile seemed to have a charmed life, continuing as though all was normal.

It was almost at the point where Athena would have to break off, otherwise she wouldn't have enough room to pull away without slamming into the side of the Heavy Cruiser herself. Though unwilling to admit defeat, Jessica clung to the missile, using every available second she had.

Yelling into her cockpit, she pulled away, catching with the corner of her eye, as the missile vanished from her view, an explosion. She had done it! Relief flooded her system, but it was short lived.

As she rocketed up, skimming so low over the battle-scarred armour plating the light from her shields and engines glowed against the *Yucatan*'s hull.

"Warheads! Port side!"

Craning her neck, she tried to see passed the side of her canopy. Sure enough, another flight of bombers was peeling away from their attack run.

Athena rolled onto the new heading. There below her, she saw a fan of eight missiles streaking towards the *Yucatan*.

She dived, aiming short so she could get the deflection angle and fired. One missile fire-balled without setting off the warhead. She switched targets only to see another friendly fighter closing on her bearing. She had to break off so as not to hit the other GTN fighter.

Shifting targets again, going for the next missile, but again, another friendly fighter got in her way.

Jessica changed direction, trying to come in from another angle, but as she got into effective range, she watched helplessly as the first warhead hit the side of the *Yucatan*.

First one, and then another. Six direct hits close together, the Heavy Cruiser heeled over with the force of the explosion.

Jessica banked, watching the grand ship as the explosions diminished, its armour plating buckled and twisted. Scorch-marks blackened a vast portion of the hull and had obliterated part of the insignia and name. Jessica could hardly stop to watch as more fighters and bombers took advantage of the lull in the defensive firing.

Swinging onto the tail of one bomber that passed her by, Jessica made short work of its shields and blasted it out of the sky.

The Heavy Cruiser started edging off station; nosing down towards the planet, Jessica saw it go as she doggedly stuck to the tail of another fighter, slowly chewing away at the fighter's armour.

"THE *YUCATAN* IS DITCHING!" one wild voice shouted over the radio.

Sure enough, the Heavy Cruiser had begun the descent towards the planet surface, navigating its way through the debris from all the other destroyed ships, both friend and foe alike.

Jessica assessed the situation around her, with the *Pegasus, Krasev, Conquistador, Halifax* and two gunships all somewhere on the planet's surface; three of their number having jumped away and a further three in full retreat. That left only two fleet destroyers and the cruiser, GTSC *Protheus*, in the fight now that the *Yucatan* was ditching.

The number of GTN fighters had dwindled, barely enough to form a full squadron for each of the remaining three ships.

Making a snap decision, she rolled onto her back and nosedived after the Heavy Cruiser as it transcended the battlefield towards a new one in an emergency descent. She throttled up and followed at full power, barely keeping up even with afterburners engaged.

"Athena, where are you going?" It was one of the two fighters from the *Pegasus* that had been fighting alongside her.

"Going to the next battlefield. This one seems to be over and we have friends down there."

"She has a point. It does seem like we are losing this one." Zatara's voice was sincere, yet still held a wild tone from the excitement of combat.

"On your wing." Malakh's voice was as even as if he was discussing the weather.

Jessica hadn't waited, dodging the debris that swirled in the *Yucatan's* wake, she had no idea where Melissa was; the last time she had seen or heard her was when she had escorted her friend back to the hangar.

Three enemy fighters seemed to have joined the pursuit, laser fire tore past her, joined by another stream of a different colour.

"Athena, I'll clear your tail," Malakh's voice still as calm as ever.

Jessica didn't reply, she just continued weaving through the flotsam that could wipe her out at any moment, the adrenaline rising, making it seem more like a race, rather than a desperate attempt to survive.

The *Yucatan* disappeared into the cloud cover, the scene below unknown. Jessica and her two comrades weaving in an intricate helical spiral. They ploughed into the clouds, the milky impenetrable world cutting visibility to nothing forcing them to rely solely on the HUD and radar. Various IFF signals showed up on the ground, highlighting a world of activity.

She identified the *Yucatan*, descending and manoeuvring into an unseen location; the *Pegasus* and *Krasev* and two gunships all showed up in a semi clustered formation.

A mass of much smaller IFF swarmed around the downed ships. The GTSC ground troops had rallied around the warships.

As Athena surveyed the hidden scene below, a lone IFF signal detached itself from the side of the *Yucatan*, a fighter. She allowed her thoughts to stray again briefly to wonder where Melissa was, but she had to push it to one side and focus on the fight at hand.

Glimpses of the ground began to show through the clouds, they were nearly through.

"Hoorah!" the war cry came from Zatara. Her wild enjoyment of the flight was genuine in the moment as they shot out of the clouds in time to see the Heavy Cruiser impact the ground.

It had fired all its boosters to decelerate as much as possible, but it still hit the surface hard enough to raise a cloud of dirt and dust that covered the battlefield. The Heavy Cruiser slid under the momentum, grinding to a halt and leaving a deep cleft in the earth behind it.

The *Pegasus* lay angled in front, the two armoured bridges a mere couple hundred meters distant. The two captains able to see each other, the ring of warships forming the beginnings of a defensive position backing onto a small rise ringed by cliffs.

The scene of chaos lit up with the ground fire glowing amidst the settling dust. An epic battle ensued around the *Pegasus*. Troops and armour swarmed like an army of ants around the devastation from the *Yucatan's* arrival which was causing havoc amongst the enemy troops, the outer fringe of which now lay crushed under the Heavy Cruiser.

It was not long before the *Yucatan* recovered, its guns coming alive and raining fire down onto the battlefield in support of the flagship.

The three fighter pilots had been heading towards the arena, but Gideon was the first to speak.

"Let's go see what we can do to help."

"On your wing, Gid." Zatara and Athena formed up. The other single GTSC fighter already engaged in combat over the battleground below.

"I'll come in from the starboard side on an attack run across the troops. Watch out for enemy fighters," Athena commanded, a matter-of-factness coming over her. It was as though she realised that even though they had survived one of the biggest battles of the entire war, their fight had only just begun!

**Lieutenant Melissa Blackwall,
On board the GTSC *Yucatan*, Heavy Cruiser,
Two days, three weeks before Operation *Trident*:**

Handing the data pad back to flight engineer, Thomas Garnet, Melissa looked up at the pyramid of engines with a frown, her breathing was heavy as she calmed after the exertion of working on the uncooperative aircraft. They had been at it since she had landed from the patrol the day before.

Running one grease-stained hand through her shoulder length, mouse brown hair, she rested her other hand on her hip, sleeves rolled up to her elbows. She looked at the young flight engineer as he rechecked the data pad.

It had been one heck of a patrol, three enemy scouts had been detected at extreme range and closing with the Heavy Cruiser, the GTSC *Yucatan*.

Melissa had been at readiness and had been launched immediately. Five fighters had spewed from the side of the Heavy Cruiser, flames and exhaust gasses stabbing like spears from the side of the *Yucatan*. It never failed to excite her: the rush of speed down the enclosed tunnel and the adrenaline of being accelerated to 'attack speed' through the launch tube before bursting out into the wide-open space, her vision obscured by the inferno as the flames overtook her, the immense feeling of speed slowly receding as the massive bulk of the Heavy Cruiser dwindled behind her.

They had closed with the approaching scouts who everyone had assumed would be relying on their superior speed as their best defence. It had taken everyone by surprise when they had turned and engaged the five fighters.

Melissa could remember the details of one of the scout's bodywork, the pattern in the paint as it flashed mere feet overhead.

She had isolated one of the scouts and attacked using every ounce of skill she had, and she had got her target, the highly manoeuvrable scout exploding with a vivid blue and purple flash, the flames that dissipated almost as soon as they had formed.

Something solid had smacked into her fighter, which reverberated through her seat and flight pedals. She had turned back to base as warnings and alarms started screaming at her in an ever-increasing number, a tremor reverberating through the flight controls.

"I don't know, Flight Sergeant. I know what I felt, and you saw the warnings before I shut down. I don't know why nothing is showing up now."

"We'll keep searching, Ma'am. No smoke without fire."

"I appreciate that, Sergeant. What's next?" She wiped an oil smear from her cheek.

The engineer watched Melissa rub her hands together; it was unlike many officers on this ship to get their hands dirty helping lower ranks with their job.

Before the flight engineer could reply, Viktor, another flight mechanic, passed close behind her, never breaking stride and , keeping his voice low as he muttered, "You better go see Athena."

It was unlike most personnel on board the *Yucatan* to disrespect their officers, the Captain had seen to that, which made this comment rather unusual from a junior officer. Melissa looked at the retreating back of the younger engineer; it was unlike him too, normally a very polite hard-working individual.

Melissa came to a decision quickly and ran after him: "What happened, Sergeant?"

"I don't know, Ma'am, but I overheard someone saying that she's in for it this time. I think it was another meeting with the Captain. Seems like he's really gunning for her this time, huh?"

"Is it still going?"

"Finished, I believe, Ma'am."

"Thank you, Viktor."

He nodded and Melissa turned back to her fighter bay. A lot of the crew liked Athena; she was friendly and easy to get on with, not to mention extremely beautiful. There was, of course, her father's history that everyone seemed to know about as well, but the Captain had never liked her from the first moment she had stepped on board.

"Thomas, you carry on. I'm going to check on something."

The flight mechanic saluted before carrying on with his task. Melissa grabbed her uniform jacket from where it hung on the wingtip and headed for the exit.

Melissa had had a bad feeling about the last operation Jessica had been on and the Captain had been absolutely apoplectic upon her return. Hurrying along the corridor, she wondered what the future held. Jessica had been in trouble many times before and so far, had pulled through, but something told her that this time it was going to be different. After all, she had publicly discredited the Group Captain, and he was an Admiral's son, as well as a favourite of the Captain, at that.

Reaching Jessica's cabin, she entered without knocking. She reckoned that if Jessica really was in trouble, she might not want company until she had come to terms with it, but she also figured that if that was the case, Jessica could probably do with someone to straighten her out, none other than a friend, a sister.

The doors slid open and she stepped into semi-darkness. There was no sign of Jessica immediately apparent as Melissa entered the room, while the door slid closed behind her.

"Icca, you here?"

With her eyes and ears adjusting to the surroundings, Melissa could pick out the uniform jacket hanging by the wash-room door, Jessica's boots by the foot of the bed. The photo of Jessica's parents stood in its frame on the desk. Her ears became accustomed to the quiet in the room and she could hear water running in the ensuite. Jessica was in the shower. Melissa undid her uniform jacket and draped it over the foot of the bed.

Something pulled her skin on her arm as she did and she twisted it, turning towards the security light, she saw a scratch that ran almost the length of her forearm. She must have picked it up when she was helping with her fighter but had been too busy to have registered it.

She rubbed it, mentally noting to wash it later.

Just then the sound of the water stopped. Melissa heard Jessica moving around; the door slid open after a while and Jessica came out rubbing her hair with her towel.

"You've heard?"

"Yes."

Jessica nodded, turning back to the bathroom. Her wet hair hung longer than regulation length, well past her shoulders, the damp waves showing more prominently.

"What are you going to do?" Melissa called from where she stood in the main room.

"Captain's seeing to my dishonourable discharge, *personally*. There's nothing I can do,"

It was unlike Jessica to give in, but Melissa could hear the venom in her voice. She really had been defeated by the Captain this time.

She knew he had a harsh reputation and had derailed several officer's careers over the years, but she did not understand the animosity the Captain held against Jessica.

"How long?" Her heart sank, while she tried desperately to keep any sign of it from tinging her voice.

"Two days." A friendship that had built so strong, was now going to be separated when they reached orbit in a little over fifty hours. The two of them looked at each other as Jessica re-emerged from the ensuite.

Melissa's mind raced, there must be something they could do that would change the course of events.

"There's still time. We haven't docked yet."

She stopped, the look that Jessica gave her cut her off. Melissa had seen that look before. Her aunt had been fighting a debilitating disease while Melissa was growing up and had struggled a long time before finally it had won. Just before the end someone had come up with a new cure. They had wanted her to try it. But her aunt had come to the end and wanted no more, just peace. The look her aunt had given the doctors, was the same one she now saw in Icca.

Jessica looked like she was giving in, carrying the same aura around her.

"Don't you ever give up? It would take something pretty monumental to stop the Captain this time. He's got the Group Captain's father to think about. After all there's no better promotion than that from a grateful Admiral," her voice dripping in sarcasm and bitterness. "Not even Squadron Leader Jacox has been able to divert the Captain this time."

Melissa went to the lighting panel and adjusted the lights to give a warm glow compared to the gloom from the security lights that had illuminated the room thus far. Moving to the bed, she sat down on the edge while Jessica hung her towel up in the bathroom.

Straightening her back, Melissa stretched her neck over to the left and the right, feeling the pull of her tight muscles.

Hearing the sound of a desk drawer opening, Melissa looked up to see Jessica sitting by her desk, her long legs crossed, baring her toned thighs.

She watched her friend as she leaned down, reaching into the drawer, her unbridled figure moving easily under the black t-shirt that hugged her upper body, her waist exposed where her shirt rode up from her black underwear.

Melissa heard the clink of glass as Jessica brought out a glass bottle, two-thirds full of a golden amber liquid that glowed reddish black when the light blinked through it.

It always gave her the sense of the cavalier, as though she were a buccaneer in the age of pirates.

"K2?" Jessica held up the two tumblers they had acquired when on leave in the Dan'Zar system before shipping out to the Raven Head system for combat training.

A wide smile lit Melissa's face. If this was really it, she'd never be able to drink K2 again without thinking about Jessica. It was a tradition they had started in flight school, to mark any event they faced together.

"One last time?"

"This can't be it. You're too good a pilot to be discharged."

"Tell that to the Captain."

"What if we went to Admiral Fraser?"

"And what? Ask him to overrule one of his Captains' decisions in order to keep an untested pilot with a black record, however unfairly blackened?" Jessica snapped back. Jessica placed the two tumblers on the desk with a solid clunk, she breathed deeply for a moment, controlling her anger, then poured out a generous dash for them both and handed it across.

Melissa took it, there wasn't much else she could say or do that would change anything.

She hated the feeling of helplessness.

Jessica leaned forwards and they clinked glasses.

Melissa watched as her friend leaned back and crossed her slender legs again, resting one arm on her thigh, the glass suspended over the floor as Jessica swirled the reddish gold liquid around in the glass before letting it rest. Over the course of their training, right up until now, many men, even some women, had been after Jessica. Melissa could understand why: her friend's looks were, as one guy had described her, "of goddess quality", but she had rebuffed all advances.

Melissa was not jealous, instead she wished they really were sisters. Melissa was slender with fewer curves, while Jessica, also slender, had delicate sensual curves in all the right places, stunning long legs and a figure that Athena's namesake, the goddess of war and strategy, would have been envious of.

It was funny that in uniform, they really did look like sisters, although Jessica was slightly more well-endowed.

It was ironic, especially under the present circumstances, that Jessica's interactions with her colleagues held more integrity than those who claimed to uphold the traditions of the service.

"I won this bottle on the Klava station, a whole case in fact." Jessica smiled for the first time since they had started talking, the smile carried the memory and the pride of the victory in it as she continued their conversation.

"That's right, you were playing 'red loca' and the guy was cheating but you still beat him."

"And then he tried to start a fight..."

"And you pulled your gun on him. He backed off pretty quickly after that."

"Until the next day when he and his goons tried to corner me at the docks. I had to get away quickly and the only choice that presented itself was their light frigate."

"I remember watching that depart, it got so many violations I'm still surprised that the patrols didn't try to shoot it down. How did you escape again?" Melissa's eyebrows raised as the memory came back.

"I locked myself in the cockpit, guided it out into open space and set the computer to jump. They figured out what I was doing and tried to stop the jump by disabling the core reactor."

"But how did you know there was a secret passage from the cockpit to the hangar?"

"I spent some time on that class of ship as a kid with my parents... So, I stole a fighter and launched before the ship jumped."

"Didn't their core go critical?" Melissa furrowed her brow, recalling the details.

"Just as I hit the afterburners and got out of there," Jessica agreed, another smile of victory touched her lips.

Melissa shook her head; she loved hearing this story.

"It just so happened that there were a couple cases of loot in the fighter's cargo bay."

"You nearly got kicked out for that. How many times have you 'nearly' got kicked out?"

"One too many now," Jessica hissed. Melissa's smile dropped. Oh, back to that, the whole reason they were in Jessica's room in the first place.

"Hmmm…" Melissa took a sip of her drink. "How the hell did you get this on board though? I thought everything in the fighter was checked."

"Well, not all of it made it to my cabin."

Melissa laughed, her eyebrows raising. "Who?"

"The Chief."

Melissa smiled, her shock plain on her face; for the life of her she didn't know why she had never asked her friend that before.

With a big smile on her face, she clinked her glass with Jessica's, shifting back to lean on the wall along the length of the bed, careful to keep her boots off the bedding.

"We made a great team."

"Yeah, I can't believe that I had to join the Navy to find the sister I always wanted."

"At least you'll still be in the service." I will probably have to sell my soul to some greasy, little cargo merchant to keep flying.

"It's not going to come to that. There's still time, something might just happen."

"You're so sure of that?" Jessica's question was more of a statement.

"No more than you were on the moon of Ka'raz."

"That was different."

"How?" Melissa countered.

She could relive those moments in an instant if she closed her eyes, as the billowing clouds of dust that enshrouded the lonely fighter as the visibility fluctuated with each gust of wind.

There were moments when she couldn't even see her fighter, even though the was touching it.

She had looked at her craft, its paintwork was already getting dirty in the blowing storm.

How the hell had she managed to land in this?

Alarms had distracted her from the surroundings as she looked down at the environmental screen on her flight suit. Oxygen was venting from her suit from some unknown location. Assessing the rate of loss, she knew that she would run out of oxygen long before the rescue bird arrived.

So too could she remember the feeling of hope when she saw the patchy shadow of Jessica's aircraft coming in to land and the sense of failure, knowing that the two of them couldn't escape in the one vessel. She hadn't wanted her friend to watch her die, she couldn't bear the thought of that...

Melissa snapped back to reality. Jessica was watching her with a keen, intense stare, no detail escaping her eyes. Their eyes met and Icca smiled; she knew what Melissa had been thinking about. The conversation carried on, covering various experiences they had together, however Melissa's mind was still working for a solution in the background.

Just as much as she knew that Jessica had never had a plan when she had landed on that forsaken planet or opened up the engine compartment of Melissa's aircraft. She knew there was only blind luck that could save her friend now. Yet, somehow, she was sure that the stars would align and Jessica would plague the Captain's temper for far longer than two days.

Jessica held up the bottle again in an unspoken question. Melissa nodded and handed her tumbler across. While Jessica poured, Melissa got up and undid her boots, pulling them off and placing them at the foot of Jessica's bed. She sat back against the wall and rested her head, staring at the ceiling, lost for direction.

As Jessica swung in her chair to face her, the flash of her sparkling toenail polish caught the light.

"You're still wearing that nail polish?"

"Yep, just like you said when you gave it to me, what they don't see, they can't tell me off for."

Melissa smiled. She raised her glass and took a sip – that conversation had been after yet another strip had been torn off Jessica. They had been roommates in flight school at that point, it had been the first time they had really spoken to each other. Before that they had been two people with the same goal sharing sleeping quarters: after that, they had been inseparable and unbeatable as a team.

Melissa sipped her drink again while Jessica, in contrast, downed the whole shot in one go, throwing her head back, her hair cascading down her back in the movement. She held the back of her hand to her lips as she swallowed, empty glass angled between forefinger and thumb, before setting it down and her gaze settled on the coloured liquid in the decanter.

"I'll have to leave the bottle with you, so you'll have to promise to remember me when you drink it."

"It wouldn't be the same without you."

The two friends looked at each other.

"This just isn't right!" Melissa said forcefully after the silence of their own thoughts had dragged out. "You've probably saved more lives by showing up that stupid manoeuvre than you could have if you had shot down everyone on the tail of the whole squadron."

Jessica just looked at Melissa. She had been thinking about the same thing – the irony about proving that the manoeuvre designed by Group Captain Walter Burke was not only incompetent, but dangerous was the final straw for her getting kicked out of the Navy.

"Don't you think the High Command will have something to say about you being discharged after that fiasco?"

"The Captain hasn't made it about this event so that they cannot intervene. It's a totally unrelated situation, it just so happens that it happened exactly after this catastrophe."

Their conversation continued, heading away from what the Captain had done, recounting happier times from training at the Academy.

*****

Melissa came out of the bathroom and glanced over at the bed. They had been talking for most of the night and now, Jessica lay asleep face down on her black sheets, her head turned away towards the wall. She was still dressed as before in her black t-shirt, the training squadron insignia between the two wings across her shoulders. Her legs were sprawled across the one side of the bed, the black sheet up to her waist, leaving one leg exposed from the knee down, her skin pale against the darker material.

Melissa watched her friend sleep for a while thinking about the past and the future.

Jessica had saved her life during combat training. Without her, she would not be here today, that was the simple truth of it. She watched the peaceful figure stir slightly on the bed before settling again.

A private moment of worry came into her heart. What if she was wrong? What if this really was the end of Jessica's service career?

She thought about the possibility of resigning her commission if Jessica did leave. It would take months before it came through and if they were deployed during that time, she would have to serve out the patrol before being able to leave. She could be gone for years.

There was of course her own career to think about. If she left, her family line and tradition would be gone, she could just imagine her father's reaction. The scandal would explode, and she would be pursued until her father's people could bring her back home.

What would her mother think, she wondered?

Toying with the idea back and forth, she knew not what she would do, but letting Jessica leave by herself was not an option she wanted to entertain.

Melissa moved her uniform jacket from the bed and hung it over the back of the chair, straightening, she ran her hand through her hair, tiredness dulled her thoughts, she needed to sleep but her mind would just not accept that she was going to lose Jessica from her life.

She walked slowly across to the bed and sat down. Jessica shifted rolling over towards her, her dark, walnut hair fanning out across the pillow, blending into the glossy blackness of the pillowcase in the room's twilight gloom.

Running her hand through her own hair again, Melissa stretched, looking down at her friend. She admired how Jessica kept her hair long, somehow getting away with not maintaining the regulation length saying that her father had like it that way, but until she got posted to the *Yucatan*, it had never been a problem. Jessica had gotten away with it. Although male and female officers alike had tried to reprimand her, they never succeeded. Even the Captain's dogged criticism and belittling had not caused Jessica to shorten it.

It had been a world apart from training when they had arrived onboard the *Yucatan*, from the very first moment. Gone was any encouragement.

Swinging her legs up onto the bed, Melissa momentarily thought about taking her trousers off as she pulled her t-shirt down around her midriff.

Her head hit the pillow before she reached a decision, eyes closing as sleep claimed her.

***

The world around Melissa exploded in motion, adrenaline pumped into her body as her heart rate shot up. She was vaguely aware of commotion above her, the bed still undulating beneath.

Her eyes snapped open and she rolled over, pushing herself up on one arm. She hadn't slept nearly enough and could feel a dull headache behind her eyes.

Jessica was by the desk already, pulling on her trousers. Melissa's tired dulled brain refusing to respond. The cabin erupted in red pulsing light as the alarms sounded, beating everyone to general quarters, galvanising Melissa into action, finally. Swinging her legs off the bed, Melissa sat up in one easy motion, reaching for her boots from under the bed. She briefly considered grabbing her bra from where she had left it the night before when she had made herself more comfortable, but rejected the idea, there was no time to waste.

"ALL HANDS TO DEFENCE STATIONS. PREP FOR SLIP-SPACE JUMP."

"What do you think this is?"

Jessica looked up from lacing her boots. "I have no idea. Let's go to the hangar and find out."

Pulling the knot tight on the second boot, Melissa catapulted herself into a run from the bed. Jessica's lithe figure slipped out the door and Melissa followed close behind, her hand slapping the security lock as she went. The door slid shut behind her receding back.

Dodging between the other people, Melissa followed the black shirt of Jessica, aware of those in the corridor turning to watch the two young officers. She could feel her figure bouncing unrestrained under the t-shirt as she ran and knew they must be putting on quite the show, but with her state of tiredness, she couldn't care less.

Ducking through one of the doorways, they ran onto the flight deck. Straying wide as they rounded one fighter into the flight lane, the scene opened up before them. It seemed as thought nearly every fighter pilot and mechanic was there, the large crowd milling around one of the havoc fighters with the senior Wing Leaders standing on the fighter about to address everyone.

As they drew nearer, Melissa could hear the murmur of excitement in the crowd. Still the crowd grew as more pilots were still joining them as the Wing Leader began.

"LISTEN UP! Command has just ordered us to join Admiral Fraser's new task force. This time tomorrow, we are on our way to the war in earnest. Those with shore leave can forget it for the time being...."

The guy next to Melissa gave a load groan, his baritone joining several other choruses echoing in the group.

"… I know it has been a long patrol with little excitement, but if the intel is right about this one, we will be the spearhead to invasion." Melissa felt her heart start racing as adrenaline started flooding her system. Butterflies churned her stomach as the realisation of the future hit home: this was what she had hoped for, a chance for a 'change' that would keep Jessica on board the *Yucatan*.

"I don't need to tell you what is expected of you..." she could feel the swell in her chest, her training, her purpose coming to the forefront of her being.

"... after we make the next jump, it will be radio silence from then on. DISMISSED!"

Melissa realised that she had stopped listening, her own thoughts taking precedence. The group started to break up into individual conversations, noise erupted in the hangar deck.

Turning to Jessica, Melissa started talking only to realise she was alone. Looking around, she couldn't see her friend anywhere, having been focussed on the immediate while the Wing Leader had been speaking. Jessica had weaved her way forward through the crowd ever since they had got there in order to catch the Wing Leader when he finished.

Melissa looked around through the throng of people and thought she could see her much closer to the havoc fighter and it looked like she was in conversation with the Wing Leader.

She ducked as one guy next to her turned around, his arms spread out as he made some proclamation at the top of his lungs while she tried to slip through the mass of people to get to Jessica.

She reached them just in time to hear the Wing Leader say, "Who knows, you may even save my life one day, breaking more rules than have been written, no doubt."

"Yes, sir, thank you, sir." Jessica's evident confusion over whether that was a compliment sounded in her voice, but the Wing Leader didn't elaborate.

"You fly until either you die or the Captain finds something else to court-martial you for."

Melissa shoved another guy away who was pushing into her with his back, turning back to Jessica, she heard the Wing Leader finish, "... no matter how much he'll hate it."

Jessica saluted, but the Wing Leader had already turned away, his attention on something else.

"You lucky she-devil, Icca. I told you things could change."

"Yeah, saved by the war," Melissa laughed at Jessica's sarcasm. "Are you sure you didn't send a false signal to High Command for me?"

"I wish I had thought of that," Melissa said.

"I'm going to tidy up. We're about to go to war and I don't even have a bra on."

They turned to leave the crowd, Melissa high on euphoria about her best friend getting to stay in the Navy. A rather rash decision formed and took hold in her mind as they walked away from the crowd in the hangar.

"You know what we should do?"

"What?" Jessica shook her head, her long hair bouncing with the movement.

"Get a tattoo together."

Melissa carried on, turning to look back at her friend who had stopped abruptly.

"Since when did you get so crazy?"

"I don't know. I met this crazy pilot who is like a sister. She taught me to really live."

"So, what shall we get?"

"What did Jethro call us in the Academy?"

"The Valkyrie sisters."

"So, how about some Valkyrie wings?"

"Sisters to the end, huh?"

"You bet."

They headed off, leaving the noise and excitement behind them as they made for the lower decks, enacting their rather rash decision straight away – both aware that neither one would go through with it if they left if for another day.

***

Waking inside her cabin, Melissa could feel her shirt shifting against the raw skin on her back. It had been three days since she had gotten the tattoo done and it didn't feel as if it was healing very quickly. The K2 the artist had poured over her back had burned way worse than she had thought possible, and even felt its searing heat again from time to time.

She still couldn't believe she had actually gone ahead and gotten a tattoo. Why did she think it was a good idea? And the design, what would her mother think? She could hardly blame Icca as it had been her very own idea which still baffled her. The size had been Jessica's fault though, of which she had followed through without thinking.

She rose slowly from where she sat on the bed and headed for the bathroom, lifting her shirt painfully over her head.

Turning, she examined what she could see of the tattoo in the mirror, reminiscing about the events that day. The design process had been fun and exciting in a nervous kind of way.

It had been as though she were designing a piece of art to hang on the wall of her cabin, not something that would be etched into her skin permanently; her nerves falling away until it came time to go through with the tattoo.

The design was intricate, and had come out beautifully on her back, but she could still feel that pause in her breathing as she walked into the room with the artist after adding the personal touches to her design while Jessica had been under the laser, especially after they had discussed where they would get the tattoo and how large it would be while on their walk to the parlour.

It was meant to be in between their shoulder blades, but high up at the base of the neck.

The detail in the design had been phenomenal and when Jessica had finally been satisfied, they had gone into the room where the tattoo would be administered. Jessica removing her shirt as she lay down, chucking it to Melissa who had then returned to the artist's station to personalise her design before the process had begun.

She had changed a few things. For one, the central Spartan helmet had the word 'Icca' forming the central nose guard. In the visor of Jessica's helmet there was a tri-engine dragonfly precariously perched on sandstone rocks, while in Melissa's visor another dragonfly was approaching out of a swirling dust cloud. The reflected sun illuminated the background, with the bluish-purple glow from the engines forming a halo around the training fighter, memorialising the scene that had saved Melissa's life.

She, too, had added the sparrow to her design, flying as if circling the blade of the upheld sword.

The real difference had been the central figure. She had gotten the artist to model the Valkyrie on Jessica herself. He had pulled up her biometrics and service record on the system and customised the woman to be similar, but not unmistakable as Athena.

Without thinking, Melissa had said she wanted it to have the same placement as Jessica's, and after the alterations, she had gone into the room to get started.

It wasn't until after she had seen Jessica laying there that she had realised the scale of the tattoo. That hollow pause within her as she made a quick decision. She had asked the artist to tweak the length of the wings to fit within the width of her shoulder blades instead of wrapping around her deltoids as they did on Jessica. Given time to think about it, Melissa didn't think either one of them would have gone through with the tattoo idea, but Jessica had been captivated by it, magnified by the possibility of leaving the Navy temporarily being laid to rest. Melissa had been caught up in the tide of events, but in a way, she was glad she had gone through with it after Jessica had. They now shared something that symbolised their friendship that no one could take away from them.

Checking to see that she had enough balm left, she contemplated whether to have a shower now or leave it until Jessica came, so she could help with re-applying the balm.

Deciding against putting her shirt back on, Melissa turned the water on and ran her hand under it.

The water burned on her tattooed skin when she stepped under it. The cool temperature lessened the sensation a little, but in spite of that she felt as though the water droplets exploded one by one onto her raw skin as they fell.

Reaching for her towel as she stepped out of the shower, drying herself, she towelled her hair dry – the regulation shoulder-length haircut would dry easy enough after that.

No matter how long she had her hair the mandatory length, she could not get used to it; it made her look much younger than she was.

Whilst at flight Academy, she had to put up with a lot of jokes, but even now she found people still treated her as though she was inexperienced for her role as an officer and fighter pilot.

Those in her squadron had gotten used to it, but they still treated her as a young woman, a junior member of the crew, rather than a lieutenant in the Alliance Navy.

She missed having long hair as she had as a girl, but she wasn't carefree enough to wear her hair long again, like Jessica did.

Drying off her legs, Melissa hung the towel up, going to her clothing closet that was recessed into the wall of her main cabin. Pressing a button on the wall, a panel slid sideways with a hiss, revealing her uniform and flight suits. Other clothing items were stacked on shelves to one side. Selecting a tight pair of black underwear shorts, she pulled them on and returned to the washroom to apply as much balm as she could manage before laying down on her stomach on the bed to let it absorb.

She had been an avid reader before joining the Navy, but flight training hadn't left much time for a consuming hobby like that. It had all been training manuals and aircraft documents, strategy and psychology. So now she read as often as she could.

She propped herself up on her pillow and leaned her data pad against the wall.

She read for a while, eventually getting up to put on the under-layer of her flight suit as by now, the balm had been mostly absorbed. She was not in the habit of walking around in her present state of undress, not even in the seclusion of her own cabin. However, as the tattoo needed time to heal, she pulled on the lower half of her under-suit only, wrapping the arms around her waist to leave her back, and her raw, etched skin, exposed.

Just then, the door in the anteroom opened and Jessica walked in.

They were going to go over some fighter drills and tactics together, revising those from flight school that the Captain wouldn't allow from pilots on board his ship.

Turning away and covering herself with her arms, she greeted Jessica from over her shoulder. Jessica went passed her into the washroom and returned with the balm.

"Lay down, I'll do your back," Icca commanded as she nodded towards the bed.

They had helped each other with the reapplication of the balm over the areas they could not reach in the middle of the back over the last few days.

***

Melissa ran her hand through her hair, giving herself a basic scalp massage as she tossed her hair while she looked in her mirror. Neither of the two jumps in slip-space had been for that long as journeys went, but it had been long enough for her and Jessica to get into the simulator on several occasions to practise. They took advantage of the times when few of the other pilots seemed interested and had flown in multiple combat scenarios over the sessions with ever increasingly hard and challenging dogfights.

Now, as she grabbed her uniform jacket before heading to the viewing deck, the Captain's recently re-enforced squadron was nearing their destination, the rendezvous with Admiral's Fraser's fleet.

Jessica had asked if she wanted to watch their arrival from the viewing deck together: Melissa pulled on her jacket, her shirt still dragging on her tattoo like sandpaper, as she slipped out of her room heading to the top deck of the Heavy Cruiser.

The double doors slid open, revealing the colourful world of slip-space; Jessica stood by the curved bay window framed by the ever-changing background that enveloped the ship.

Entering, Melissa called out her greeting, but Icca didn't respond. Melissa knew that her friend was still worried about her future, her fate undecided once they reached Admiral Fraser's fleet. Transfer was still possible as their length of orbit was unknown and Fraser's decision unpredictable, she knew it had been playing on Icca's mind for some time now, although Melissa had done what she could to distract her from her worries.

Admiral Fraser had a reputation of legendary status in the GTSC, his accomplishments during the War of Ascension made him a first-class fighter pilot and tactician; however Melissa didn't know enough about him to be able to reassure her friend on this matter. He was a wild card, his dealings with two Captains previously had shocked the GTSC when he had court martialed them, and yet he had been lenient to another whom had crashed a destroyer in a training exercise.

Crossing the room to the large, curved bay windows, Melissa tried again.

"You OK?"

Jessica turned to look at her, her eyes distant, lost in thought.

"You wondering about what will happen when we rendezvous with Admiral Fraser?"

Jessica nodded. She knew that Melissa understood.

Melissa understood, really understood and smiled, changing the subject she asked: "Just like at the Academy, first on the parade ground." Melissa came across to where Jessica stood. "How are you adjusting to the tattoo?"

"I still can't believe we went through with it."

"I especially can't believe that I was the one to suggest it," Melissa breathed out a big sigh, "What will my mother say?"

"I know, right? We're fully trained fighter pilots, and yet we're still scared of what our mothers will think," Jessica smiled.

"That'll probably never change."

Silence fell between them as they stared out into the unreadable future.

The tannoy blared, interrupting their thoughts.

"All hands, stand by to exit slip-space."

Melissa felt the engine pitch change as the soft thrumming whistle of the hyper cores came to an end. The spiralling world unwrapped like watching giant petals unfolding from a multi coloured flower. For an instant, Melissa felt as though they were moving backwards, the deceleration and changing visuals messing with her senses for a moment before she could reorientate as the stars and planet sprang into view.

Before them lay a force of warships that was impressive by the sheer magnitude of power; the centre was dominated by the large bulk of the grand constellation class battleship GTSC *Pegasus* as it towered over those ships closest to it. Melissa examined the columns of ships;

she could see evident gaps in the formation that looked strategically placed for the new arrivals.

She had heard that Admiral Fraser liked to organise his fleet in a way that the fleet could work as a whole as opposed to the more traditional strategy of allowing the individual squadrons work together, forming a fleet by sheer numbers. He must have had a good reason for his decision, but no doubt Captain Allers would contest it as soon as he could gain an audience with the Admiral. The Captain hated any potential threat to his power, even if that power was temporary in nature.

One other important thing she noticed was that the fleet looked as though they were impatiently waiting to leave. The newcomers would have just enough time to load the last stores on board before they moved out. She could see the glow lighting the engine cores. Yes, someone was very impatient to be underway.

Melissa examined the formation as the squadron split up into their new positions. The fleet looked like it had been thrown together with haste. Whilst its combined firepower would be formidable, it looked as though it had been assembled out of some forlorn hope for testing the strength of the enemy forces and trying to punch a hole through the front lines for others to follow.

The last of the supply ships waited just outside the fleet. It seemed evident that their squadron was the last to arrive at the staging ground for war, the next time they jumped would be the last for many of them.

Traversing all that had come, Melissa's mind had jumped forwards to the battle that lay ahead. She was imagining what it was going to be like flying along the length of the flagship while all its guns were firing.

It had been some time since they had been in formation with any warship larger than the GTSC *Yucatan*.

The tannoy broke her line of thought as a message sounded, "Lieutenant Wind-Hawk, report to the bridge." Melissa looked at Jessica who was staring at the speaker as though she was expecting more to follow. She had no idea how her friend must be feeling, but she felt like a war hammer had just dropped on her, the sting of the tattoo all the more apparent now as it felt like her shirt was sticking to an open wound.

"Better go see what that's about," Melissa said, catching Icca's arm as she tried to head for the door, Jessica spinning around from the force to face Melissa.

"It's going to be OK. You wouldn't have gotten this far only to be court-martialled now. Look at the level of preparation! The fleet is ready to depart!"

"Let's go see, shall we?" Icca said.

Melissa nodded, she knew her friend and at times of deep worry or sadness she closed up. This was her way of asking for support without wanting to expose just how vulnerable she felt, even though Melissa could read it as plain as day in her expression.

At a time of great display for a ship of war, it was odd for the Captain to be absent from the bridge; and that's exactly what Melissa was aware of as she stood behind Icca in the doorway to the command nerve centre of the heavy warship.

There was a general air of efficient professionalism as the Heavy Cruiser drew into the final position in the formation next to the flagship.

Something of critical importance must have taken him away.

She had felt her heart lift. There was no way the Captain would let someone else have the pleasure of sentencing Jessica which meant that she was most likely still in the clear, for now at least.

"Lieutenant!" The XO called from where he stood next to the navigation command across the bridge; Melissa followed as Jessica weaved through the command terminals. She watched the XO as he stood with his back to them; his posture one of relaxed power, knowing that for the time being, he was the most powerful person on board the ship, but his folded arms and the way he held his shoulders, told Melissa that he was also very aware of the huge responsibilities such power holds.

She had never had the same impression about the Captain on the several occasions that she had been in his presence. His had always been a bravado that demanded complete attention, rather than admitting to his responsibility and role as a leader. The Captain's power was for his own glory alone.

As they drew closer, the XO glanced back over one shoulder at them, but still not turning to face them yet. In their whole time on board, Melissa had never really got a read on the XO. All she knew was that he had come from a naval family like hers, but she did understand one important thing: to survive as long as he had, he must hold the Captain's favour, but he had never been outwardly hostile to Jessica despite the favour bestowed upon him.

"Lieutenant, you have been ordered to report on board the *Pegasus*," he remarked as he held up one hand to stifle any protests or questions.

Melissa's attention was divided. She partly listened to what the XO was saying, but also examined the navigation screens behind the XO. She could see their position and the fleet's telemetry mapped out on the screen. A single transport shuttle's IFF separated from the side of the *Yucatan*, heading away in a curved path heading for the flagship.

Melissa turned her head to watch out the great front windows, she didn't have long to wait before the blue glow from the twin-engine cores scored its path across the blackness of space.

She existed in two worlds at once; one being focused on the *Yucatan*, gaining as much information as possible from all the screens and command units, but also watching the shuttle, so small now, as it tracked its way to the flagship; the other was focused intently on the XO and learning the fate of her friend.

She had never experienced anything like it before, but she soaked up information like a sponge.

The XO was telling Jessica that the Admiral had sent orders for her to report to him as soon as the *Yucatan* was on station.

Jessica had become very still at that point and as the XO kept talking, Melissa knew that Icca's heart rate was pounding like a war drum.

Her own reaction was yet one of puzzlement: it was unlikely an Admiral would waste his time confronting a junior officer if he'd already made a decision to court-martial them. That task would be delegated to a shore-based panel, so what was going on?

***

Melissa hefted another box onto the growing stack filling the ammunition locker room. She had been working in the hangar ever since Jessica departed for the flagship, that had been three hours ago.

"Chief!" She called across the bustling flight deck, "where do you want all these boxes?" Melissa waved her arm at the growing tower of boxes that was leaning against one stanchion.

"In the munitions locker."

"It's almost full!"

"Against the back wall then."

Melissa watched as another supply shuttle flew in high above their heads. The hangar was running out of room, as no doubt, were the rest of the hangar bays and all the storage spaces in the ship.

Supply vessels had been swarming around the new arrivals like bees around their queen: they were packing in so many new stores, it felt as if the ship was going on a campaign deep into uncharted space, rather than preparing for the next advance.

Pushing a stack of crates into place against the wall, Melissa stood up, "Thank you, Corporal," she said, wiping her hands together.

The deckhand nodded, already heading for his next task. Melissa pulled her black shirt away from her body. It was hot working in the hangar, even with the extractor fans going. The heat blasting from the supply ships' engines as they continually worked only added to furnace the situation, and they had been at it for hours now.

Neither Melissa nor Jessica had been on board a major warship preparing for a campaign before: there was an electrifying atmosphere she had never felt before, the prospect of real action was exhilarating.

Engines on low power echoed throughout the hangar, Melissa looked up as yet another shuttle glided passed. She thought about the other shuttle that had come in to land about an hour earlier, it had swung around, positioning to land and she had stopped to watch it, wondering if it was Jessica, but it wasn't.

The brief moment of excitement that had risen was soon crushed as the door had opened and the Captain had disembarked. His gaze swept across the activity on deck until his cold glare settled on Melissa. Anger flared in his eyes before he deliberately turned his head away, ignoring her completely. The Captain climbed down from the shuttle and onto the deck. The OOW had saluted him, but the Captain had only given a flap of his hand as he walked away.

That was really weird! What had just happened? Melissa thought, she had never seen the Captain being that openly hostile in public before, he was acting like a petulant child.

But what had happened to Jessica? She had been gone for a good length of time now.

The encounter with the Captain had shaken Melissa to the core. His meeting with the Admiral evidently hadn't gone the way he had wanted it to. No doubt Jessica would bear the brunt of his displeasure upon her return.

***

When Jessica eventually did return, the two of them had hugged on the hangar deck before going back to her cabin for her to get changed, then they headed for the viewing deck.

Melissa stood, leaning on the railing, looking out into the vast panorama of space; the lines of the fleet almost at odds with the planet behind: the colours of the landmass lit in the sun, the curve of the planet dropping away into night. There was a lot playing on her mind, but she allowed her focus to drift and sort itself out.

"Are you OK?" Jessica's voice cut into her floating, disconnected thoughts, pulling her out of her reverie.

"Yeah, why?"

"Your hand was cold," Jessica sounded concerned, but there was something else in the question. Melissa had the faint shadow that there was something important she had just thought of, but because of the interruption, she couldn't pinpoint it.

"No, I'm fine, see?" Melissa touched Jessica's hand. Her mind racing with trying to find that thought again, but then she noticed Jessica watching her.

Melissa smiled, "What?"

"Nothing," Jessica shook her head and looked out the window again.

Melissa turned to the window as well, but like a dream after waking, her previous thoughts remained illusively out of reach, vanishing every time her mind tried to pinpoint it.

"Let's go to the simulators, get as much practice in as we can before we get there. This is everything we have been training for since joining the Academy."

Melissa paused before nodding; she took a deep breath. Icca was right, they were going to a very different scale of war, one that they had not seen before. Practice was definitely a good idea, but her friend's training regime was going to prepare her in a way that would keep her breathing long after others ceased. "You're right. It shouldn't be any different from chasing those enemy scouts on our patrols when we joined the conflict on Thermopylae prime, but every bit helps."

***

One week later

Launching through the archway into the hangar, Melissa sprinted for her fighter as the alarms continued to sound, the hangar deck jumping underfoot with each new impact sustained by the Heavy Cruiser. It was like trying to run across moving sands.

She had drawn ahead of Jessica, dashing towards the next fighter bay along. The deck lurched again, sending Melissa sprawling across the hard metal, her body rebounding off the flat surface as it heaved beneath her. She tucked her arms in and allowed herself to roll with the motion of the *Yucatan*.

As it subsided, Melissa lay on her back, staring at the metal gangway one story above her. She rolled over and pushed herself up with her arms, her senses dazed from the suddenness of the shock.

Clarity came back to her as she recovered, the thrum of engines thundered through the bay to her right as they burst into life. Jessica's fighter came alive like a bird of prey awakening, the smell of blood in the air. Heat blasted through the fighter bay, filling the air with the sweetly acrid stench of burning plasma that wafted over her as the engines warmed; a fine cloud of soot billowed in ever-shifting black and blue clouds. The rich tang of burned plasma filled her senses and it electrified her just like it had that first day at the naval airbase as a kid, standing by the railings looking out over the landing pad, the wind blowing the faint bluish plume from the landing fighter towards where she stood with her family.

Jumping to her feet, she covered the remaining distance, vaulting up onto the wing in one easy leap.

Her flight engineer appeared beside her as she settled into her seat, lifting her shoulder harness over her and handing her the buckles as he grabbed her helmet while she snapped the harness in place.

It was a routine they had practiced so many times over the last year and it worked seamlessly, as her engineer jumped down from the wing in a matter of seconds. He gave one last sweeping glance over the fighter, checking the ordinance was all secured and, seeing it was, he gave her the thumbs up. Melissa thumbed the switch and the fighter came alive under her. It rose from where it stood and shivered in the hover like an animal seized by adrenaline before a hunt.

All of the fighter's systems came alive, screens alight with an array of colours as the aircraft ran through its diagnostics.

Jessica's fighter was moving out of its fighter bay already. Melissa looked across, their eyes met for an instant, then Jessica was gone, the large vessel gliding forward as though it was a bird of prey, born for the hunt. It looked magnificent, the sight of which she would never forget. There had been so much in that one glance, a bond only sisters could share, now to stand the test of war.

The blue plasma from the engines burned white-hot as the temperature rose. Iridescent blue ion clouds billowed in the heat emanating from the engines as Jessica had throttled up. Chills ran through Melissa, goose bumps forming over her whole body as the scene unfolded before her. She watched the fighter enter the flight lane, lifting higher, turning as it picked up speed, the high bypass Hyperion plasma cores accelerating it effortlessly while the speed was exaggerated in the close confines of the hangar superstructure.

Watching the fighter go past, Melissa eased her own out into the open 'ready' area in front of her bay. Other fighters along the hangar were starting up and getting ready to launch. She looked down the length of the flight deck, Jessica's fighter was travelling at real speed now and had almost reached the giant plasma shield that covered the mouth of the hangar with a glimmering iridescent aqua blue wall. Her engines burned bright blue with purple tongues reaching back as the pilot boosted power, while the jets left traces of black smoke as the oil burned off to the optimum lubrication. From the corner of her eye, Melissa saw the Squadron Leader climbing onto the wing of his fighter, face red and an ugly expression masking his features. She knew he was yet again ticked off by Jessica's disregard for his authority.

Looking around for her flight engineer, Melissa lifted from the fighter bay as he gave her a partial salute, enough to convey the message he wanted her to see.

A faint private smile touched her lips, Jessica had always managed to annoy the Squadron Leader with his constant insistence that people acknowledge his rank. As Jessica always used to recount her father's saying, '*A lion doesn't need to tell anyone its a lion.*' Just like her mother used to tell her about officers in the GTN, there are always two types, '*A leader with a title and a leader with a mantle.*' For the first time, Melissa truly understood what her mother meant.

Guiding out across the open expanse before she entered the flight lane, she suddenly felt settled, at peace in that moment, as her nerves dropped away.

The canopy was closing as she slid forward, but Melissa caught the strong tang of burned hydrocarbons from the drifting smoke. It had been one of her favourite memories about being at the naval base with her father. Seeing, hearing, and especially smelling, the fighters leaving on a patrol or training exercise had filled her with an excitement that she could hardly contain, much to her mother's disappointment, despite her also having had a long career in the GTSC.

She had longed for the day that she could fly one of those sleek machines that looked so graceful and yet so purposeful. Now, it filled her with the same excitement that built from her core with the settling aroma in the cockpit until her whole body felt alive like she had never experienced before. Today, she was joining the ranks of her past generations on both her father's and mother's lines; today, she would be tested in the fires of Ares transcendence. Her mother had cried when she had received the news of Melissa's deployment, but it had been tears of understanding, those only a mother in uniform could truly comprehend.

Turning the fighter on the spot, she could see the Squadron Leader glaring up at her as he grabbed the straps of his harness.

Never one to previously break the rules, Melissa had always been shocked by her friend's unique way of existing in the Navy. It had gotten her into so many tricky situations, but now, that touch of recklessness that Jessica always seemed to have when she flew also filled Melissa, settling on her like drifting colourful ion clouds.

Ordinarily, the Squadron Leader preferred all of his pilots to wait for his lead and then depart together, with him at the head of the tight Vic formation, but with Icca heading out to war by herself, Melissa was not about to let protocol prevent her from covering Icca's wing.

She engaged the thrusters and accelerated down the length of the flight lane, the close confines of the hangar seeming very small as it went flashing by, exaggerating the feeling of speed. She weaved slightly to keep separation from the metal stanchions, travelling not nearly as fast as her friend. Finally, she slid through the plasma shield at the end, much slower than Jessica had done, but still much faster than regulation speed. She turned towards Jessica's fighter and engaged the afterburners. She was free: free from the ship, free from the politics, free to spread her wings. Despite the pressing need for combat, Melissa once again enjoyed the same exhilaration she felt every time she left the hangar.

***

The sheer magnitude of the raging battle struck her with a surprising jolt. She knew they were going to war, but seeing the large warships pitched in battle, their powerful weapons firing constantly, while short and medium range weapons deluged the arena between, was a sight beyond her imagination.

Dogfights lit the darkness with colourful streaks of laser fire as the smaller aircraft danced with each other in the ultimate ballet of life and death.

It was both beautiful and terrible: who amongst them would catch it this day?

She spotted Jessica's fighter, the range holding constant as they matched in speed.

"Athena, on your six, closing." On the radar she could see the range decreasing as she started catching up, knowing that Jessica must have eased up a little to facilitate this.

Off to one side, the capital ships were firing upon the *Yucatan*, the heavy rounds and beam cannons targeting the grand Heavy Cruiser. Melissa watched, taking in as much as she could to understand the battlefield as best possible, hoping to glean some detail that would help her in fighting this battle.

It was hard, but she tried to block out the radio chatter as much as she could, the background filled with calls from the other fighters and bombers.

"Athena! Mila! Get your asses back into formation. NOW!" Squadron Leader Rex Barnwell roared on the radio. Melissa watched Athena's fighter, but she never turned back so Melissa continued closing on her fighter. Her correct position was on Jessica's wing; the Squadron Leader would have to wait.

The empty void ahead of her on one quarter filled with tiny pinpricks of light, their spirals building in size and colour — sixteen of them.

She recognised what they were: a squadron of enemy fighters jumping in.

"Mila, form up!" Jessica's words were unnecessary.

She would stick to Athena's tail for as long as possible.

Their war had just begun!

***

Melissa rolled away as the stream of fire tore past her cockpit; she had lost track of time; her world revolving around attacking and defending, one dogfight after another.

A GTSC marauder flashed in front of her, its rear shields lit up, frosted white as yet another enemy fighter followed hard on its tail.

Instinctively, Melissa turned to give chase, but unlike the enemy pilot, she held her fire as she closed the range. Opening up with a direct burst and launching one of her few remaining missiles, the enemy fighter exploded seconds later.

Ultimately, it was a numbers game. If they managed to shoot down more enemy fighters than were shot down from the GTSC fleet, they would win, but as she watched the marauder arc away towards another engagement, its engines streaming smoke from the punishment it had taken, she saw in the distance behind it another squadron of slip-space ruptures lighting the dark sky with diamond bright blue and white signatures. She knew that this campaign was stacked heavily in favour of the enemy forces.

Warnings sounded in her cockpit, flashing on various screens, demanding attention. Melissa pulled her fighter around, feeling the aircraft stagger with the effort and the crushing weight of the force pressed her into the seat as a missile shot passed.

Melissa hit the afterburners as she straightened out; the offending fighter that had fired the missile was coming head on. Melissa opened up, her stream of tracer lighting up the enemy fighter, flashing in the darkened canopy as it struck home just forward of the engines.

With the minutest movement of the controls, Melissa directed the shots into the cockpit and the fighter was lost, as its engines lost power and the hull drifted under the momentum of its trajectory.

More shots flashed overhead, Melissa rolled her fighter inverted and pulled through, diving into another dogfight whilst escaping from the previous one.

She had only two missiles left, and her weapons cores were starting to show high temperature readings.

It was not long now before she would have to either call for a resupply vessel or she would need to make her way back to the *Yucatan* and refit.

She had no idea where Jessica was, having been separated in the first engagement, their entire squadron broken up into individual fighters desperately trying to survive the chaos of the battle.

Seeing a flight of bombers heading for the *Yucatan*, Mila continued her turn and dived on them, rapidly closing the distance. She fired one missile at the righthand-most bomber, tearing through its shields with her guns before switching to the next, repeating the attack. Both craft exploded, one after the other, as she chewed through the shields of the third. The fourth had dived, seeking refuge as his three friends fell prey to their attacker.

Melissa wasn't put off that easily.

She followed it down, punching though its shields, however the pilot had other ideas. It rolled away, throwing off Melissa's deadly stream of fire.

Determined to launch his ordinance, the bomber pilot doggedly hung onto his mission.

Mila closed in behind it. She could see charring around the engine cones, the blackened scars and torn holes that her guns had made in its wings and body. She saw two warheads detach from the underside of the enemy bomber and speed away, streaking for the *Yucatan*.

Emotionless, unfeeling, her body cold, she depressed the firing button. Melissa raked the bomber from nose to tail, igniting the damaged engine cores, watching the bomber break up, she could see the legs and arms of the pilot flailing about as his existence ceased.

Her attention switched to the missiles that had just cleared the bomber and were rapidly diverging away from her.

She fired again, catching the closest. It ignited, blowing up and detonating the other.

The combined blast hit Melissa's fighter, forcing it up as though propelled by a giant hand, something smacked into the belly of her fighter and warnings screamed at her on all the display panels.

She needed repairs and fast.

Adding as much power as she dared, Melissa weaved her way towards the hangar, leaving the scene of chaos and death behind as she slipped past the protective blue plasma shield into the safety of the hangar, only to be greeted by another scene of chaos.

***

Hitting the afterburners, Melissa sped towards the battle once more. It was amazing how much could change in such a short time. Her attitude and thought processes had changed. She found that she was turning towards the battle without the nerves she had experienced before, viewing it in reality, grown up, taking that major step across the line, maturing into battle-hardened adulthood.

The refit hadn't taken too long initially. Melissa had grabbed something to eat while the Chief got his people working on the damaged fighter. Teams of erks were crawling over broken-down fighters, making repairs as fast as they could and cannibalising from others that were too damaged to be put back into service again.

Melissa had wanted to help as much as she could, but she also needed to rest before heading out into the battle again. The Chief had kindly, but very sternly, ordered her off his flight deck while they fixed her ride up.

The maintenance team had been fantastic, swarming over the fighter like a pack of wolves that hadn't eaten in days, tearing at a carcass in a frenzy.

"You really took a beating out there," one mechanic commented as she walked past him to go to the hangar med bay as she had been ordered to.

Heather stood in the doorway, bracing herself as the Heavy Cruiser rocked underfoot from another blast, behind her were stacks of containers that thankfully were housed in grilled crates.

When the deck righted itself underfoot, Melissa crossed quickly to the med bay.

"Ah, Mila, you're back. How long are you on board for?"

"Just a short refit, then back out."

"Eat this and come find me before you launch," Heather said, handing Melissa a bar of something wrapped in silver.

"What is it?"

"The equivalence of the last three meals you just missed. Now go get yourself sorted and report back here before you launch, Lieutenant."

By the time she returned, things had drastically changed in the hangar. Flames beat at the access way. She had to raise her hands to protect her face but the inferno was fierce as it burned around the archway.

Two other crew members came stumbling around the corner on the far side, they were junior deck crew, terror showing on their faces as they scrambled for freedom.

Shouting at them, Melissa ordered them to give her a hand, but they broke and ran. She ran to the nearest extinguisher housing and grabbed the equipment then punched in the emergency code for damage control to see and know that there was a fire in this part of the ship.

Taking the extinguisher to where the fiery tongues licked at the archway as if from a beast trying to claw its way through, Melissa started combatting the advance as best she could on her own.

"Hey, grab the hose!" a voice shouted behind her. "Sir, skip and I will use the hose, you can stand back."

Looking over her shoulder, Melissa saw two men in black t-shirts and combat trousers; they were evidently part of the soldier detachment on-board the *Yucatan* that hadn't dropped yet.

One was pulling a hose from a rack in the wall, the other was closer, yelling over the roar of the flames to be able to talk to her. She nodded at his friend wrestling with the hose, he left to help.

She kept fighting the fire until the two soldiers returned, manhandling their hose between the two of them, directing a jet towards the archway that overtook the much smaller spray from the extinguisher Melissa held. It was nearly empty anyway so she retreated, replacing it in the housing and connecting the pipes that would refill it.

Running past the opening, Melissa headed for the next extinguisher further along the corridor, but as she was passing abeam the archway an explosion detonated inside the hangar bay, flames erupted out into the hallway, almost engulfing her form. She ducked away from it, dropping to her knees and sliding along the floor diagonally into the wall. Arms raised to protect her face, she scrambled to her feet and ran.

Two extinguishers were better than one, but she didn't have the strength to hold the hose by herself under the pressure of the fire-suppressing foam jetted out with such great force. Instead, she hauled the hose out and dragged it across to where the two soldiers held their ground, laying it against the wall for when other helpers hopefully came to their assistance.

Fetching the fresh hand-held extinguisher, Melissa joined the firefight once more.

Melissa replaced the emptied cylinder in the wall for its automatic refill, then grabbed the hose. No one had come to their aid. Bracing herself against the wall, she turned on the hose. It kicked back at her and would have knocked her right over if she hadn't propped herself up against the wall to stabilise herself while she fought to control the direction of the flow.

With two hoses going, they finally started making progress and it wasn't long before the two soldiers were right by the entrance of the archway, the world of flames and smoke filling their view.

Through the thick flames and dense black smoke, Melissa could just make out figures on the far side of the fire engaged in the same desperate attempt to stop its spread.

Shutting off her hose, Melissa moved directly opposite the archway and set up again. Turning her hose on, foam jetted past the two soldiers into the thick flames. She had no idea what exactly she was aiming at, just that it was going to help in the long run.

As they beat back the furnace, the two soldiers moved into the hangar, the overhead stanchion had buckled and twisted from the intense heat, the walls blackened, adding to the smoky darkness. It was just as well the extractor fans still functioned otherwise dense acrid smoke would have been flooding the hangar and corridor and spurring on the inferno.

As the two soldiers disappeared through the opening, Melissa turned off her hose to move position again.

An explosion cut through the flames, the shockwave flattening her against the wall, knocking the hose from her hands; her hair flying as she whacked her head on the unyielding surface. Several objects slammed into the wall next to her, missing her by mere inches. She looked into the shimmering darkness. The two soldiers had not come out. As their hose snaked across the ground like a writhing snake, she grabbed the refilled hand-held extinguisher from the rack and ran into the fire enclosed space.

Smoke clouded her senses, heat beating at her face and bare arms, the whole area a shimmering hellish dreamscape. She could smell her singed hair, as the stench of seared flesh filled the darkness.

Firing off the extinguisher, she sprayed at the spreading flames that licked across the floor towards her. The two soldiers were close to one side having been cut down by more shrapnel from the explosion. The hose thrashed under the pressure as it sprayed the edge of the fire in an erratic motion.

Fighting through the fire, Melissa knelt to check on the soldiers. One was clearly dead; a large piece of metal jutted from the man's neck, blood leaking from his ears and the corners of his eyes and mouth. She moved towards the second. Looking at the flames, Melissa rolled the soldier over, her hands coming away sticky with blood. He had a pulse, although faint at best.

Throwing the extinguisher towards the door, Melissa seized the soldier's arm and belt and dragged him to the archway and the relative safety of the corridor. Laying him down against the wall, she ran to the fire station. Wrenching it open, she hit the med-evac button before turning to dash back into the blackened scene. Damage control and the medical parties would know that someone needed assistance in the hallway.

The fire continued to rage and was spreading once again. The hose bucked and kicked as it thrashed out its contents indiscriminately, almost knocking her down as she squeezed passed through the archway.

The second soldier's shirt smouldered, and Melissa could see wisps of smoke rising from him as she drew closer, the metal grill walkway above groaned, threatening to give way and collapse on top of them.

Grabbing hold of his arms, she dragged him out, his blood leaving a long trail, staining their path that mixed with the black soot from the charred hangar.

Melissa laid him down along the wall by his comrade before locating the empty fire extinguisher bottle from where she had thrown it and fitted it back in the rack to be refilled, hitting the med-evac button again while she was at it.

Turning, she faced the furnace alone once again. Plunging through the blackened archway to wrestle the firehose and take up her lone vigil from within the chaos.

***

The fire had only been burning for twenty minutes before they got it under control and started making progress in extinguishing it, but it felt like hours. The damage it had caused was incredible: the whole fighter bay was black and deformed.

The Chief watched as his men worked around the burned-out carcass.

In a sense, he thought, it was lucky that it had crashed the way it had. If the pilot had managed to turn the fighter around as he had been intending, then the fighter would have backed into the bay engines first, hiding the fire from their efforts, exposing it to the unprotected access ways and hallways that ran along the length of the back of the hangar. That would have had dire results and could have potentially cost them their ship.

Sergeant Thorn had been quick to react, sensing the danger and calling for hoses before the danger had materialised. The Chief turned away. He would recommend that the Sergeant be put forward for a decoration for his actions, going above and beyond. It would give his family something to be proud of.

Two more mechanics lay off to one side, patched up and waiting for the medics to transfer them to the sickbay, they had all been caught in the blast when the munition boxes along the stanchion had exploded.

Out of the chaos of the fighter bay emerged a familiar figure, with messy mousy hair and fire-blackened dishevelled clothing, face and arms smudged with soot, blood on her hands and wrists and smeared on her clothing. The Chief almost sighed with relief at the sight of her standing against the wall, the hose now turned off, hanging in her hands.

"Lieutenant, it's good to see you made it through that mess. Might I suggest a different door next time." A slight grin cracked his hard expression.

"Hey, Chief. What happened?" She breathily asked, exhausted from her vigil.

"That fighter had a damaged engine. Luckily, the core didn't ignite. The pilot lost it as he tried to dock, and it dived into there…" he pointed with his fingers where the aircraft had collided with the stanchion. "The engine was practically on fire as he settled, but the fuel cell exploded as the fighter rolled over."

He looked at the state Melissa was in. She had grown up since he had seen her last, the young pilot who had launched all those hours earlier now had an aura around her, one that transcended any belief that she was too young to be in this role.

"You should go clean up before getting back out there," he said as he nodded towards the battle beyond the great plasma shield at the end of the hangar where, yet another fighter came streaking in, smoke and flames trailing from two of the engines.

"How's my fighter?"

"No good just yet. I've got a team working on it. I have another that's good to go, but if you go clean up, it will give me a bit more time to apply some modifications we're adding."

"Sure thing, Chief. You got it."

She headed off, her head still spinning from the adrenaline. The clean interior of the Heavy Cruiser at odds to the scene she had just been involved with.

She stood in her shower, feeling the prickle of her skin as the sonic waves passed over her. It was not as relaxing as having a hydro shower, but it would put her into the fight quicker and that's where she was needed.

Every time she closed her eyes, she saw fighters exploding or flames licking the hangar entrance and the explosion that cut down the two soldiers. This was only the beginning, the nightmares would follow; of that, she was sure. For those lucky enough to survive long enough to have nightmares anyway. It had been the same in her father's war.

****

Subtle differences in the fighter's handling characteristics made the craft more nimble, and slightly skittish, under her control thanks to the unsanctioned improvements that the Chief had made. It felt great to fly as though she had changed to a fresh thoroughbred mid race. She even had a slightly greater weapon loadout now, but it was strange leaving the flight deck. So much had happened between leaving the battle to face dangers just as real in the sanctuary of the *Yucatan*.

Melissa seemed to have relaxed a little, maybe it was the shots the doctor had given her after she had returned to the hangar the second time. Performance-enhancing meds brought a clarity to her thoughts in a way she liked. So many things were falling into place, lessons learned solidifying into knowledge that she could draw upon.

A fighter flashed passed her being chased mercilessly by an enemy fighter that sat close on its tail. Melissa didn't even think about her reaction, she just gunned the afterburners again, opening up with her main armament. The enemy pilot would barely have had time to register the threat before the fighter exploded.

Melissa rolled away from the shrapnel and dived into another engagement.

****

Melissa's attention was diverted from the scene as a GTSC fighter spiralled across her nose, trailed by four enemy fighters in hot pursuit. Hauling the fighter over, she dived on the procession, lighting up the trailing one in a short spray of flames as her guns ripped through the shields and made short work of its armour plating.

Chasing down the procession, Melissa clawed her way from one fighter to the next until the GTN fighter was free, twisting away from a drifting segment of the GTSC *Ohio,* the bright visage of the GTSC *Cossack*'s insignia emblazoned on the side of the fighter.

The large destroyer had been in close combat with one enemy cruiser in company with the GTSC *Halifax.*

It had suffered significant damage and turned to retreat, but the enemy cruiser continued to pummel it. The *Ohio* hadn't lasted long after that.

Turning to follow the fighter that flew the squadron colours for the GTSC *Cossack*, Melissa saw out the one side of her canopy the blood-chilling sight of the GTSC *Halifax* drifting: engine cores dull as it swung end on, guns still firing, while the bulk of its hull sustained more punishment from the enemy cruiser.

The length of the destroyer swung faster as if accelerating in the turn. The enemy cruiser evidently saw the danger as well, its bow swinging away in a hasty course alteration as it took evasive action. It was not enough. The front of the *Halifax* swung around, slamming into the side of the larger vessel, crumpling the armoured plating of both warships. The side of the enemy cruiser opened up as though it were soggy cardboard rather than hardened plating of the pressure hull.

The damage was instantaneous and catastrophic; internal fires breaking out, personnel and equipment jettisoning out into space with the sudden vacuum.

The *Halifax* kept swinging around and as the prow came back into view, the fore section was missing, torn jagged metal marked where the nose had once been.

Melissa stayed on the tail of the GTSC fighter as they arced around another drifting segment of a warship. She was flying totally on instinct, her eyes fixed on the sight of the damaged destroyer as the *Halifax* began to drift down out of the line of battle, direction unsteady and wavering in its descent.

The pair of fighters came along the far side of the grand battleship, the GTSC *Pegasus*, flying up over the top and into the hellish storm once more.

There were at least three ships attacking their flagship, however the cruiser, GTSC *Attoris*, had positioned itself in front of the Admiral and took a brutal punishment for having done so.

Melissa stuck to the wing of the fighter as the two of them ducked and dived through the anti-aircraft barrage. The pilot seemed to be trying to get into an attack position, but once they had retraced the full length of the cruiser again, she was about to break off and head back into battle when they were attacked from a section of six fighters diving from above.

She turned into them straight away, but the lead fighter turned to run. It was a mistake. Five of them took up the chase, clinging to his tail. The sixth never saw what hit him. Melissa had raked his fighter on the first pass, and it went spinning out of control only to explode off to her starboard beam.

Reversing course as hard as she could, Mila took up the chase once again, working hard to clear the tail of the unknown pilot.

This time he wasn't so lucky — his fighter was badly hit before Melissa could clear his tail, but as she doggedly hung onto the last enemy fighter, she saw the friendly fighter get winged badly. Sparks and smoke poured from the one engine and stabiliser.

She poured out a torrent of laser fire, the twin streams of bright blue flashes scored a line between the two craft, the enemy fighter seemed to fly right into it as if drawn like a moth to the light. The fighter faltered and fell, its nose dropping and the engines catapulting overhead as if the pilot was trying to reverse the fighter on the spot before it disintegrated in a cloud of coloured plasma.

She could see the damaged friendly fighter approaching in a tight arc towards one of the *Pegasus'* landing bays.

Not everyone who wears the uniform of a fighter pilot is cut out for war, how many times had her father said that when recounting his stories. She turned back into the fight once again.

***

She had no idea how long it had been, but since clearing the tail of the fighter from the GTSC *Cossack* it seemed like there was a fleet of bombers launching themselves at the *Pegasus*. She hadn't seen another friendly aircraft for quite some time, it felt as though it was just her against the whole darn enemy Navy.

Bomber after bomber had set up attack runs, and time after time, she had shot down as many as she could before breaking off to chase down the warheads before they made contact with the flagship.

It vaguely reminded her of when she had been a kid, playing games on the simulations at home, each wave had a set time limit to deal with the attacking force with a short rest period between sets to rearm and reposition, only this time, there was no reset button, nor was the target just some helpless cargo ship — rather, it was a powerful warship carrying close to ten thousand people within its armoured pressure hull.

Behind her the panorama of the GTSC *Attoris* shielding the space between itself and the *Pegasus* from the bombardment would have been impressive if it were not so sad. Bright flashes of light outlined the destroyer every time another impact from the enemy vessels hit home.

It couldn't withstand much more punishment, surely?

Her thought was interrupted by a beam cannon from an unseen warship that hit the side of the destroyer, causing it to reel from the force. The powerful beam burst through the hull, shooting out the near side to the flagship, ironically sweeping aside three bombers making their next run.

The GTSC *Attoris* started drifting, its bows dropping towards the gravitational pull of the planet; engine cores going dark. The punishment didn't stop there: shot after shot smashed into the hull, ripping its corpse apart. There was no mercy in this war — it was a lesson Melissa was going to remember throughout her posting to this theatre.

The destruction of the *Attoris* seemed to make no difference to the determination of the enemy warships, they simply shifted their focus to the flagship and kept up their onslaught.

The *Pegasus* had been heavily engaged for a long time and the bombers that Melissa hadn't been able to stop had definitely caused a few extra scars that would not help the balance of this next fight.

Melissa kept up her defence along the exposed side of the *Pegasus*, but it was a losing battle that she was now caught in.

Clearing the skies of each bombing run was Mila's priority between the vicious dogfights that came with each new escorting fighter.

Rolling way from a stream of laser fire, Melissa pulled hard, turning into her attacker; this fighter pilot was more experienced than the rest, his determination to get his target was showing. She had a hard time shaking him off, but before she could, she felt the hard impact on her havoc fighter. Dark scorches appeared on her wings as his shots landed. The hammering of each blow reverberated through her rudder pedals while a string of slogging impacts punched into her engines. She felt the fighter go soggy. The top mounted engine had flamed out, too much internal damage for her to be able to reignite it.

More flashes tore past her cockpit and several hits struck her fighter. Three holes opened up in her wing and she could see the glow of circuitry and sparks flying as damaged components still tried to function.

Pitching over the aircraft's nose, Melissa allowed the fighter to slide backwards with her momentum, firing at the rapidly approaching enemy fighter. The pilot's nerve broke and he pulled up, allowing Mila to rake his fighter from nose to tail. She felt the rending crash, the fighter, all but dead, collided with the top of the vertical fin mounted on her top engine.

She didn't see the demise of the fighter, but rather from the corner of her eye, Melissa saw one bomber diving for the engines and she gave chase. If it managed to damage the engines, the proud flagship would be crippled at the mercy of the enemy fleet. None of the GTN fleet would be able to take her in tow, not in the midst of a pitched battle.

Hard on the tail of the bomber, she cleared the last of the armoured hull in time to see the throbbing glow of colour from the bright engine cones. Turning, the bomber was angling for a shot. Two of the engine cones went dark, the ship visibly slewing as the nose yawed off course.

Melissa tore a stream of fire across the bomber's path, the need to stop the pilot from launching was tensing her body as she tried with all her might to get her target first.

The bomber launched the warhead, peeling away as it did and flying straight into Melissa's shots and exploding in a sudden burst.

Switching targets, Mila opened fire on the warhead, but it was a race she was destined to lose. The heat from the remaining engine cones triggered the detonator, the explosion damaging the remaining engines, but far less than if it had struck home.

To her horror, the great bulk of the battleship dipped out of formation, changing course away from the battle. The flagship was ditching. The battle, as hard as it had been, just got a whole lot worse.

Outnumbered already, the enemy fleet had just disabled the most powerful ship of the GTN fleet.

One of the enemy battle cruisers was no more, the other streaming plumes of fire and only half the guns firing while the other battle cruiser was still locked in combat with the flagship of the GTSC.

A single broadcast seemed to momentarily silence all others. "THE *PEGASUS* IS DITCHING!" yelled one pilot, his voice battle-crazed.

Staying close to the *Pegasus*, Melissa covered its retreating stern as more bombers and even the odd overly keen fighter tried to have a go at the wounded beast.

***

Wheeling off to one side of the formation, Melissa knew that she would have to get back to the *Yucatan* as soon as possible.

It had been a joyous moment when she had heard Jessica's voice on the radio, like a angel speaking from heaven. She had pushed all thought about fellow comrades from her mind as the battle had increased in ferocity all those hours ago. *Had it really been yesterday morning that they had first engaged with the enemy fleet?* They had been in the thick of it when Melissa had last seen Icca's fighter peeling off after an enemy, five or six on her tail.

'Next to a battle lost, the saddest thing is a battle won' — the quote from history class came back as she dodged around another dead fighter. The drifting remains were all that marked the former life of another luckless pilot.

Those that survived this monumental engagement would be hard-pressed to forget it; the memories would live on far beyond the dangers of the macabre ballet of war.

Warnings screamed at her as a wall of fire lit the side of her shields, four enemy fighters had come in line abreast, seemingly from nowhere, all firing together.

Instinct kicked in and Melissa twisted into a dive, the four fighters giving chase. Between them, they kept Melissa on the defensive as she tried to outrun them. She flew as hard as she had ever flown before, her arms heavy and drained of energy, as perspiration poured down her body inside her insulating flight suit.

The five aircraft weaved and twirled, carving a passage through the battlefield; Melissa had no idea how long she had been evading her attackers. Power warnings were lighting up on her instrument panel and as good as she had flown, the enemy fighters were relentless, constantly shooting, her shields depleting and several shots were getting through, punching into her fighter's armoured wings and body.

Try as she might, it seemed impossible to shake off her attackers.

"HOORAH!" came a shout over her radio. Melissa caught a glance of her radar; Jessica was close behind the procession and one less enemy fighter lit her radar screen.

"Welcome back. If you don't mind, we could do with a hand dealing with these pests." The sarcasm in her voice was strong.

"All yours, Mila. Lead the way," came the reply from Athena, her voice light and flamboyant, totally at odds with the nature of their engagement.

Melissa dived into another swarm of fighters, Jessica close on her wing. Her mind took in small details as they flew in formation, the clean appearance of Jessica's fighter compared to the scarred wings of her own.

The ensuing dogfight was savage. Melissa threw the fighter this way and that, Athena sticking to her wing as though she could read Melissa's mind, knowing what manoeuvre was coming next until a head on attack forced them to separate.

Melissa dodged and weaved, hard on the tail of an enemy fighter, well aware of the two close behind her, but she wasn't about to let them regroup and try another attack.

As she followed closely, chewing away at the shields, she could feel her fighter behaving soggy beneath her as it refused to respond with the slick ease of earlier.

A great ball of fire surged past as one of the GTSC *Protheus*'s medium range weapons fired at the nearby enemy destroyer. Under different circumstances it might have scared her, the kind where the heart beats a million miles an hour and the throat feels hollow and limbs hardly function as the mind races to catch up, but she felt nothing but that cold sensation again. Death was waiting, stirred by the breath of war, smiling at her from the other side of the thin veil, ready to part and let her through.

"Your tail is clear!" Icca called over the radio, her voice as hard as steel. Melissa's own target ignited and blew up with a beautiful smoke circle that formed a hoop for Melissa's fighter to pass through. It erupted with the vivid flash of the jump core going critical; the rest she did not see as she and Jessica turned back towards the fight.

What seemed like a wall of laser fire struck them both broadside. Her systems and screens freezing for an instant as all the systems tried to cry for attention at once, overloading the computers and paralysing the fighter for a brief moment. It felt to Mila like a living thing, the pain virtually reaching her own nerves as well.

An entire new flight had joined the fray, taking advantage of their distraction.

Jessica turned into the attackers while Mila looked out of the fractured canopy, her fighter turning sluggishly, the soggy feeling from before replaced entirely with a lack of responsiveness.

She had enough control and sheer bloody-mindedness to persuade anyone thinking that she was an easy target to think again, but that was it. The first one that came across her bows vanished in a ball of flame as it disappeared from view.

It was taking a great deal of effort to keep her havoc fighter on an even keel, let alone launch a full offensive as she had done previously.

Realising the full extent of her situation, Melissa had to make a quick decision: leave, make a run for it, try to get back to the *Yucatan* now while she still potentially could and run the risk of being shot down as the fled, or turn and fight. The latter was death assured but running was not such a certainty. But leaving now meant resigning Jessica to her fate, outnumbered, and out gunned. *How could she run and risk her friend's life like that?*

"Head for the *Yucatan*! I'll cover you!" Jessica's voice close to a shout over the radio.

Knowing Icca was right made the decision no easier, but she turned, boosting power, asking the damaged fighter for everything it had left, one last ditch effort to make it back safely.

Ducking and diving not nearly as vigorously or as nimbly as before, Melissa made for the light blue plasma shield across the hangar entrance on the armoured side of the Heavy Cruiser and the promise of safety within. Her range decreased, but time seemed to drag. With each new attack from the enemy fighters, time seemed to slow further. She struggled to maintain control. However, the tempting safety offered by the bulk of the *Yucatan* was drawing nearer.

Even at the last, the enemy fighters nearly had her. She flew as fast as the fighter could carry her, around a dead bomber and in towards the plasma shield — one fighter hard on her tail, guns hammering while Athena dealt with another one. Melissa's shields faltering as the energy surge drew too much power, the engines winning the priority struggle.

Shot after shot slammed home into the unprotected, damaged fighter. A panel close to the front of the fighter broke free and cascaded backwards over her canopy, but the enemy fighter had tried and failed to shoot her down. The welcome plasma shield slid over her, engulfing the damaged fighter, welcoming home one of its own.

Melissa had never been more grateful to be back on board the *Yucatan*, seeing the stanchions sliding past. Her limbs started shaking uncontrollably with the sudden release from certain death, while tears ran down her cheeks as she fought to retain control of herself. To lose it now would be unforgivable.

Engaging the thrusters, she slowed the fighter for the last time, seeing the fresh damage in the hangar. Scattered entrails littered the deck. Five more fighters adorned various spaces of the flight deck and fighter bays. Two bombers lay crippled and broken against the far wall, their hulls already being pulled apart.

Fewer mechanics were present on the flight deck — a heavy price had been paid here as well. Allowing herself to absorb the sight, it sobered her to the reality of how lucky she was. Pulling herself together, she flew with every ounce of skill she had left.

Handling the fighter as best as she could, she briefly glanced at the remaining flight mechanics staring at her as she glided past. She swung the fighter, lowering it down to the deck where it dropped the last few feet, slamming into the unyielding deck, tipping over onto one short, stubby wing. Shaken by the undignified landing, Melissa had a sudden thought of fire, flipping every remaining switch off to safe, she unlatched her harness, pushing hard against the canopy that refused to open with ease. She stood up and climbed over the side, sliding down the lower wing to the flight deck where she stumbled, as her legs gave way and she collapsed in a heap, propped up against the wing.

The Chief and two other mechanics came running over, one carrying a fire extinguisher in his hand in case the fighter went up in flames.

Melissa dragged at the small ledges on the wing, pulling herself up. The Chief grabbed her elbow and helped her up the last part of the way, holding her by the upper arms, steadying her. He looked at her with visible concern in his eyes.

"Are you alright, Lieutenant?"

"Yes, Chief." He didn't seem to believe her, but took a step back, still holding her up, but relaxing his grip so that she held more of her own weight on her feet.

Pain shot up her one leg and she buckled slightly before the Chief caught her again.

"Look, Lieutenant." He nodded back at her fighter.

Not only was her canopy starred and fractured, but blood-spattered on one side.

Red speckled the far wing along with streaks reaching backwards over the control surface.

She looked with surprise. She hadn't felt like she had been hit, but she had also known of people to be in shock, feeling no pain, right up until they died.

She looked down at herself. She had definitely been hit, but how badly? Nothing to warrant this much blood spattering.

The savage scars of jagged metal from where she had been hit. She could see material caught in the torn plating.

When she pointed this out to the Chief, he grabbed a device from his work belt and zoomed in as far as the tool was capable of. Sure enough, there was part of an enemy pilot's flight suit caught in the jagged shards sticking up from her fighter's damaged wing.

"Lieutenant, you know you have guns to get rid of the other pilots. You don't have to physically fly through them," he smiled at her, softening the gruff tone in his voice. "Well, Chief! It's becoming that kind of a war."

"I sure as hell hope not."

"You'll be sending us up with bows and arrows next."

A cold, veiled smile was turned her way.

"Go get yourself cleaned up, Lieutenant. Your original fighter is back up and running so we will get that ready for you to fly."

****

The wound in Melissa's leg was nothing serious — just a piece of shrapnel from inside her cockpit. The doctor extracted it in the hallway to the med-bay, the ward overflowing with the wounded and dying.

She had not complained, rather she had been grateful to get out of there. The medical bay was not somewhere she liked hanging out. Her uncle was badly injured in the last war and she had visited him with her father and mother. It left a lasting impression on her — one she was very keen not to repeat for herself.

Heather had helped her to get to her cabin where she had a quick shower to get rid of the stress and sweat from the battle.

She wished again she could have a hydro shower, but there was not enough time and it would have soaked the dressing encasing her thigh.

Heather remained in her cabin to reapply the combat boosters for the next round of duty. She had protested when Melissa had told her that she was going to launch again, but she found it pretty hard to refuse an order from a wild pilot with the light of battle still in her eyes — that and the raging battle that threatened their survival.

Stepping out of the shower, her thigh hurt badly, aggravated by the sonic waves. She pulled on fresh black underwear and bra, heading out into the main room of her cabin, grabbing a new under layer of the flight suit from the wardrobe when Heather's voice came from behind her.

"You've got the same tattoo as Lieutenant Wind-Hawk."

"Not quite the same."

"Can I see?"

Melissa turned around, unhooking her bra to reveal the full picture.

"Nice."

Fastening the strap again, she shook out the under armour and laid it out on the bed.

Heather grabbed her arm as Melissa stumbled, her leg buckling under the pain from her weight.

"You really shouldn't be flying again, Lieutenant."

Melissa shot her a glance that stopped her protest.

"Here, let me help you."

Between the two of them, Melissa managed to get dressed in her under layer. The tight compression from the active suit was painful, but at least it helped stabilise her leg and increased her range of motion. Heather administered the combat boosters before sealing the tight layer of clothing.

Melissa could feel the energy surge beginning to work, revitalisation coursing through her body and the tiredness that she hadn't been aware of clouding her mind. She began to clear, her thoughts sharpening with a razor sharpness that she found astonishing. After a while, her leg seemed less painful as well.

Accepting Heather's help, Melissa made her way back to the hangar where she parted ways with the young medical officer.

"Good luck, Lieutenant," was the last thing she heard from Heather as she headed for her fighter bay in the hope that she would find her fighter ready to go.

She had barely crossed half the flight deck, weaving her way through the broken wreckage that now littered the hangar when she felt the deck shudder underfoot.

Guessing at what was coming next, Melissa looked for the nearest stanchion or solid object that she could hang onto.

Sure enough, the explosions could be felt through the soles of her boots with the detonation from each warhead impact. It was a tremor, a ripple under her feet, then the shockwave hit fractions of a second later. The deck lurched and heaved her off her feet, bodily slamming her into the flight deck, as she rolled with the momentum.

Catching hold of a stanchion as she slid by, Melissa swung on her arm. The dead hulk of a crashed fighter slammed into the metal support that shielded Melissa from its trajectory.

After what felt like a full minute, the Heavy Cruiser rolled back the other way as the stabilisers in the autopilot corrected the ship's spatial orientation, the angle of the deck less severe, but she held onto the stanchion, watching the chaos unfold.

As life returned to a passable normality, she rolled over and lifted herself to her feet, continuing her run towards the promised fighter that was hopefully still undamaged in her fighter bay.

***

The Chief had both arms outstretched, raised as though ready to launch into flight. His ordered world and immaculately clean hangar was now a dishevelled scene of chaos and destruction. It was the first time anyone on board had been in a battle of this magnitude and his team had done well, but the devastation was still marked by all the debris that littered the length of the hangar deck.

Behind the mechanic, who was talking to him, there was blackened scoring from where one of the damaged fighters had ditched, its guns lighting up before the pilot could react, stitching a line of laser fire across the flight lane into the wall beyond, cutting down three erks as it did. Blood still stained the walls and deck from various encounters, the worst being when two pilots had run for their fighters that had been manhandled into clear space for their launch. The two had passed behind a fighter that was being worked on to fix the engine cores.

He hadn't ever seen two men vaporise into blood and tissue before, but it was a sight he would not forget — of their entire bodies liquifying and spraying against the stanchion and across the floor. One of his mechanics had thrown up almost instantaneously and another had been so shocked, he stopped in mid tracks only to be cut down by a fighter that had been out of control.

The fight had been bloody and as bad as it had been for them, he knew that it was far worse outside.

"Chief, is my fighter ready?" Melissa called over the din of rivet guns and welding torches that sent a storm of sparks skittering across the deck.

The Chief snapped out of his reverie and looked at Melissa, his mind adjusting to the present conversation.

"I thought you were grounded?"

"How the hell would that help the situation?" Melissa limped closer.

The Chief turned back to his mechanic, "You'll have to figure it out. Get the Hyperion core from the locker and jimmy-rig it. Until we can get a team to focus on it, that'll have to do."

Nodding, the rigger walked off. He was a good officer but was crumbling under the devastating environment. The Chief didn't mind too much. With a bit of guidance, he would turn out to be a very decent mechanic after this situation — if they survived that was.

"Lieutenant, your fighter is pretty much ready, we have kitted it out like the last one, but I can't let you launch just yet."

"Why not?"

"I have three that are blocking your fighter. We need to shift them out of the way..." In that instant, they both felt the deck tilt, angling down at the bows.

It did not take a detective to put two and two together. The Captain had ordered the Heavy Cruiser to ditch after that last attack. The warheads must have done some serious damage to the ship.

"Chief..."

He looked at her but didn't answer her. "Vik, Erris! Let's get a move on it!"

"Chief!" Melissa shouted again as he turned away.

"On it, Lieutenant!"

Melissa hurried to her fighter, making sure her flight equipment was in her aircraft before taking enough time to check her fighter for serviceability.

Once satisfied, she climbed into the cockpit and got herself strapped in.

"ALL HANDS, PREPARE FOR EMERGENCY LANDING! STAND BY TO DITCH!"

"Chief! Get me in the air!" Melissa shouted from the cockpit.

"MOVE IT, PEOPLE!" the Chief shouted at his crew. Some were breaking off to find as safe a place as they could to brace for the impending impact, but there was enough of a band of faithful crew who stayed to clear the blockage that hemmed Melissa's fighter in.

"GOOD LUCK, LIEUTENANT... GO!" the Chief yelled as he swung his arm down the length of the flight lane, pointing at the closing door at the end of the hangar, the diminishing gap of the blue plasma shield reducing as the huge shield doors slid shut. "... and God speed," he finished under his breath as he watched the fighter lift. The canopy closed as Melissa swung the fighter around, boosting power and accelerating down the length of the hangar. It felt as though he was watching Athena, the wild manoeuvres precise in every element. How much Melissa had changed and matured over the last two days of hard fighting, he pondered.

***

The close proximity of the stanchions and hangar walls accentuated Melissa's speed as she boosted down the flight lane, the light blue plasma reducing at an alarming rate, it was the ultimate game of chicken for her short life. If she miscalculated, the doors would shut and her havoc fighter would slam into the unyielding armoured door and explode.

Her throttles were fully open and she was approaching attack speed, far faster than the recommended maximum for passing through the plasma shields.

Nearing the end of the hangar, Melissa did a mental calculation — she was not going to make it, nor did she have enough distance to bring the fighter to a halt in time. She hit the afterburners and felt the sudden jolt as the fighter shot forward. In space it was hardly noticeable, but here, in the enclosed confines of the ship. It felt as though she was flying dangerously close to the maximum structural limit of the airframe.

Focusing all of her shields to the forward quadrant, she punched through the pulsing blue sliver that remained. The event passed in a fraction of a second, but her mind recorded it as if in slow motion, pausing on the great lines that marked the edge of the door, where blue plasma fluctuated like jelly as the power generator nodes between the great armour plates of the door shimmered with iridescence. Great runners where the doors slid along top and bottom of the opening were marked with indented tracks.

Her fighter's shields flared blue, purple and then white as the energy absorbed the impact from hitting the plasma shield at such speed — it had the same effect as being hit with a beam cannon, her shields were wiped out and her fighter felt like it had come to a stop for a fraction of time, but then she was through, speeding away from the Heavy Cruiser. It was only then that she took note of the dense cloud that engulfed her, flames surrounded the fighter as the sense of falling became rapidly apparent.

She was no longer in space; she was falling, her exact location unknown, but presumably within the planet's atmosphere already. Maximising the shield regeneration, she turned the fighter, her HUD picking up the horizon and leveling her orientation.

The bulk of the GTSC *Yucatan* was lost in the impenetrable clouds, only its IFF signature showing on both her radar and the HUD.

With nowhere better to go, she turned towards it and hit her afterburners. She might as well see where it landed so she would know where she had to return to.

The scene she emerged into was no more heart-warming than the battle in orbit had been.

Six ships were already on the ground, clustered around a small rise that led up to a clifftop plateau, the vessels close enough together to form the beginnings of a defensive position, but still a vast distance of open ground between them.

To plot a landing as they had done while descending at terminal velocity was no easy feat. The time was minimal and the distance, apart from high altitude, was little more than decimals of a degree of difference.

From a quick assessment, Melissa noted that the first to ditch must have been the gunship sitting atop the tall cliffs from when the ground troops had been unloaded.

This being ground zero made it ironically poetic.

The *Yucatan* hit the ground hard enough that Melissa saw the shock wave pass through the upper surface of terra firma. Billowing clouds of dust and dirt mushroomed out, covering the scene from view as the massive bulk slid to a halt; that was until the disco display of laser fire illuminated the battle that raged within.

Diving on the battlescape, Melissa saw the IFF of friendly fighters streaming out of the downed ships to join those that already patrolled the sky above the crippled warships that had just become fortresses of the newest GTN beachhead.

**Jacqueline,
On board the GTSC *Queen of Hearts*, Black Ops Cruiser,
Six years, seven months before Operation *Trident*:**

Jacqueline eased the controls a fraction, as the stealth fighter glided sideways a little further. The view of the formation of ships changed in the front screen.

If a single one of the fighters in formation before her happened to turn around, she would be in a world of pain.

'Observe and scan' — that was the nature of her mission, but the 'safe' distance that she had been given was too far away. She had hardly picked up anything on the scanners and none of the information looked useful. Closing the distance, Jacqueline flew the aircraft as though it was an extension of her own body, her thoughts translating into movement without conscious effort. The stealth fighter, although still relatively new to her, having only a few hundred hours experience flying it, gelled with her as though it had been designed for her alone.

The present scan was finishing and she knew she had to depart before the situation changed. She had already pushed her luck beyond all reasonable chances, but something still held her there.

She manoeuvred the stealth fighter closer to the cruiser; something about the way the engines glowed and weapons were mounted on the side sparked her curiosity. She wanted to get closer, but knew she was increasing the risk of detection.

She set up additional scans and kept watching as the cruiser began to transform before her eyes. Large segments broke away, repositioning.

By the time she figured out what she was looking at, it was too late!

Her instincts kicked in — those of a Black Ops pilot surviving behind enemy lines for as long as she had. Reversing course, angling the scanners behind her, Jacqueline accelerated away.

As she cleared the suggested safe distance that her briefing had detailed, she reached for her boosters, preparing to jump away as three fighters jumped in, line abreast in front of her.

She had been compromised!

Putting the fighter into a spiralling dive, she flew with wild, reckless abandon, they had known she was there, expecting her to jump to safety so they could follow her.

If she could only reach the transmission distance, Jacqueline figured she'd transmit the data so that she didn't endanger the cruiser as well. She had fought and survived so many battles, becoming a key member of her squadron, and yet she knew that she was expendable.

Flying to the outer limit of her skillset, she rolled and dodged, weaving between the attacking fighters. More jump signatures lit the background. This was going to be a battle as hard as ever she had faced.

Triggering the long range encrypted transmitters, Jacqueline watched the message finish before reversing course and opening up in the first engagement of her skirmish.

She attacked with a ferocity of one doomed to play out one last macabre ballet — her epitaph would become legend. Even if her side did not know about it, the enemy would speak of this day for generations to come.

Oh, and so they would!

Boosting power, she tore through the remainder of her turn, guns hammering as the first two fighters fell before she had even got to level flight.

Charging straight for another that came head on, Jacqueline deluged the cockpit in fire, watching the fighter disintegrate. Her breathing was even, the huntress within had risen like a conquering angel spreading its wings ready to do battle, like in the stories of old, when the heroes and champions set foot on the battlefield, their swordsmanship rivalling all others. She fought with the skill of Athena, goddess of war, the cunningness of Loki and brutality of Ares — there were few in the history of the Alliance that could rival her in this battle.

***

On board the Kane class cruiser, GTSC *Queen of Hearts*, stunned consternation filled the bridge as the full extent of the message came in and was decoded.

The detailed scans were beyond the expected and the final closure of the message killed the excited chatter on the bridge.

"... make use, good luck, goodbye."

Their pilot knew she was going to die; she had sacrificed herself for their survival.

With that the Captain gave the order and the cruiser moved out of its position and angled away, gathering speed, preparing to jump.

Removing his cap, the Captain stood silently looking at the blip on the screen, the brave pilot who had just given her life for the information was swamped as more fighters swarmed around the lone GTN IFF signature.

He kept watching her, knowing he needed to tend to his ship, but he refused to leave her to her fate alone — someone had to keep watch. More IFF surrounded the lonely marker, but he also noticed that a number of enemy signatures were disappearing as well. If she were going to die this day, she was evidently going to take as many with her as she could.

Just then an entire squadron lit up the screen, their IFF indicators different to those of the enemy fighters. The Captain studied them, the information broadcast on the screen was basic at best.

"HELM BRING HER ABOUT! LAUNCH THE ALERT FIGHTERS! NAV PLOT A COURSE TO..."

The XO was by the Captain's side. "Sir, what are you doing?! She's dead, don't make the cruiser suffer the same fate."

The Captain turned back to the screen, his anger boiling over for not being able to do anything, his eyes dark as he turned back to his subordinate. He knew the XO was correct, but the futility of the situation made him seethe. Jacqueline had been one of his very best pilots too, the stealth fighter experimental based on captured designs. At least before she had a fighting chance to make her mark, now the lone IFF was swamped in enemy signatures.

***

She had been engaged for a good length of time, the stealth fighter behaving like a dream with movements sleeker than any combat vessel she'd ever flown.

Shrapnel punctured the hull as the stealth fighter punched through the cloud of remains, vivid flashes of bright colour lit her cockpit as the flames vanished.

How many did that make? Did it matter anymore? For some strange reason, to her it did. All she knew was that she had been surrounded, outnumbered, outgunned, and ordinarily speaking, outmatched, but there was nothing ordinary about the situation.

She had been engaged long enough for the secure connection with the *Queen of Hearts* to be lost, they had jumped!

She had lost count at twenty-six, her gun cameras recording for her. With no idea how long ago that was, she battled on, fighting to survive in an arena she knew there was no surviving.

Shifting targets as her quarry disintegrated, Jacqueline pressed home another attack, her arms and legs were getting tired, her flight suit drenched in sweat.

More shots skimmed low over her canopy. She turned towards her latest attacker, opening up and obliterating the enemy fighter.

Out of the corner of her eye, she saw a wall of jump signatures, diamond-bright pinpricks of blue and white light up one side of the dogfight. She was about to have company, as if her job was not hard enough already.

Four fighters dived on her as she turned, her shields misting over from the impacts of shot.

Her next attacker flashed across her nose and she opened fire, leading her target perfectly; the enemy fighter never made it past.

Angered by another of their number falling to their enemy — the lone fighter that had the audacity to attack them after trying to spy on their clandestine project. They redoubled their efforts to shoot her down.

The other squadron engaged as Jacqueline was hard on the tail of another fighter, but, to her surprise, the newcomers launched their attack on everyone — these were not friendlies to her enemy. *The enemy of my enemy is my friend*, she thought, *or at least no more of a threat than the original battle*. The divided attention afforded her enough breathing room to become even more lethal.

She attacked anyone and everyone who attacked her, every enemy fighter that crossed her nose.

Some of the new squadron attempted to take her on, but she made short work of them.

She had lost all track of time. Her gun cores were running low and her missiles had long since run out. The battle had been savage and showed no signs of abating.

The last jump signature disappeared from her screen as the final capital ship jumped away. Two squadrons of fighters remained, their comrades having either retreated or been destroyed. There was so much wreckage in the arena of open space they had been fighting in, but it was not over yet.

Jacqueline pressed home the attack with determination and a ferocity that belied the length of the battle.

It seemed the etiquette of a dogfight was to gain the upper hand and then allow the others to withdraw. Jacqueline had no such inclination. They were still outnumbered three to one, but Jacqueline attacked as though it were an even match.

The enemy numbers dwindled to just a handful, a few having escaped but the majority destroyed. As two more met an abrupt end, Jacqueline spotted the last one heading away from the dogfight, she pulled her fighter around in a savage turn, accelerating to maximum speed, she chased it down latching onto its tail just as it engaged the jump drive. The fighter levelled its course and started its acceleration run into the blue and white spiral opening up before it. Just as it was about to slip through to safety, Jacqueline's guns tore through the armour plating and hit the engine jump core as it spooled up to maximum. It exploded, mere feet from the promise held beyond that elusive slip-space spiral. The vivid flash of white as the fighter spilt apart; the engine cores going critical.

Jacqueline's fighter was thrown over onto its back from the force of the explosion. She was fighting the controls to regain level flight.

Another fighter flashed across her nose, a sudden fear rose sharply within her. She had thought she had shot down the last one!

Fighting for control with desperation, she levelled the fighter and turned towards the one she saw, it was flying a wide arc away. She turned her fighter towards it when another came alongside her, flying level, she could see it intended no threat.

The pilot visible in the cockpit as he signalled his neutrality. Getting the message Jacqueline stepped down from open combat and not a moment too soon.

Her whole body was shaking with adrenaline and fatigue.

Staying on the wing of the fighter, she followed it back to where the other fighters were forming up.

Surrounded by the remainder of the squadron, Jacqueline followed the lead aircraft. Her arms ached and heart still pounded wildly from the exertions of the dogfight, but she still had one trick up her sleeve — the stealth fighter had a self-destruct function that tied into the hyper core. If she set it, then the explosion would tear apart any warship up to the size of a medium battle station.

Having already come to terms with death, the details of how it would happen didn't really bother her anymore.

For now, she followed the lead fighter of the formation into an asteroid field, weaving between the floating masses of rock as they tumbled in the gravity field.

Jacqueline watched with fascination as the procession worked into a clearer area at the centre of the asteroid field. A fortress of a battle station was built into the side of a large central asteroid.

Towers and spires rose from a central construct, much like the castles of old back on earth.

Large gun emplacements were positioned throughout the station. Anti-aircraft batteries lined the buildings, as numerous as leaves on a tree.

It was an intricately built city, its entire purpose being war. Its guns were ready and tracking the closest targets, but the station seemed to have a shield around it, technology so far unheard of.

Surrounding a heavy warship was doable, but it took a fair amount of power. This however, was an entire battle station, the shield not only protecting it, but with enough of a clear area to facilitate a combat patrol around the station within its open space.

Jacqueline could imagine how ferocious the attack would be once enemy fighters managed to break through the outer defences. Once inside the shields, it would be a living hell of anti-aircraft fire.

She noticed floating gun platforms stationed around the installation, even hidden ones on the asteroids that she could now identify were in geostationary orbit with the fortress, pulled by some artificial gravity well.

As the formation rounded the last asteroid before beginning the approach run, Jacqueline saw a frigate entering the shields, evidently heading to a docking bay while a mid-sized cruiser was in dry dock, the clear covering exposed to the heavens, Jacqueline could see a multitude of tiny figures swarming over it. The apparent size was thrown into sharp relief. The station was huge.

She followed the leader as he led them through the maze of buildings and tunnels — each one looked a lot like the hulls of former warships and freighters, now re-purposed into the station structure, she could see the distinct differences now that she was closer up. These must be pirates, Jacqueline came to the conclusion, if that was the case, there was an outside chance she could get out of the station alive, but go where? That was a problem for later.

Coming into land in the hangar bay, Jacqueline slowed her fighter and landed where the deck crew were indicating. She saw a swarm of people massing around her fighter. There was very little time to act, her activities hidden by the darkened canopy. She activated the self-destruct function and then hid it in the framework of the fighter. If anyone tampered with the aircraft, it would detonate, she had also coded her biometrics into the unit, so if her heart stopped beating or brain signal ceased, the trigger would be set off, detonating all the engine cores with enough force to destroy the entire station.

One of the soldiers surrounding the fighter gestured for her to open the canopy. She unclipped her harness and pressed the canopy release switch, thumbing another selector that would close the fighter up once she was more than a few feet away. Once she was escorted away, no one would get in unless she was close by.

Waiting for the next instruction, she remained seated, assessing the crowd without moving her head. They all seemed ready for a fight, one she was very keen to avoid.

The same soldier made another gesture with a clear meaning: get out.

Standing up, she stepped out onto the wing, lowering herself to the deck, the canopy closing behind her with a satisfying sucking thump as it locked.

She just stood there, assessing the scene while no one moved. The first man gestured again for her to move away from the fighter. As she stepped away, a purple flash covered the fighter and vanished. The shields were back up, she turned, facing the one giving the orders.

It gave her the chance to assess the crowd some more. There was one man, standing in the shadows on the balcony that lined the far wall of the hangar. He wasn't interfering, but somehow she knew he was the one she needed to talk to — he was an officer in uniform backed by two others.

The speaker, a young man in his mid-thirties with an over-dominating expression, clearly wanted her to think he was the one in charge of the situation.

"Remove your helmet!"

Slowly, she lifted her helmet, shaking free her wet hair and holding the helmet against her side with one arm, running a hand through her hair. She had cooled off a lot during their flight here but was still badly in need of a shower and a change of uniform. Conscious that she was visibly a mess, she didn't let it alter her composure.

Another gesture, all the soldiers had their weapons ready. She watched the man giving the orders — despite his outwardly tough appearance, he was nervous on the trigger. She could see the indecision as his finger twitched. He didn't seem to know what to do with her calm demeanour and the confidence under the present situation.

She stood. Waiting for him to make the first move.

It took a while before he made his decision, but it was not the one she wanted.

"Faethel, secure the prisoner. Take her to the brig, I'll interrogate her later."

One of the gun hands to her right lowered his weapon and came forward. Turning to face him, she spoke up, loud enough for her intended target to hear.

"I am not going to the brig. I will only speak to the commander of this base and the lead pilot that brought me in!" She cast her view up to where the officer stood. He watched her intently but she could not read his expression.

He turned to the person standing next to him, speaking quietly and then left.

"Faethel, I gave you an order!"

Jacqueline looked at the tall, well-built man in front of her; he made to grab her arm, but she stepped back out of reach.

Faethel stepped back, raising his rifle, the whole ensemble raised their weapons again, tension mounting in the room.

"I will go with you, but not like that."

Faethel advanced again, his weapon still raised. With one hand, he gestured for her to come towards him. She slowly stepped forwards and he moved aside to let her past, following her with his weapon ready.

Keeping her stride even, she walked with more confidence than she felt. The crowd opened up to allow her through, Faethel guiding her at a slight distance.

"She tries anything, kill her!" the gruff voice of the first man broke the silence as they passed. His eyes glaring orange red at her; she ignored him.

As the door closed behind them, shutting the hangar out of view, she turned to the soldier. "Listen, Faethel, I need to talk to the Commander and lead pilot. It is vitally important that I do so before that other man gets to me in the brig."

"I don't have that authority." He motioned for her to keep moving. "Best I can do is go see the Commander and tell him you want to talk."

"Then please do that." She didn't struggle after that, she had to trust in the word of this soldier. After a few minutes, Jacqueline realised that they didn't seemed to be taking the most direct route to the brig, rather their path meandered through the corridors across the base. After a short while, three other soldiers came around the corner, walking intently towards her. The lead figure was an armoured, efficiently beweaponed woman whose scar traced down the side of her face, along her neck and down below her armour into her uniform, making her look every inch the mercenary that she was.

"Faethel, the Captain wants to speak to the prisoner."

"What took you so long? I've been wandering around half the base waiting for you to show up." Turning to Jacqueline, he said, "Go with these men and woman. The Captain will see you."

Jacqueline turned and saluted Faethel before being escorted away. The three new soldiers took her on the most direct line to the Commander's quarters.

The Commander's quarters opened from an initial entrance landing to a spacious area lit from the light cast down from huge aquariums that lined one wall. A doorway led off to parts unknown, and a study was in one corner of the room.

The trio stopped and waited. Jacqueline in the centre of the triangle they formed.

When the Captain entered, he was not a tall man, but his well-kept appearance commanded respect in an oddly naval way. He had a steely expression that seemed to look right through her.

He gestured for her to approach. She moved further into the cabin, which opened up into a wide-open space, furnished by a sunken square in the centre with cushions arranged around the sides. Open bookshelves adorned the walls and a desk lined one corner.

Once she passed him, the Captain nodded to the three soldiers who backed up and left the room, the cabin door sliding shut behind them.

Turning around, Jacqueline saw the base Commander watching her, more like, analysing her. The room was empty, the others were gone and the door shut, leaving them alone.

"You are a Black Ops pilot of the Alliance." It was not a question, more of an opening statement and Jacqueline took it as that.

"Why did the majority of your pilots not attack me when they jumped in?"

"The enemy of my enemy is my friend."

"You're at war with the Shadows of Kane, too?"

The Commander nodded. "It's complicated, but we have been operational since the end of the War of Sigma Prime."

She watched his eyes. He was an officer and a gentleman, his behaviour told her that much, probably former Alliance on a Black Ops programme that got left behind on a brief that exceeded most clearances.

"Why are you out here?"

"I was on a mission that got compromised. The cruiser left with the information that I had gathered."

"What were you scanning for?" He saw her expression, holding up his hand before she had time to respond. "No matter." He paused.

"How did you know we were there, and the enemy forces did not? The *Queen of Hearts* hadn't heard of your installation even existing in this area." Jacqueline questioned.

"We have been on a Black Ops mission for so long, it has become a way of life. The threat of discovery with nowhere to retreat to, but rather to face total annihilation, has left its mark on us. The clumsy die and the weak crumble; only the discreet have made it this far, but not without severe cost."

Indicating for her to sit down, they retreated further into the room.

"Will I get to meet the pilot who brought me in?"

"Yes." The Captain studied her.

"What do I do with you?" It was a rhetorical question that he let linger in the air for a moment, but moved on before she had chance to suggest an answer. She was pretty sure he had already made a decision and just needed to confirm it before he gave it voice.

"How long have you been in this base?"

The Captain looked at her intently, not answering, as she went on, "I thought I noticed several hulls that made up the structure."

He nodded, a quickening within him, as he replied, "Former ships, those who surrendered or were captured. It's been a long war. Only a few still remain from my original crew."

She looked around as though she could see the rest of the fortress from inside the room.

"We have the equivalent of a small armada living here on the base," he explained in response to her unasked question.

They talked for a good while before it got to one significant point of their discussion.

"You evidently don't want us examining your aircraft, hence the reason you have armed the self-destruct function." He paused, one foot tapping ever so slightly as he watched her, "What is it that you want from us?"

"Right now, this beats dying. What I want to know is if there is a chance to work together to harass the enemy?"

"Join forces? What can you offer me? My people will be wondering why you are getting special treatment."

"You are basically pirates out here?"

"Yes, unofficially. We have a file back at the *Hill*, but no doubt it's either been lost or so its far down the directory that no one even remembers what our mission originally was, or that we were out here in the first place. I'm sure our file reads 'Missing in Action', if anyone cared to look."

Jacqueline was a little shocked by the Commander's mention of the *Hill*. The only other times she'd heard of it were in connection with the rumours and stories that floated about a secret organisation running the Black Ops, so covert that they were shadows amongst the night, fairy tales in the military branches. Supposedly the formal name for the headquarters of this organisation was Mount Olympus. It was the stuff of legend and secret societies; myths that only the impressionable believed, yet here was a former Alliance officer who claimed operational status with Mount Olympus.

"Most of your people are not operatives, though?"

"No. There is a very small handful of people who know the truth of our original mission. Some surviving crew members who think that we got stranded after our mission went south with no way of returning home, but outside those, the rest think that we are just pirates, and to a great degree, we are." He leaned forward in his seat.

"And what do I do with you?" he asked again.

"I will fly and fight as one of your pilots. For all intents and purposes, I am already dead."

"This isn't like flying for the Navy. You'll basically become a pirate and that will taint you for the rest of your life."

"What other choice do I have?"

"You'll need another call sign. Everyone here must not learn the truth about who you are. The only people you trust are those who know about Mount Olympus."

"Understood. Who do I report to?"

"For the time being: me!"

Jacqueline nodded. She stood and made as though to leave.

"Lieutenant, as far as you're concerned, you're now a Captain, consider it a battlefield commission. Watch out for Jan'Dyr, he won't take kindly to you being here, nor that you're of higher rank than he is."

"He's the guy on the flight deck?"

The Commander nodded, "He has been behaving like that ever since he came into power several months ago."

Jacqueline nodded. She had known people like him before.

"If you'll permit me, I would like to go over your fighter with my most trusted mechanic, he'll exclusively handle your fighter. After that I will devise a plan to get you active immediately."

"Ok, if you can give me a couple trustworthy people to help get me sorted with guidance and jump nodes, I'll get studying."

"One more thing, Captain: you're call sign and therefore your identity here will now be Zatara."

"What does that mean?"

"Driftwood."

"Hmm, apt, I guess."

"Get familiar with all the fighters here, you'll most likely need to be able to fly them all in combat at some stage."

Walking across to his desk, the Commander keyed a switch, "Get Fischer and Carlzone to come to my cabin. And then I want to see Wynter and Shea after that."

"Michael Carlzone is one of my operatives from Mount Olympus. Fischer is the best Chief Engineer I've ever known. They will help get you sorted. Fischer and I will be the only two to deal with your fighter. Wynter is Navy intelligence and has been with me only a few years. As former Alliance, she will help you a lot when you get her alone. We picked her and Shea up when their long-range destroyer was attacked two jumps from here, they were part of a handful of survivors from a company of nearly a thousand. They will get you settled and help you with the day-to-day operations..." He looked Jacqueline in the eye, making sure she understood the full weight of his words. "You're former Alliance Navy, you don't know the nature of your mission out here. Don't trust anyone, do you understand!"

She looked at him, taking in his eyes, seeing past the mahogany brown with emerald flecks, seeing the Special Operations Commander who had been fighting on his own since the previous war.

"Yes, sir." She nodded and saluted.

There was a knock on the door from the entrance and the Commander went to go answer it.

Jacqueline looked around the cabin. There were a lot of books, classic literature as well as philosophy, with a fair few on the art of war. Three that stood out were *The Count of Monte Cristo*, with two being holobooks, recreations from the old world libraries. She wished she could read them. Reading was one of her most enjoyable pastimes. She could still remember the first time at school she had read war and peace from the old civilisation as part of a project.

The Captain walked in, taking note of her interest in his books, but said nothing.

"This is Michael Carlzone, one of my operatives on the station. He knows everything that happened in the Insurrection War, he knows about Mount Olympus."

Jacqueline absorbed the information, the Commander's former statement about not trusting anyone still ringing in her ears.

Carlzone wasn't tall but had a stocky build and a stony authoritarian silence that demanded respect. His experience was almost a physical presence in itself, but there was something about him that made her wonder just how loyal he was.

The Captain explained about Jacqueline being the fighter pilot they had captured and that she was coming on as part of the crew. Jacqueline watched Carzone's eyes as he took in the news, his expression flickering briefly at one point, but his mask never changed from the stony expression he had entered with.

She had noticed that the Commander had skipped over several details from their conversation; she did not try to interrupt him. There was an element of trust, one that she would not betray. Still, she had a lot to learn about the dynamics of the place.

"The Chief and I will deal with her fighter directly. You will be the only other person that she is going to share anything with."

Michael shifted his focus to her for a second and then back to the Commander.

The door opened again in the anteroom. The Captain sidestepped so he could see into the lobby.

In walked another man, much younger than Jacqueline would have thought; his dark hair wavy and obstinately unruly, keen dark eyes and his slightly olive skin gave the newcomer an exotic look. His wiry frame was no doubt strong, but he was lean where Carlzone was muscular.

The Commander explained to Fischer that Jacqueline would cooperate and assist where needed with her stealth fighter, but that he would be the only engineer to work on it.

After a short while, Carlzone and Fischer left the cabin only to be replaced by Wynter and Shea who were waiting outside.

They came in and the Commander introduced Jacqueline as Zatara, explaining her background as much as he wanted to and gave Jacqueline a quick order with just his eyes, she understood and kept silent.

When the Commander was done, he told Jacqueline to come back the next day, but for now, to go with Wynter and Shea.

"They will show you to your cabin and get you settled."

The armoured doors slid shut behind her, the two young women already heading down the corridor as though they expected her to follow them. Young and bubbly, their innocence untainted by a mercenary way of life and yet they were no strangers to it, fully aware that they were on the dark side of central rule, where friends were people who didn't shoot at you and life was a pendulum swinging in the balance.

***

Six years later
Lieutenant Gideon
On board the GTSC *Paladin*
Seven months before Operation *Trident*
Somewhere in the Herri-Gawa sector:

Pushing through the ion clouds of the nebula, the GTSC *Paladin* ran at sub-light speed: as part of the Hunter Killer group, its mission brief was to sweep the sector for long range scouts, enemy Black Ops ships and pirates that had been harassing the supply chain to the front lines.

High Command had ordered them to try and find the base of operations, if any existed in the region.

They had been out on patrol for several months now, but the most excitement they had found was only a few small skirmishes with a couple of scouts and two or three pirates.

All supply chains had been rerouted out of the area, which left no enticement for any raids or strikes to take place.

Lieutenant Gideon Ben Ra'am walked down the corridor towards the hangar. He had another patrol in an hour and wanted to make sure everything was ready. The familiar walls and familiar faces all blended together as he moved through the depths of the ship. Unlike his last posting, the GTSC *Paladin* did not feel like home, not even after ten months on board.

The Captain didn't like him, that much he knew; and he really didn't care about it either.

The hangar was a spacious cavern after the confines of the corridors. He looked up at the stanchions that lined the walls, reaching up to the ceiling like the pillars of an Athenian temple.

His fighter was one of the 'alert' six positioned near the ready room where other pilots sat and waited for an immediate scramble.

Circumnavigating the aircraft, Gideon made his way to his fighter without disturbing the mechanics and armourers that were sorting the last-minute details.

Their patrol today was much the same as the time before and the time before that: launch all six fighters, break off into pairs and fly for four hours before returning to the cruiser.

Chance of any activity was unlikely, but they would still have to be alert, attacks could happen without warning.

Checking his guns, he made sure that the mechanisms were all correct and connected up.

Since arriving on board the *Paladin*, Gideon had hardly seen any combat. Facing routine patrols, and flying operations that would have kept junior pilots busy, but really didn't take much of his focus.

It was not that he was better than anyone else, simply that his last posting had been right in the thick of it, and the end of the first and only patrol had been a baptism of fire that very few had survived. Now the rigors of duty had lost the wonder lust that it had held for him during flight training.

Happy with his pre-flight inspection, Gideon clambered up to the cockpit. The T6 *Trojan* was a sturdy craft, built in the aftermath of the previous war, it still owed its design to that era to a large degree. It was a solid fighter and could sustain huge amounts of punishment and keep flying. Slower in handling and less responsive on the controls than his previous aircraft, the *Trojan* showed its age in its armament and powerplants.

As such, it was commonly found on board aging warships that typically were used to protect the forward bases behind the front line.

When the time came, he started the engines and felt the fighter rise and wallow in the gravity fields of its engines. The other five fighters were all doing the same, the six of them manoeuvring from where they hovered into the launch tubes.

It was his favourite part about the patrols, the tight launch tube that would flash past before being catapulted into the wide-open expanse of space.

As the sense of speed fell away, Gideon turned his fighter to follow his flight leader, forming up on his wing in textbook formation.

That was one thing he had been noticed for: the precision of his flying.

Beauty amongst the stars never failed to excite him, but for the first hour of the patrol, that was all there was to look at. The scan Gideon was running, reported back blankly as all sensors picked up nothing except background radiation.

"Red flight, we're picking up two signatures in your area, about ten o'clock, angles four five, range fifteen thousand. Investigate."

The two of them turned their aircraft and headed towards the coordinates they were given. Their radar screens still not showing any reports.

As they closed on the reported location, two blips appeared on their radar.

"Bandits, eleven o'clock, angels two three, heading away."

"Any back up?"

"Negative, they're only two small craft."

"Chase and engage."

Gideon started wondering about the pirates, the GTN signatures would be appearing on the pirates HUD and ordinarily they would try to blow out an engine just to get away, fleet fighters were formidable opponents for the less trained, but these pirates were not running.

"Red One, there's something wrong."

"What is it, Red Two?"

"They're not running from us this time."

"Nonsense, it's the ion cloud interfering with their systems."

Gideon frowned, he didn't like it at all, there was something really not right about this and the flight leader was making reasons fit his own preferred scenario.

Inexplicably he pulled up to gain height over the pirates they were chasing.

"Get back in formation, Red Two!" the flight leader shouted a fraction before opening up with his main guns.

"We're in range, open fire!" he cried.

Gideon saw it in the flash of an instant: Red One in perfect firing position below him, the shield behind the closer pirate flashing blue, white with the impacts from the laser fire. Five white sun bursts were spiralling with blue supernova edges, five fighters jumping into perfect firing position behind where they both were.

"Red flight, we're detecting multiple slip-space ruptures in your vicinity. Get out of there!"

Before either of them could do anything, the five that jumped in, opened fire, the deadly streams of bright coloured laser flashes converging on Red One, the fighter exploding in a vivid flash of red and purple.

Temporarily mesmerized by the sight of his compatriot fire ball, Gideon saw in the corner of his eye the other two aircraft turn back. Their job as bait was finished.

In ten months, the most he had faced was a small group of three pirates with backup, but right now seven fighters were closing in on him.

He had a momentary sense of fear, a vestige left over from a previous skirmish; but momentarily only. The first volley of shots tore past his canopy, colour drained from his face as ice ran through his veins. Time slowed down as twelve more slip-space ruptures tore the sky apart in front of him.

"Red Two, re-enforcements on their way, get out of there!" Gideon heard command over the comms again.

Moving as if on a training exercise, Gideon engaged his shield regeneration control, the T6 slowing down from the energy draw away from the engines. He would need his shields if he was going to survive.

Rolling onto his back, he dived onto the closest fighter, tearing through its shields and pulled up firing a missile just as it reacted with an avoiding manoeuvre.

He had no intention of listening to the Captain's orders, this dogfight was an ambush. Engaging in close combat again brought back that last battle on board the GTSC *Bellerophon*. A calm came over him, peace like he had not felt since he was a boy standing on the banks of the Varèdoré river on his home world.

Gideon switched targets, not waiting to see the results, somehow, he just knew that it would explode — and it did.

As the pirate fighter disintegrate, a slight smile touched his lips, the voices of his silent friends ringing in his thoughts.

Shards of that fighter sprayed onto the one next to it, the pirate rocking from the explosion, the pilot barely registering the loss of his friend when his systems started screaming from taking a deluging fire that tore through his shields and punched into his hull.

Gideon flashed through the turbulence of the second explosion as the other seventeen fighters turned towards him.

This was going to be a fight like he hadn't experienced in a long time. Learning and understanding surfaced from his subconscious, lessons learned from combat in a realm of hell. It was a clarity that few reached, and fewer lived to experience again. His old flight instructor had been a veteran and a hero of the previous war and had imparted a lot of wisdom and technique to Gideon over the course of his training, but one phrase came back now: "Fight as though you are already dead." It was the same truth that had saved him the last time.

Turning into the oncoming mass of pirates, he isolated one target and let loose.

The pirates attacked en masse, but one after the other, the fighters fell to his guns.

The re-enforcements from the *Paladin* were boosting their engines to the maximum to reach the lone comrade that had turned to face the pirates single-handedly.

The leader was giving instructions to his squad, but they kept changing. He was assigning targets so that they would know who to tackle first, but first one then another fell silent on their displays.

"More enemy fighters detected jumping in, get to the fight black squadron!"

As they watched, another twenty signatures showed in their HUDs as more fighters joined the dogfight.

Gideon flew with a skill that his comrades had never known he possessed, fighting with a ferocity that could only match that of a divine wind, or a man possessed.

He had no idea how many he had shot down, nor how many were left. All he was aware of was his depleting missile quantity, and the increasing number of warnings and messages on his systems as the *Trojan* took punishment.

Another pirate latched onto his tail and started firing, his already depleted shields started issuing warnings with the energy drain. He turned into the attack, the fighter flashing overhead. Gideon reversed his turn and followed the fighter, blasting the shields away and hammering the thinnly armoured plating until the engines ignited.

The T6 *Trojan* rocked with the explosion as he flew through the blast. It seemed as though there was no end to the enemy fighters. His automatic targeting picked out the next closest target but, as he turned, one strange fighter appeared in his forward view. In an instant, Gideon realised that it hadn't shown up with an Indication of Friend or Foe. Gideon flicked his guns onto the energy drain shots and let rip, he saw the fighter move, but he got in close following its every move and blasted away until the fighter skewed sideways and started drifting. It was disabled for now and he could return to fight the other enemy aircraft.

His HUD showed only another five fighters left. He put his fighter into the tightest turn he could muster and was just in time to see one on his tail go flashing past. He was just about to go into another turn to follow, but an explosion rocked his fighter, something solid slammed into the side of his *Trojan*. Alarms sounded and red warning lights started flashing in a manic desire to get attention.

Taking the briefest moment to switch to an auxiliary power source, he kick-started the fighters damage control. More shots fanned overhead before hammering into his fighter, the canopy splitting, sliced with jagged fracture lines.

Gideon checked his flight suit readout on the system. There were no leaks. Ignoring the warnings, he boosted his shields and turned to avoid the next incoming attack.

The fighter flashed passed, he followed, but his fighter wasn't producing as much power as before. The enemy fighter was drawing ahead, but Gideon poured a stream of fire into the fighter. It exploded just as four fighters came in on a head on attack, but three of them exploded from a wall of fire that came from behind him. Gideon looked at his HUD. The signatures of his incoming friendly squadron showed up. He breathed a sigh of relief. It was none too soon. The last pirate was heading off in a desperate attempt to escape, but he didn't get far.

Gideon turned the aircraft slowly; he was looking for the fighter he had disabled during the fight.

"Well done, Red Two, return to base with Black Squadron."

"Thanks, Command, there's a fighter that I disabled during the fight, request recovery."

"We didn't pick up anything on the scanners. Are you sure?"

"Yes, I'm locating it now and will standby until the recovery unit gets here."

"Negative, Red Two, return to base. Black Squadron can take care of it!"

Gideon ignored the last order, there had been an edge in the voice that hadn't been there before. He flew back to where he had marked the HUD, there was floating debris, the wrecks of fighters created a maze of death, but in amongst all of that, he found the strange looking fighter that had given no radar signature. He brought his fighter to a stop and turned on all his lights. The search beams centred on the drifting vessel.

"Command, I have located that fighter, send a recovery vessel."

"Recovery vessel on its way. Return to base, Red Two."

Gideon acknowledged but remained on station until he could see the recovery vehicle closing in on his location. None of the other fighters had come any closer, so there wasn't a great chance of the recovery vessel finding the disabled fighter either.

After a lengthy wait, Gideon called again, "Command, status on that recovery vehicle?"

"It is on its way, Red Two. Return to base."

"Negative, Command, not until that recovery vessel gets here."

"You were given an order, Lieutenant!" sounded the XO's voice, brittle with anger.

The two of them had never been friends and now it was starting to affect operational activity. Gideon had never outwardly disliked any superior, but the XO had been different from the beginning. Always questioning the report of his last patrols, querying his medal and abilities. The Captain had even encouraged it from the XO.

Gideon didn't reply to that; he knew a stone wall when he saw one.

In the last year since joining the squadron, he had noticed an attitude on the ship that he didn't like. Everyone for themselves, there was constant competition amongst those on board.

Being well aware of that, he knew that the simple fact that he had stayed to fight would be a sore point for a lot of people on the ship. Black Squadron would not be in any rush to help him get the fighter back to the ship after his exploits, taking on a much more superior force single-handedly that Black Squadron would have struggled to handle together. Capturing that fighter would be an impressive feat for anyone, let alone against the odds he had faced.

No, they would not help him out.

Repositioning, Gideon targeted the fighter, he couldn't see the pilot inside, but no doubt they were watching intently. He did a quick scan of the fighter, locating a strong point and fired a tow cable that secured the two fighters together. Only then did he turn the aircraft and slowly increase power until the tow was fully extended.

Dragging the fighter behind him, he made his way back to the ship.

Not bothering to make a report, he knew what he would be told, and he wasn't about to obey anyway.

"Black Squadron, return to base."

Gideon flew at his maximum forward tow speed, watching the engines of black squadron draw ahead, dwindling into the background stars of the nebula.

The flight back in his damaged fighter was slow, made slower with the dead weight from the fighter he was towing. It gave him plenty of time to think, relive the engagement and learn from the dogfight, or begin to, at least. He knew that his subconscious would take advantage of extracting details his memory couldn't pinpoint at the moment. Vivid dreams would colour his nights for the next while, after the alarms and warnings had sounded mid fight, he had gone deathly cold, his mind so sharp and clear while his fear seemed to evaporate as though he had never been scared in his life. He knew he was most likely going to die,

"Detach your tow and land in bay two."

Gideon ignored the order. He was heading for his usual bay where he knew the ground crew.

"Red Two, detach your tow and land in bay two."

As he drew closer, his trajectory made it evident that he wasn't going to comply. The great armoured doors started sliding back in place across the landing bay in front of his fighter. Increasing the thrusters, he sped up, endangering the tow line, but he judged that he would be able to get through the remaining gap by the time he reached the doors. It would just be an impressive task to slow himself down and the fighter in tow once inside.

Again, the cold sensation came over him, he felt nothing, no fear, no panic and that scared him.

Angling his fighter through the remaining sliver in the armoured plating as the doors shut, his manoeuvre swung the fighter in tow wide, narrowly missing the hardened armour door by mere feet.

Gideon boosted thrusters, pulling the strange fighter in line behind him before hitting the reverse thrusters. He had dangerously little room to play with, accelerating was the last thing he should be doing, however, if he had slowed down too soon, the fighter on the tow line would have slid straight past, pulling them both into the bulkhead at the end of the hangar.

The fighter caught up to the decelerating T6 *Trojan*, slamming into its back, their momentum driving them on together.

Applying full reverse power, Gideon brought the two fighters to a stop meters from the end wall.

The strange fighter caught in the T6's gravity well, suspending them both as Gideon manoeuvred his damaged fighter back to his bay.

As he spun slowly, turning the two aircraft, the second craft slipped, sliding out of the gravity field and slammed down on the deck where it would remain until the deck crew could manage to lift it.

With a nonchalance that belied his junior status, Gideon swung his fighter around and settled in the bay. He switched off and climbed out to find the Chief Engineer walking towards him while looking at the pirate vessel.

"I brought you a gift."

The Engineer looked at the young lieutenant and back at the fighter.

"And what do you suppose I'm going to do with this broken-down hunk of junk?" His voice stern, but he secretly liked the young pilot. He had a very different way about him and was never too proud to learn more. How many hours had he spent in the mechanics bay helping pull the fighters to pieces or asking questions?

"I'm guessing it's got some new tech on board. I didn't pick it up on the scanners during the fight."

"Yet you shot it down anyway. I heard you caused quite a storm in central command." He didn't wait for a reply, rather went towards the silent hulk.

Gideon climbed down following the Chief to check out his prize.

"Marines, at the ready. Dirk, grab the guns, arm the men."

The officers and mechanics assembled around the fighter, cradling their weapons with nervous fidgets. It was rare they saw an enemy fighter let alone had one within their midst.

Two engineers connected external power to the craft that would drive basic systems only.

The Chief gave the order, and two marines went forward to open the canopy. It slid open with a soft sucking sound and then a hiss as it equalised with the atmospheric pressure, before they even reached it.

The ring of soldiers who stood with levelled weapons was hopefully enough of a deterrent for the pilot not to try and avenge his comrades in a suicide grand finale. Gideon watched with interest, this was the first enemy pilot he had ever seen up close as ordinarily they were the aircraft in his sights, not differentiating between pilot and fighter.

The pilot sat perfectly still, not wanting to provoke the soldiers into firing.

"Who is the one who shot me down?" The voice was mechanical, produced through a distorter.

The Chief Engineer looked at one of the officers to his left and nodded.

Gideon stepped forward, aware this could be a trap, a self-sacrificing gesture for the fellow comrades who had been killed.

"I am," he said simply.

The pilot slowly stood up, leaning forward to step out of the cockpit. "Then I surrender to you. I will talk only to you."

The Chief Engineer stepped forward, beside Gideon, and said, "Come forward, hands behind your head."

"I pose no threat, but I will only surrender my arms to the pilot who beat me."

Gideon stepped forward, closer to the aircraft.

"I accept your surrender. Please step forwards and hand me your sidearm."

The pilot had on a dark flight suit with dull gold trimmings, a helmet that had a V-shaped black visor, the helmet extended up into pointy wings or ear shapes giving the whole outfit an oddly black owlish appearance.

Reaching behind his back, the pilot withdrew a small compact pistol; Gideon could feel the tension in the room tighten, the rifles levelled that little more accurately. Without flinching, the pilot spun the pistol around and handed it to Gideon, butt first.

Gideon took it and gestured for the pilot to step forward for the soldiers to surround him.

Gideon turned to the Chief Engineer, "I'll go with them to the interrogation room, but start having a play with the craft before you get any interference from above. I am convinced there is something we can learn from this craft."

"What gave you such a strong conviction?"

"As I said, it didn't show up on radar, so when I saw it, I figured it can't be there for a good reason."

"So, you shot it down."

"I only used the depletion rounds. Hopefully, I haven't fried the sub-routines too much."

"Lieutenant, you captured a fighter with stealth capabilities after taking on a squadron of fighters single-handedly, brought it back with a damaged fighter, completely in contradiction to your orders. I'm pretty sure we'll find something."

Gideon smiled, "Maybe best if you don't share your find straight away." The Chief nodded and Gideon turned and followed the soldiers who were marching their captive out of the hangar bay.

The Chief watched the procession walk away.

"Gar, Fin, give me a hand with this!"

It took several of them, but the Chief's team manhandled the fighter into Red One's empty bay.

"Ok, my beauty, what secrets do you hold?"

Looking at the two trusted erks, he said, "Not a word of this to anyone."

They nodded and the three of them started crawling over the strange craft.

There was a great commotion as soldiers and officers came pouring into the hangar bay. They surrounded the fighter bay and levelled their weapons on the mechanics.

"Stop what you are doing!" ordered the most senior officer in the party.

The Chief looked up and saw the situation, but he ignored it, knowing the officer in charge was a spineless excuse for a man, only doing this to curry favour with the XO and Captain.

"I gave you an order!" shouted the officer.

"Not on *my* hangar, you didn't!"

The Chief, who outranked the officer, stood leaning on a protruding component near the top of the fighter, looking down at the thin figure in a shiny uniform.

"I have orders from the XO!"

"Then the XO can walk his pompous ass down here and give them to me himself! Now, get off my hangar before I throw you out the airlock!" And with that he turned back to the fighter, leaving the officer standing there, indecision written all over his face.

"Time is ticking. Make your mind up or I'll pick for you" The Chief glared down at the dithering officer and saw him cave.

***

In the interrogation room, Gideon sat opposite the pilot who still had his helmet on.

"Can you remove your helmet and tell me your name?"

Slowly, aware of the guards in each corner with guns raised, the pilot detached the helmet, lifting it clear, shaking out her long hair, letting it fall around her shoulders.

Gideon was shocked by her appearance, definitely not that of a pirate.

A small scar ran diagonally along her left cheek bone. Her brown eyes were alive and bright, taking in every detail.

She was a few years older than Gideon. Ordinarily in the GTSC, someone of her status would have been higher up the command structure.

She watched him examine her. It would have made her self conscious had she not been used to it.

"What's your name and rank?"

"I am called Zatara. I'm a Captain in the Alliance Navy's Black Ops programme."

If Gideon was surprised before, then this one shook him, yet he never revealed anything.

**Lieutenant Teresa Palmer,
On board the GTSC *Achilles*, Black Ops Heavy Cruiser,
Three days after Operation *Trident*:**

Her boots rang out on the metal grill gangway that crossed the hangar to the flying bridge quick access way. Suspended close to the pipes that traversed the width of the cavernous enclosure, the echo of each footstep was lost to the mechanics far below as they worked on the fighters and bombers. Drivers sounded with jack hammer reverberations and welders sent sparks flying with the zing and crackle of high electricity as compression clips were put back in place and final repairs were completed. Only the alert fighters were separated from the rest, the pilots casually lounging around on the weapons cases or munitions boxes.

Theirs was a very different war from the regular fleet — they couldn't just call for help or spares whenever they ran into difficulties, rather they had to maintain their own fighter and bomber force, but also rebuild broken down aircraft and even build new ones when necessary.

Casting her eye down to the deck, Squadron Leader Teresa Palmer could see five new aircraft being finished and another thirteen undergoing routine maintenance.

The height of the gangway gave some people vertigo, aided by the thin metal railing that only came up to her hip.

Those people would take the long way around, but not her — she had faced her fear of heights long ago and had won her freedom because of it.

The shadows of her past lingered in her eyes and her dreams. Upon her first steps onto any high grating, she would see the twenty-second-storey drop to the street below, the narrow ledge that she stood on, but it would vanish as she crossed the open expanse, holding no power over her now.

Reaching the ladder at the far end of the gangway, Teresa climbed up to the flying bridge with ease, her agile body lithe with practise. It was one of her favourite places on board the GTSC *Achilles*; the wide-open space with plotting tables and vast, floor length windows, it was very easy to feel detached from the rest of the ship while up here: somewhere she'd come when off duty to get away from everything.

Commander Chasin Micah stood by the plotting table, his eyes down, fixed on a data pad he had placed on the corner, his back to the door.

Everyone called him Maximus for reasons he never fully explained.

He didn't look up as she approached him, rather just kept scribbling away on a data pad next to him.

"Hello, Teresa."

"You sent for me?" She was still surprised, no matter how many times she witnessed it, how Maximus always knew who was approaching without apparently looking at them.

She had managed to read a segment of his file that she had once come across in a rather unorthodox way. Most of it had been redacted, more black ink than actual writing, but what she had gathered was that his ascension to the rank of Commander was after his role as a vanguard Wraith and his posting to another unit whose name had been obscured. Thereafter, there were very few words that had not been redacted.

All Chasin would ever say about it when anyone asked him was, "I'd have to kill you after I told you."

No one ever argued with that, there was something about him that gave this statement an underlying weight that implied it was more than a joke, but Teresa had seen the long scar that ran down the length of his forearm. He was not old, but carried his age like his uniform, it had a lot of history, but looked brand new, as though it had just been issued: and he was always presented immaculately.

"We're being redeployed. High Command has something special for us."

"Do I have to ask the Captain, or will you tell me?"

"We're going to re-enforce an invasion."

"One ship? A Black Ops Heavy Cruiser? Isn't that what the fleet is for?"

He glanced up, continuing, "Half the invasion fleet ditched onto the planet; the other half was destroyed in combat. From all accounts, it sounds like a show not to miss."

Teresa shook her head. After six years as a Special Operations pilot, she had a fairly sarcastic opinion about the fleet and their pilots that got to run to safety after an operation was completed. As a Black Ops Heavy Cruiser, theirs was an existence of constant danger, fighting with a ferocity that could deter the determination of most enemy forces.

She turned at the sound of the main door opening, light spilling in from the corridor, a long thin shadow bobbing as it extended into the room like a flame flickering in the wind, until the door closed.

"Wing leader Teagan Blythe, thank you for joining us." Again, Commander Chasin had not turned his head to see who had entered. This never ceased to amaze Teresa.

She watched her superior officer walk to where they stood. She was not a tall woman, but not short either, her frame slight, yet she held herself with an air that gave magnitude to her presence. To become the Wing Leader of a Special Operations Unit and gaining nearly all of her experience in Special Ops, was virtually unheard of, especially with the average life expectancy for a Black Ops fighter pilot being rather low.

"Commander," she saluted, a bizarre formality between these two, Teresa observed.

This whole crew had lived together for the past three years, the only friendlies they had seen in that time was the surviving crew they had picked up from the GTSC *Nova* just over two years ago.

Yet these two held to the formalities of the service, their relationship complicated, a friendship that had grown strong, they complimented each other well in their roles.

"Have you told her yet?"

"No, I thought you'd like to explain it the way that you told the Captain."

Wing Leader Teagan Blythe looked at the Commander, her gaze both formal and fond of the ex-Black Ops soldier. Theirs was a friendship that had a best-selling story in it, thought Teresa. Most people on this ship had stories to tell.

Looking at Teresa, the Wing Leader began. Her direct formality laying opinions to rest, only the bare facts would remain standing: "High Command has decided that our mission priority has changed. Admiral Fraser lead a fleet on an invasion in a new sector. The GTN pulled as many vessels as they could on short notice and sent them in. It was not enough as it turned out." She looked at Chasin who was still busy with his data pad. "Seven ships were forced to ditch onto the planet's surface. Thankfully, someone had the brains to cluster the vessels and they have formed a base of operations at a place called Hal La Fe'ir. The remainder of the surviving fleet had to retreat as they were heavily outnumbered. They too have ditched on a nearby planet in the system."

Teagan looked up at Teresa to make sure she was following.

"We have been ordered to provide support to our forces at Hal La Fe'ir." Teagan was about to say something else, but Chasin stood up and looked at the two women in turn.

"We are going to do a close jump to get in and bypass as many defences as we can to minimise the risk of being intercepted by the enemy fleet before landing." He looked at Teresa.

"We will be deploying three of our four wings. The *Achilles* will keep one defensive wing onboard for the return journey home. Your job will be to lead one of the wings for the deployment. Once on the ground, Group Captain Andrea Garcia will be in overall command of our forces; he will liaise with Fraser's forces to coordinate the defence of the area. You will hold the rank of Wing Leader but expect to be on the front line on a daily basis. Any questions?"

"What about the *Achilles*?"

"The *Achilles* will recover some key personnel and evacuate the wounded before making a jump for the Polaris system. There we will refit and join the next wave of re-enforcements before heading out on our own again."

Teresa felt a little off balance. She was being promoted, posted, and sentenced all in one conversation, but the resounding thought echoing inside her mind was that she was leaving the *Achilles* — leaving home!

Chasin carried on: "It will also mean that we will need to train up an entirely new group once again..." he trailed off, looking at Teagan as he finished.

"It's more than just a new group, Maximus."

"I know." He cut her short.

Turning his head to look at Teresa he changed the subject: "It's time to earn some new stripes again. From the reports we have managed to obtain, it sounds like we will have a rather hot reception. Our forces are under constant attack by vastly superior numbers from an enemy that is proving quite relentless."

"Do you have any questions, Squadron Leader?"

Tonnes! thought Teresa, but she coolly replied, "No, sir, not right now, I will go through the intel and formulate the relevant questions."

"You trained her well," Chasin smiled at Teagan.

"We both did." Teagan gave a rare smile, her features softening into those of the bride she had once been long ago, although the tired sadness didn't lift.

The three of them gathered around the planning table, Chasin pulling up a hologram of the battlefield from the data he had on the pad. There would be a briefing with the other Wing Leaders before the squadrons will be informed, but for now the three of them poured over the information, trying to gain every detail possible for the briefing and ultimately, the battle looming ahead of them.

"You said we would be landing, are we deploying our troops?" Teresa asked after Teagan had pointed out the weaknesses in the defences of the GTN formation.

"Our troops will mostly be deployed. Only those who will be required to train the replacements will remain on board. You know the Captain takes pride in his people: there's a reason the *Achilles* has been so successful over the years," Chasin stated, "and in no small part due to the efforts of the future Group Captain here."

Teresa looked at Teagan and replied, "Congratulations, sir."

"Thank you," Teagan nodded, a deeper sadness coming through again.

Teresa wondered about what they were not telling her, for all intents and purposes, this was a major step for her, but she was withdrawn as though she wished it wasn't about to happen.

***

Pulling up her data pad, Teresa studied the images of the seven ships and the terrain that they were on, whomever had picked the area as the place to ditch had been either extremely lucky or had enough foresight to envisage the battle that was to come.

She had her own data pad next to her as she sat at the desk in her cabin, making notes of her thoughts as she detailed the place for possible locations to land the *Achilles*.

Hers was an interesting role onboard the Special Operations Heavy Cruiser. Although she held the rank of Squadron Leader, it was almost an honorary title as she was not in charge of an actual squadron — her full title was Squadron Leader of Special Operations and Tactics. Besides her vast amounts of experience as a Black Ops fighter pilot, she was a genius at thinking outside of the box. By the time the Group Captain gave his briefing to the rest of the pilots, she would have come up with a plan that would baffle the enemy forces and give them the advantage of surprise, or at least that was what they were all hoping for.

Teresa flicked her pen back and forth between forefinger and thumb as she examined the images. Every idea was plagued with other thoughts, the cryptic conversation that had been passing between Commander Chasin and Teagan Blythe kept coming back — the way they kept referring to training re-enforcements. It seemed as though they were not expecting many to be retrieved from the planet on their return trip.

But if that was the case, then what was in store for the landing force?

Teresa worked for hours on various plans that could be used until finally as she was drifting, her head nodding and her eyelids heavy.

The pen fell from her fingers, clattering onto the desk before dropping, landing on her foot before crashing to the floor, jolting her back to consciousness.

Whether she had been dreaming, or whether it was the jolt from the pen falling on her foot, she did not know, but an idea struck Teresa with enough momentum that her eyes flicked open, and her mind was back to full consciousness.

If they wanted crazy and out of the box, she'd give it to them; so far out of the box, even, that she didn't know if anyone had ever tried this in the history of the GTSC or the wars previously. She pulled up her data pad link searching for the information she had stored. Nothing new from the GTN data banks.

She got up from the chair, quickly pulling on her socks and boots, grabbing her pen and pad, she made a few notes and hurried from her room, not bothering to dress further than her trousers and t-shirt.

Hair flying behind her, people in the corridors scrambling out of her way, her figure bouncing unrestrained, she ran down the hallways and up gangways, scrambling up ladders, she covered the distance from her cabin to the flying bridge in record time.

Bursting into her favourite space, she made for the hologram table where Chasin was still standing and working on his data pad.

The Commander was taking this next mission even more seriously than normal. Again, the bizarre conversation between him and the wing leader came to her memory. Not only because it was his job, why was the Commander taking even greater care of the details of their operation?

As if expecting her, Chasin didn't turn or jump when Teresa pushed open the door; rather he waited until she was almost right next him, "What have you got for me, Squadron Leader?"

"I've got it, Maximus, I've got how we bypass the enemy fleet, get our forces off loaded and bring significant damage to the enemy force in a major way," she said breathless with excitement and from her exertions.

The Commander stood up, looking at her for a long moment, his decisive eyes observing every detail; he took in the strands of hair that hung lose, out of place from the rest. The partitions in her hair from where she had run her fingers through to straighten it out after her run. She had gold flecks in her green eyes, a rosy glow in her cheeks and her breathing was elevated after her run, but she was not panting out of breath. He took in the simple gold chain that showed just above the hem of her dark blue t shirt and the pulse that jumped in her neck.

"So..?" He asked his eyes questioning.

Turning to the planning table as she talked, Chasin pulled up the hologram of the battlefield.

"We were talking about trying to get past the enemy fleet. You said that they have reenforced their numbers since you first were informed about the situation."

Chasin nodded almost imperceptibly.

"What if we were to do a close jump?"

"Get in between the fleet and the planet surface?" Chasin said in a questioning statement.

"But then we still have to possibly contend with any forces the fleet launches, not to mention the time they will have to amass enough ships to make it impossible for us to leave." Teresa forecast.

"Your solution?"

"It will sound insane..."

"Most of your suggestions do."

Teresa looked at him as she continued, not sure if that was meant to be a compliment or not.

"We calculate the jump to re-emerge here." She used her pen to indicate a position just outside of the enemy grounded forces.

"You're talking about a jump into atmosphere?"

Teresa nodded.

"That's insane?!"

"I know it has never been done before, but all the research I've found says that it can be done. It will give us the chance to get close to our forces, deploy the fighters and complete the landing very soon after the jump. What's more..." she indicated towards the hologram again, and continued, "my research on atmospheric re-emergence shows that the exit from slip-space in atmosphere is not only possible, but it will tear a hole in the atmosphere, causing humongous damage to the immediate surroundings. If we jump in just above the enemy forces, it's highly likely that it will crush anything or anyone in the near vicinity, the same as if a hyper core went critical, only larger."

"We'd have to be exact in our calculations otherwise it will plunge us straight into the planet instead of close orbit above the surface!"

"Yes, I know, but it would be no different to when we jumped into that convoy, the navigator plotted our re-emergence slap bang on target to ram that destroyer, taking it out before we even started.

There would certainly be more factors involved, but it would be no different."

A slow smile spread across the Commander's face. "It is insane, but it might just work if we plan it right."

She knew he had taken to the idea. She had seen it enough times before when she had come up with crazy schemes in the past for different operations. That silent approval when she knew the operation was about to be accepted, when he gave that faint smile.

They started planning her idea in more detail together, working out the exact location that they would propose.

***

Teresa awoke, raw dream-filled consciousness dulling her mind as she fought with the sheets entangling her, tearing away from the dream to grasp reality. Breathing heavily, she could still see the man's face leering down at her as she lay crying on the floor, the memory clinging to her like the damp sheets that dragged over her clawing skin, heart pounding, her chest heaving and the sound of her pulse tapping in her ears, she sat up in bed, the sheets bundled around her waist, the cool air prickling her bare skin wet with sweat. She was slowly coming to terms with it being *the* nightmare, although from previous experiences she knew that it would linger in the shadows for most of the day.

Teresa hated mornings. It had been like this for a few months now and each time she woke up, her past was there to haunt her.

It had been that way ever since they had been ordered to an outer rim world for supplies. The settlement had been under attack from raiders.

After so many years, to return to the planet she had grown up on like this brought back all her memories that she had unconsciously blocked out.

It was as though she was experiencing a double existence, approaching the settlement in her fighter, their formation at full boost to reach the settlement in time. Yet as they drew near, Teresa also knew the layout of the streets — déjà vu in a way that she had never experienced before.

Diving into combat she tried not to think about the visions that clouded her mind. Onto the tail of one raider and she accounted for it quickly, raiders being even less capable than pirates, who were typically no match for Special Operations fighter pilots.

She fought with the same skill, but her confidence had been knocked badly. Weaving through the tall buildings, she dived into the street behind another raider that was close on the tail of one of her comrades.

Dropping down to tree height, she tore up the street at full power, guns hammering, and then it happened: the lead fighter pitched and rolled, inverted, over a five-storey building into the street beyond.

The raider followed, firing a missile as it pitched up — the projectile streaked away, the star-bright base lighting its path as the lead fighter disappeared below the buildings, the missile tracking the engines, angling down, slamming into the top floor of the building: the one with the bright red shutters.

In that moment, time froze. Teresa flashed back to when she had been a little girl. The memories flooded back: her parents, life on the rim world, the red shutters on her room windows that overlooked the settlement and the square.

The surreal sense of déjà vu clarified into memory.

Watching the raider chasing down the street; the explosion that killed her parents. Other memories flooded back — unwelcome memories.

She had watched the burning buildings flash underneath her as she shot over the top, following the raider.

She finished him off, but it felt as though her eyes were glued to that burning building, the one with the red shutters… her building, her childhood home, filled with all those happy memories, memories that simultaneously returned and yet were lost forever.

There were also other memories, darker memories, that had returned with them.

Sitting on the bed in the dark, she slowed her breathing to a long rhythmic pattern. She could feel her heart rate returning to normal.

Ever since that raid, she had been getting nightmares of a very different nature, ones that left her rattled on a daily basis.

Throwing off the sheets, she got up, sliding to her feet; her towel mixed in amongst the black sheets. She had a vague recollection of working late on the plan until she had gone for a shower.

Hydro showers were strictly rationed on board a combat Black Ops warship — they were total luxury. Less than a quarter of a percent of water used during a hydro shower was unable to be recycled, but for a company of the size of the GTSC *Achilles* on deployment, their water supplies would not last long enough.

She found that after a late night of working, a hydro shower normally relaxed her and send her off to peaceful sleep, but recently, nothing helped.

She must have fallen asleep while her hair dried, wrapped up in the towel.

Grabbing the towel from the bed, she dropped it over the back of her chair to properly dry.

Sinking to the floor, she began her exercises that had become her routine every morning after her nightmares.

She pushed herself harder than normal, enjoying the freedom of her attire.

Running through the various sequences, she finally collapsed to the floor on her back, her chest heaving out of breath, legs and arms sore, her whole body shaking from her exertions, feeling like the remnants of a bad night out, the nightmare skulking in the shadows once more. She lay on her back, staring blankly at the ceiling, her mind once again on the operation, as she allowed her breathing to settle at its own pace.

She found that her thoughts were clearer, and several issues were sorting themselves out in her mind.

Levering herself off the floor in a tuck curl, she allowed the momentum to carry her on into the washroom. This time she used the sonic shower, it was quicker, but seeing as she didn't have anywhere to go immediately, she could afford the time to use her lotion afterwards. Sonic showers always left her skin dry and if she didn't take care of it now, other skin issues would develop as she had witnessed others suffer with over the years — she could not afford for that to happen.

Switching off the shower, she grabbed the pot of lotion, a concoction of her own design and went to her desk chair and started applying it to her bare skin. She had the hologram playing on repeat while she spread the lotion, allowing the information to sink in and her subconscious to work things out.

Finishing off in front of the mirror in the washroom, she washed her hands from the lotion. It would take time for it to fully absorb into her skin and thus give her time to work some more before having to face the rest of the ship.

Finally sitting down on the towel, she picked up her data pad to note down her thoughts about the operation. Her mind was working overtime, assessing the task from multiple angles and finding the details that could easily be overlooked, jotting them down to research later.

The message requiring Teresa to report to the flying bridge illuminated the com-link on her desk. She glanced up at it before returning to the holo image, making sure of what she had been looking at before making note of it on her data pad.

Finishing, she stood, grabbed her towel from the chair and chucked it into the washroom. *How long had she been working?* She had no idea, only that the movement gave much needed relief to her muscles. That was always her problem when planning an operation.

Getting dressed quickly, she glimpsed herself in the mirror, checking her hair was in place before pulling on her uniform jacket.

The figure staring back at her was wearing her uniform but was otherwise a stranger. The eyes that looked back at her in the mirror were haunted; it was as though someone else was wearing her skin.

Shaking her head, she looked down at the sink. She would need all her faculties about her over the next several weeks, as the operation had all the hallmarks of a major campaign.

Leaving the cabin, she headed for the flying bridge and the awaiting audience that were there to give final judgment or approval to her plan. Commander Chasin had agreed to it, now she just had to convince the heads of every major department and the Captain himself.

***

"You want us to do *what*?" Chief Navigator Yarik asked in surprised horror as Teresa outlined her plan.

"Hold on, Nav, let's hear all the details first," the Captain turned to Teresa, continuing, "the floor is yours. You've come up with some crazy operations in the past that worked perfectly, what have you got for us now?"

Teresa spent a good hour going through her plan, Yarik was shaking his head for most of it, but by the end he had a quizzically bemused look on his face.

"Well, Nav?" the Captain had seen the change too, "what do you think?"

"I still think it's completely insane, *but...* I'll see what I can do about getting a jump to be that accurate, give me a day, and I'll report back."

"With your permission, Captain..." Teresa looked at Captain Qadir Vasilios across the table who nodded, "I'll help you with the calculations to see what works best." Teresa added, directing the rest to Chief Navigator Yarik. "I can run through a few things with you after this briefing; I have done some calculations already."

Yarik nodded.

Gathering everyone in one last look around the group, the Captain summed up the meeting: "Commander, are you ready to deploy with the troops once we have landed?"

Teresa looked at Chasin, knowing that he could read the shock in her eyes, but otherwise her face remained emotionless.

Her mind was piecing together every conversation between Maximus and Teagan, it began to make sense, the sadness that Teagan had tried to hide.

The Commander was going to war, taking up his former life as a Black Ops Wraith; leading his troops into a war where the projected survival rate was low or even unexpected.

"Yes, sir, I have handpicked those that will remain on board to train the replacements; the rest are being prepped as we speak."

The Captain nodded. There was definitely something in his expression that indicated that he wasn't keen on losing his XO, but there wasn't anything he could do to stop it, orders from far higher up had evidently come into play.

"Group Captain, your preparations are underway?" the Captain looked at Teagan.

"Yes, sir. I worked through each wing that will deploy and like the XO, I have pulled those pilots who will be needed for training the replacements." Teagan looked across to Maximus for a brief moment, and said, "I have been working with Thames, those that will remain onboard will be split into a rotation. They all will know the specifics of their roles for training the new pilots before we arrive home."

The Captain nodded, "Good work! Let's make this operation the magnum opus for this crew and this ship, for generations recruits will speak of this operation."

The group broke up, Teresa turning to go with Chief Navigator Yarik when the Captain called her over. He stood by the large windows that spanned the flying bridge.

"Squadron Leader, walk with me, I need to talk to you, but I also need to grab something from my cabin. Nav," the Captain called across to Yarik who came over. "Go get started, I will send the Squadron Leader to find you in over-watch once she has finished her task for me first. Trust her judgement on this one." There was a greater message in his eyes that Yarik seemed to understand.

"Absolutely, sir," Yarik saluted and left.

The two of them left the bridge together as Yarik headed off for the spacious yet clandestine planning room.

"Do you think this operation has a chance to succeed?" the Captain asked as they entered the hallway.

"Yes, sir. I think we shall be able to plot the jump to give surprising results. We are deploying a serious number of our forces, and combined with those already on the ground, we should be able to hold the line until the *Achilles* returns."

Reaching his cabin door, the Captain opened it and entered, gesturing for Teresa to come in. He crossed to his desk and picked up a small box.

"I won't be able to do a presentation the way I would like to. Here." He held out his hand, presenting the box to her, "but I wanted to present this to you personally."

As she took it and opened it, Teresa saw the insignia of a Wing Leader. "I know that the XO informed you of the pending promotion."

Looking up at the Captain, she could see the sadness in his eyes.

"Congratulations, Wing Leader," he said as he saluted.

Returning the salute, Teresa locked eyes with Qadir, not wanting to miss anything he was trying to convey.

"I want you to work with Rebekah, she is the only one on board who has any experience of a jump into atmosphere. Her knowledge and experience will be very useful."

Teresa nodded, she had planned on using Rebekah as a resource, but having the Captain's blessing made it much easier.

"I know you two are friends. You did wonders by taking her under your wing and helping her grow. Let her help as much as you can, but remember, this is strictly confidential until we make the announcement. And try to look after her down there, we are going to lose a lot of good people as it is."

She nodded, emotion showing in their eyes.

The Captain turned to his desk, picking something up before facing her again.

"You're the longest serving female pilot in the suicide kings, one of my best pilots. The paperwork has to go through the official channels, but I've already submitted the recommendation, I've also put you up for a Victoria Cross. The green light came today."

She looked at him, *had she really heard correctly?*

He held up the item he had picked up, another small box.

"You've earned it, Wing Leader." He held out his hand. She shook it, lost to the reality of what it meant.

"It has been a pleasure to have you serve on board the *Achilles*. Remember you're a member of this family. Stick to your training and keep on using your ability to think outside the box, it will save your life down there, and no doubt, the lives of many others."

Watching him, she waited, knowing he would continue.

"You've heard us talking..." he went and sat on the edge of the desk. "We are deploying almost all of our forces. Commander Micah will be leading the black forces when we land. He is going to resume his posting as a Special Operations Commander once on the ground. Group Captain Garcia will coordinate the aerial defence of the region with Admiral Fraser's forces..."

He paused and looked up at her. "The *Achilles* will be returning with a full complement, trained under Group Captain Blythe and Commander Sanchez…" Another pause, then, "Based on the intel, we are not expecting to retrieve many, if any, of our forces when we return with the re-enforcements." He finally finished, "I wish you the very best, Wing Leader, and do so hope you will be one of those we pick up once we return."

Teresa stared at him; they were being sent to a war that was likely to be their last.

Well, she thought, *their squadron was known as the Suicide Kings for a very good reason*

"Ours is not to reason why… sir," she saluted.

"Let's hope not, Wing Leader, let's hope not." A heaviness seemed to come over him, all energy draining from him. He knew he was living with a false hope for his people.

***

By the time she left the cabin, she had a lot more respect for her Captain. It must have been one of the hardest decisions to follow that order: to sentence a crew that he had moulded into a family to almost-certain death.

She walked down the corridor, her thoughts lost in the future and the past. She didn't see an inch of the way. Sadness overwhelmed her for the man who had led them through operations on a path as treacherous and precarious as a knife's edge.

Life and hope had overcome death and despair under his careful leadership with unprecedented success. Now, he was sending so many lives, he had initially saved, off into a hell hole that almost guaranteed, certain death.

"Do you have a minute to talk, Squadron Leader?"

Teresa looked up at the young officer who had fallen into step beside her.

"Rivkah..." she pulled herself back to the present. "I was going to come find you."

"There's quite the rumour going around about a new operation."

"I'm not surprised, there's always rumours about new operations."

"No, this one is *big*. There's talk about invasion."

Teresa looked at Rebekah, this young officer was an outstanding pilot, her story as clouded as the murky lakes where the Mosas lurked in the depths by Teresa's childhood home. Her life experience was such that any ordinary person would have been crushed by it.

Over the last two years, they had become fairly close friends, Teresa having taken her under her wing, helping her develop her skills and guiding her as an officer and tactician, but also learning from the wealth of experience the young woman had.

She had already been an outstanding fighter pilot when they had rescued her from the GTSC *Nova*. Over time, Rebekah had opened up and the two of them had grown as friends, sharing stories, rather than just as mentor and student.

"Walk with me."

The two of them talked about various subjects as they made their way up to Over-watch, Teresa careful not to talk about the operation while in the hallways.

When they reached the corridor, Teresa ordered Rebekah to remain outside in the corridor before heading in to find the Chief Navigator sitting with several charts laying out in front of him.

"The Captain has given me permission to work on this with Rebekah. Once we've gone through several things, I want to check with her, we will come and plan with you." She said when the navigator looked up at her, his expression plain that he had no idea where to begin.

"If you can plot the rest of the jump, we'll all plan the re-entry together."

Nodding with exasperation, the Chief Navigator never said a word. Teresa watched him return to his charts with more enthusiasm than he had when she had entered. She left the planning area.

***

It was customary for junior ranks to wait for an invitation into a senior officer's cabin, and although Teresa and Rebekah were friends and had spent a fair amount of time chatting in her cabin, Rebekah stopped respectfully, waiting for Teresa to permit entry upon reaching her cabin.

Flicking on the lights, Teresa hit the selector that made the door slide shut and lock. Traversing the open space, she started up the holo programme and pulled her data pad out of the holder. She gestured for Rebekah to come over and join her by the desk while she reached into another draw to pull up a data pad for Rebekah to work on.

She unfastened her jacket and hung it on the hook by the washroom door.

Rebekah came across to the desk, undoing her flight suit also and tying the sleeves around her waist.

She had gotten used to her friend's withdrawn nature, the 'true' self that only fully materialised behind closed doors.

Her antics had told Rebekah that it was going to be a while before she would leave and followed Teresa's suit in getting comfortable.

Their pasts had made them closer, despite being totally different, the adversity they had experienced was a common bond.

Taking a seat by the desk, Teresa looked at her friend. "What we are going to discuss cannot leave this room until the official briefing, otherwise if you join a discussion it will be in a secluded environment."

Rebekah looked Teresa in the eye, the intensity of understanding clear in her brown eyes.

The images, so familiar to Teresa, jumped into view; the ring of ships on the ground with a makeshift barricade and fortifications. The images included the storm of fighters in battle for the heavens.

It was a shock for Rebekah to see and then she made out the moving land was in fact the tide of ground troops swarming the area.

"Is that where we are going?"

Teresa looked up at her. The expression in her eyes told Rebekah all she needed to know.

"When is the briefing?"

Teresa gave an imperceptible smile that barely touched her lips. Rivkah was good like that, she could be trusted with anything and it would not get spread around the ship.

"Two days' time." Their eyes met.

"It's dangerous, isn't it?"

"Let's just say we'll be making GTSC history."

Rebekah nodded, she knew what that meant, that was what Sebastian used to speak about. She closed her eyes, picturing his face for a moment, opening them again, bringing herself into the present.

Rebekah's face had flickered with an emotion that confused Teresa.

"You're going to jump into the atmosphere! Bypass the fleet orbiting the planet."

It was less of a question, but not quite a statement.

Teresa felt like she had just been punched. Rebekah had always been quick at catching on, but that conclusion, at that speed, was astounding.

"When I was on the *Ulysses*, we used to do that over short distances when we would jump the fighters in to attack settlements."

"Do you think it can be done with a ship the size of the *Achilles*?"

"We jumped the *Ulysses* into atmosphere once."

"How did it go?"

"The navigator plotted it wrong. He wouldn't allow anyone to help, so he never corrected for the inertial momentum from the jump, spin of the planet and factored time difference in the jump clock. He didn't account for the gravitational well from opening a slip-space rupture in close proximity to another large body and the pull of the planet's gravity."

"And..?"

"We ended up jumping in too close to the surface and off target. The *Ulysses* was partially crushed upon entry. The engines couldn't catch us in the descent in time before it slammed into the ground, partially crippling itself."

"What happened then?"

"We completed the raid while the Captain tried to get the ship off the ground. He managed it too. We were limping away when an Alliance warship ordered us to stop. The Captain went ballistic, ordering us to attack. I think he had inhaled too many cryo fumes from the pipes that had burst. He was acting very weird."

"That's how you ended up on board the *Repulse*?"

"That's right, the Captain decided to fight instead of running, not that we would have got very far. We were venting atmosphere into space from the crash."

"What can you tell me about a jump into atmosphere?" She knew that Rebekah had been part of the bridge team and had helped with navigation as well as flying fighters while she had been on board the *Ulysses*.

"Well, the first thing you have to remember is time. The predicted jump coordinates need to be adjusted for the fact that the planetary body will rotate by the length of time spent in slip-space. Next, the gravitational force of the planet and third, the density and composition of the atmosphere itself." Rebekah pulled up the data pad while Teresa made notes on hers.

Soon there were graphs and drawings all over the screen.

Calculations littered the open spaces and they had only just begun.

Five hours later, Teresa emerged from the washroom rubbing her eyes. It had been an intense planning session. Her uniform hung from the hooks in the wall, her boots tucked tidily by the far wall.

She looked at Rebekah who had also gotten more comfortable over the last few hours, her flight suit folded at the corner of the bed, her boots by the door.

Seven plasma glass scrolls were stretched out over the desk. Both data pads had writing filling the screens, the holo table still glowing with the images of the planet and the battle.

Rebekah picked up her glass that was by her hand on the desk, swirling the amber liquid around in it before taking a sip.

She was still head down, working intently on a calculation, as Teresa walked over to the desk again picking up from where she had left off.

Teresa was in only her black t-shirt and underwear that she had been wearing under her uniform, but her presence of mind was as though she was already in the cockpit during the operation ahead.

Rebekah looked up. She too was only wearing the under armour that all flight crews wore beneath their flight suits: a form-fitting razor back sleeveless top and equally fitted shorts. The knife that she always wore when ready to fly lay on the bed next to her flight suit.

Teresa paused with her pen raised, mid-thought.

"If we could calculate the telemetry, could we launch the fighters directly after re-entry?"

"We should be able to while the *Achilles* is still descending."

The two young women kept discussing as they worked on their ideas.

Teresa was getting pretty satisfied that they would have enough to take to Chasin and the navigator soon.

Another couple of hours passed before Teresa and Rebekah gathered up all the plasma glass rolls and data pads that they would need to take with them to see Yarik. Rebekah redressed in her flight suit while Teresa checked the data link one more time to see if there were any new messages about the situation on the planet. She pulled on the combat trousers she wore off-duty and they headed out to find the Chief Navigator in over-watch where he sat with his own calculations spread across the plotting table, the majestic array of slip-space lighting the background beyond the vast plotting table.

Looking around her with intent amazement, Rebekah took in the view of the clandestine planning area that she had, thus far, never set foot in.

As they crossed the open space, Teresa noted the work that the Chief Navigator was putting into the operation. All that for plotting a jump, and now for the difficult part.

"Nav, shall we plan the unthinkable?"

He looked up from his work.

"You really know how to come up with some crazy ideas, don't you?"

His eyes flicked to Rebekah and back to Teresa, "Let me ask you one thing. Do you genuinely believe this is possible?"

Teresa smiled, ushering Rebekah forward with her hand.

"Let us show you what we have come up with so far."

***

Visions of dark fighters streaking low overhead, guns flashing like droplets of fire along their curved wings. This was how every night started...

Pain lanced through her side as another blow knocked the wind out of her. She was tiring from her fight, her back raw from scraping on the hard surface beneath her. Harsh breathing and the stale rank stench of alcohol and cigarette smoke filled her senses, robbing her of breath and lessening her ability to fight back. Somewhere a woman laughed, her maniacal cackle, rasping from a life of substance abuse, rang out hollowly in the room that was out of sight behind the greasy hair that hung like a curtain around the face above her, hiding it in shadow. Only his eyes, bright pale dots of evil, were visible as they glared down at her. All she could feel was the sandpaper roughness of his unshaven

face chafing at the soft skin of her wrists with every movement as she tried desperately to keep him at bay.
The more she fought, the more he was strengthened by it, enjoying it, while the lancing pain split her apart!

She came abruptly awake, fighting the tangled sheets that suffocated her damp skin, dragging at her legs, restraining her, her panic rising as she could not move.

Heart pounding hard enough to escape her chest, Teresa fell to the floor off the side of her bed. Finally finding enough purchase to free herself from the dark sheets.

Forcing herself up, she perched on the edge of the desk, looking down at the sheets, seeing only the memory. Breathing hard, breaths coming in gasps as though she had been running hard for a great distance.

***

Dressed in full uniform, Teresa emerged onto the flying bridge, the Captain was already underway briefing the Squadron Leaders and other wing leaders on the upcoming operation, standing around the holo table, the Captain was talking earnestly. She took a deep breath and headed over, the Captain nodding to her as she joined, never breaking sentence.

Before her was the scene of the raging battle, the ground troops heavily engaged and fighters in a swarm over the scene.

It looked like the fortifications were being overrun, but some heavy equipment had been deployed, that was for sure. It must be that the very latest intel to have arrived, it looked a lot more detailed than what she had seen before.

"... re-enforcements... next wave... deployed... squadron deployment..."

Teresa was examining the map and not really listening. She noticed the precarious position that the defenders were in.

"What's the ETA?" asked one of the Squadron Leaders.

Switching her attention to the conversation, she was in time for the Captain to detail their part in the situation.

"Six days! The instant we jump in, all fighter and bomber squadrons will need to deploy. The *Achilles* will then jump out again." Taking a deep breath in, he continued, "The *Achilles* will make its way home and then join the re-enforcements for another wave." he scanned the group, looking everyone in the eye. "Group Captain Blythe has devised a training scheme for those staying on board for the re-enforcements while Wing Leader Palmer has detailed a training plan for the mission. All crews will be in extensive training until zero hour."

He looked around the group again, then stated, "Commander Chasin has also come up with both training and deployment plans for all ground troops and Wraiths."

Teresa knew what was coming next but to hear it again, the clarity in his voice seemed to seal her future with finality. Time slowed down as she waited for the Captain's next words, "You will be on your own until re-enforcements arrive. I do not know how long that will be... you all have served the *Achilles* well. I know you won't let her down now."

They all nodded, there wasn't much else to say when the Captain who had built the ship and squadrons up to what they are now asks for such a sacrifice, and they all knew that was exactly what it was... *a sacrifice!*

They all saluted.

"I will go through some more details with you once I get a response from High Command and then I will address your squadrons, but for now, keep this under wraps; we don't need everyone to know just yet."

Again, they all nodded and started heading out.

"Teresa, wait behind please."

She looked at the Captain, who had moved over to the side where he grabbed a data pad from the bench and came back to the holo table. He stood there watching the scene displayed in a kind of trance.

"Are you set?"

"Yes, sir. Just about. A few more things to check with Nav, but I believe we are ready."

The Captain nodded. "I will need you to finalise those, but you are also a Wing Leader now. You're effectively taking over Teagan's role as she steps up."

Teresa nodded; she would have to look after her wing's preparation now as well.

"I got a reply back from High Command about your idea."

She looked at him, realising he had lied earlier, and she was about to find out why.

"They freaked. I've never seen such a reply to any communication in the history of my time in the GTSC."

"So?"

"I'm authorising it on my own accord."

"Thank you, sir."

"It is the only tactic that will prevent severe casualties to our forces." he looked at her; "It is absolutely crazy, but you've proven in the past that crazy works … I'm going to miss having you plan our ops. The others will just seem boring from now on."

Teresa smiled. It was a legacy she was going to be remembered for. Her final mission and it was her best: the plan was ground-breaking, monumental in the history of the GTSC.

***

Walking the halls of the *Achilles*, Teresa took in the level of activity, people hustling this way and that. Her mind roamed every detail of the operation, making sure that the plans were as complete as possible. She knew, deep down, something would be out of place, but it was

195

unlikely to surface. Next was making sure that her wing was ready. Of the two, the latter was the one she was most concerned about. Her new role held the lives of her pilots. It was strange — the mission held the lives of so many more, the whole ship in fact; however, she was less concerned about that, that was her forte.

Heading down the corridor that led to the female quarters for the Suicide Kings, Teresa was thinking about the training regime that she and Rebekah had devised. But something about the programme had made her wonder about Rebekah's ideas. She had hit the simulators more than anyone else so far.

Rounding the corner into the cabin Rebekah shared with the other female pilots of their squadron, she saw Rebekah, standing by her locker; her shirt was dark from her exercises.

"How did you do today?"

Rebekah looked around, "Good, I think. Managed to fend off a couple of fighters for a little longer."

"From what I've been told, you're running the black level sims, delta clearance. The ones designed for squadron practise."

Rebekah just looked at her.

"You've been beating squadron records single-handedly on a daily basis."

"I wouldn't know, just want to be ready and there's nothing better than practice."

"Don't overdo it, I need you strong for the actual fight."

"I'll be alright."

Teresa watched her for a short while but decided to let it go. There were still a few days before they would be in range to jump into the system.

"I'm going to need your help organising things. I've asked the Captain if he will consider promoting you to Squadron Leader to make it official."

***

196

Breathing easily, Teresa rounded the corner onto the hangar deck, keeping pace as she ran across the bustling yet open flight deck. It was nearing the end of the longer route she took around the Heavy Cruiser. She felt good, the plan had been laid, with last-minute details being worked out as further intelligence came in, but for the most part, all that was left was the systematic training of everyone involved. They had been running drills around the clock for all fighter and bomber pilots and she knew Maximus was doing the same for all ground troops. The paces the Commander put them through were stringent, but he led them from the front, no one holding a higher score than himself.

Teresa had seen them on occasions and joined them on others as they ran the length of the cruiser, but today she wanted one last long run around the ship. The next two days would be hectic to say the least, and it was her way of saying goodbye to a ship that was the first home she had since her parents had been killed when she was eight. She was leaving more than just an operational posting, this had become the reality, the world she understood and a family that had accepted her. She was leaving her home.

She remembered the pain in the Captain's eyes as he had explained the situation to her, he was their Captain, their protector, and in many ways, he was her architect, guiding and encouraging her to think through a problem to far greater depths, learning to eliminate the devil hiding in the details, pushing her natural ability to think outside the box to new heights. She owed him so very much.

She maintained a fast pace despite the length of her run, choosing lines to run around the obstructions in her path as she weaved through the fighters that were undergoing repairs and improvements. She preferred running the length of the ship rather than the exercise sims that most used, it was more mentally stimulating for her.

Each pilot was taking minimal personal belongings, the rest being stored in the *Achilles'* hold for when they either returned to the ship or to be send to their next of kin in the actuality of their predicted deaths.

Teresa wasn't taking much. She came to the ship with very little, the rest left behind in her aunt's house when she had finally managed to escape on her thirteenth birthday. By the time she joined the Navy, there was nothing left for her there.

However, life on board a Black Ops battle cruiser didn't allow room for much anyway. A pilot's personal effects were usually able to fit inside the cockpit for storage in any case. Thinking about her parents and their house back on the settlement, they had been happily comfortable, but by the time she had joined the Navy, she had only a few photographs saved from her aunt's destructive tendencies; the Navy had given her the rest that she now owned, save for her mother's dog tags and her father's pendant, retrieved from the wreckage of their building.

Teresa pushed on, faces and memories flashed before her, the last few years running through her mind, friends who had transferred or been silenced forever in the battles they had been through. She remembered Veikko as she ran; he was the first fighter pilot she had seen running the decks upon her arrival. They had quickly become friends, running together. She had mourned his loss greatly but had kept running alone, until Rebekah, that was.

Hers had been a happy existence in this Special Ops Heavy Cruiser, although touched with sadness when friends failed to return from a mission.

Reaching the stairs at the far end of the hangar, she seized the railing and scaled the steps fast, one last time. At the top, she never broke stride, launching from the uppermost step towards the door at the end of the gangway. Pushing it open, she burst into the flying bridge and across the entire length of the open expanse, coming to a stop at the far side in front of the large windows that curled down under the deck.

There was a glow of light green by the planning table, the ship's AI at rest, reflected in the window.

She stared out at the colourful world of slip-space, her thoughts as numerous as the shifting shapes in the display that enveloped the ship.

They were set to have a party that evening, one last time. She knew that the other pilots were expecting her to say something, explain, reassure, tell them why they had been picked and not asked to join those that would stay on board. She could feel it in the ship, everyone was mobilising to be on top line as though they were joining the invasion fleet, but instead everyone on board seemed to share the conscious awareness that they were departing the ship — 'stepping off' as it was known in the service.

If that was the case, then the Suicide Kings
would go out in style, she decided.

She had seen it in everyone's faces, the uncertainty. People all over the ship were taking the remaining opportunities while they existed. Newfound relationships had started, one-night stands between friends who danced around each other for the last few years, seizing their last chance. She was painfully aware that many of their number would never see home or each other ever again.

"Yit'rô! Everything ready?"

The green glow disappeared and a figure in naval uniform appeared.

"Yes, Wing Leader."

Teresa stepped closer to the planning table.

"The issue with supplies has been resolved?"

"Yes, sir. They will be transported using the sparrow hawks to get them over to the *Pegasus*."

Nodding, Teresa pressed a button, calling up the hologram of the battlefield; the last images and clips that had been received from the ground base as they got closer to the planet came alive, showing once again, the stark reality of what they were going into.

Pressing a soft key on the screen, one of the clips started again. Screaming and automatic fire could be heard in the background, the heavier crump of larger cannons shook the ground while the person filming panned the scene. It could have been night-time — the sky was filled with black, billowing plumes of smoke that rose from all over the area. The land was scarred with scorched earth and debris, broken mechs and tanks that still burned, and then a fighter appeared through the smoke, guns hammering, blue flashes lighting up the scene, as it shot low over the area and the sound of its engines screamed until it vanished from view.

This was going to be a war like no other they had ever seen during their service on board the *Achilles*. She sincerely hoped they were ready.

***

Heading down to her cabin from the flying bridge, Teresa took the longer route that would take her past Rebekah's cabin. She wanted to check on the young officer as she had been pushing herself a lot with the training. Teresa had seen her out running and exercising as well as logging lengthy sims and yet still had managed to keep up to date with all the organisational prep that Teresa had asked for help with.

Reaching Rebekah's dormitory, she stopped by the door and looked in. Rebekah was there, fast asleep on her bed, face down, wet hair to one side. Teresa smiled. Rebekah was a good girl; she knew how to listen to her instincts better than anyone Teresa had known before.

***

"Tomorrow morning we will arrive at the planet. Then, ladies and gentlemen, you are on your own."

Silence reigned on the bridge. Those in the small knot of people absorbed the news — it was not new, but hearing it put so black and white gave an edge to it.

The bridge staff around them were frozen, trying not to move so as not to be noticed. They were all listening to the briefing, all accepting the news in their own way as final. A cold reality faced those that remained on board — a long trek back to safe space from behind enemy lines with a skeleton offensive crew and their ability to protect themselves heavily impaired. If they were attacked in force, it would be a desperate struggle to survive, let alone win, and, when they returned with re-enforcements, they were unlikely to see the majority of the crew they had lived with for the last several years ever again.

The Captain was the one to break the spell, barking, "Zero hour is just over twenty-seven hours away. Let's make sure that we have everything prepped and ready for a seamless deployment."

They all saluted and headed for their respective departments with the meeting breaking up, it was as though the bridge had come back to life. Noise and activity erupted into efficiency — personnel walking between stations, officers giving orders and the rank and file being a lot more streamlined in their activities.

Heading out of the bridge, Teresa wanted to check on Rebekah after she had seen her asleep that morning; she needed her at full strength for the coming operation.

Heading to the cabin she found Rebekah on her bunk still, a book in hand and reading.

"How's it going?"

Rebekah looked around the page.

"It's going pretty well."

"Are you ready?"

"We'll find out, I guess."

"I need you strong. Will you be ready for departure?"

Rebekah watched Teresa as she spoke; the genuine concern and care was something she was still not very used to.

"Already packed, just one last run around the ship tomorrow morning and then it's go-time."

Teresa nodded.

Teresa assessed Rebekah, she knew that she could count on the young woman, an unwritten honour code that she seemed to live by gave Teresa confidence, not only was Rebekah a friend, but she was a valuable person to have by your side in a bad dogfight.

***

Teresa's fighter lifted. The thrum from her engines hummed through the hull as they warmed up, the dials on the screens changing colour as the cores reached optimum levels. The instant response on the controls was comforting but was again a reminder that she was leaving more than just a ship, their maintenance crew had looked after the aircraft better than she had ever seen anywhere else in the service manage to do.

The *Epirus* fighter was not a new generation fighter, but it was tested and true, its service in the GTSC Black Ops programme had success records that out classed most other fighter classes.

Gliding into the flight lane, she was aware of the rest of her wing manoeuvring into the lane behind her along the length of the hangar deck. They would form up for a squadron take-off, each squadron sectioned off, with Teresa's fighter at the head of the formation.

The Chief Mechanic was standing prominently by one of the main stanchions, he was going to watch his fleet depart, probably forever. She saluted him and watched him return the mark of respect.

The great timers displayed the countdown to their re-entry. The clock had nearly run out, mere minutes remaining before they would emerge from slip-space and Teresa and the other pilots would launch into the unknown. That certainly churned her stomach into a storm of butterflies that she worked hard to stifle, so as not to betray her outwardly composed demeanour.

Any exit from slip-space carried a tremor of turbulence felt throughout the whole ship, but emerging into the atmosphere of a planet, the speed and gravitational pull combined with the huge bulk of the Heavy Cruiser rupturing the natural realm would prove severe. Only Rivkah had any former experience of what that would be like, but her knowledge was coloured by the *Ulysses* slamming bodily into the planet's surface, the hull being partially crushed by the force and the dissipating slip-space rupture.

All they could do was expect severe turbulence and hope it wasn't going to be immobilising.

"All hands standby to exit slip-space!"

The announcement electrified the crew in the hangar deck. Everyone finalising their preparations before the armoured door to the hangar would slide open.

Teresa looked across to where the Chief Engineer stood, he was facing away, one hand to his ear, listening to instructions over an earpiece that he was wearing.

Returning to face Teresa, he raised both hands, fingers spread, then closed his right fist with curled fingers facing Teresa and pointed one finger to the ceiling while circling his hand anticlockwise.

Teresa nodded. The message gave her ten seconds before re-entry. As soon as the tremor started, she would lead her formation down the flight lane, that would give them plenty of time to accelerate, along the length of the hangar, for the armoured door to have opened for their passage into a Valkyrie's paradise.

A murmur rang through the ship, felt rather than heard. Teresa picked up on it as some of the deck crew started looking around them.

Then she could see equipment shaking to the tremors. Ten seconds were up, she lifted the *Epirus* fighter up into the flight lane, knowing that the rest of the wing was doing the same, section by section.

As she began accelerating, she saw the sudden rise in turbulence becoming markedly severe, the deck crew being jolted around, stumbling as they scrambled for safety.

The huge door at the end of the hangar started sliding open, the shimmering blue of the plasma shield extending as it sealed the opening, keeping the hangar airtight. Flames engulfed the entrance, burning violent orange and red against the perpetual darkness beyond. The world around them erupted in commotion, the deck shaking violently as its crew went sprawling, cables and lanyards swinging through the open spaces, their pulleys sliding on rails across the ceiling.

It was beautiful and terrifyingly surreal seeing the familiar world moving around them as the fighters remained safe, suspended between ceiling and floor, the fighters weaving to keep from colliding with the stanchions and other obstacles as they presented themselves.

Ninety-six fighters poured out from the side of the *Achilles* like a stream of flares, their engines bright in the engulfing flames that surrounded the descending Heavy Cruiser.

The *Achilles* still sinking from the pull from the planet's gravity; dust clouds billowing up from the shock wave that covered the battlefield below in an impenetrable cloud in the thick darkness. Plumes of dense black smoke towered over the scene that surrounded the *Achilles*, covering the whole arena with an acrid blanket that blocked out the sun.

Far below was a scene of chaos, the enemy forces in disarray from the sudden appearance of the Heavy Cruiser. The gravity well from its slip-space rupture acting as a concussive blast that had crushed the armoured mechs and tanks. No doubt the soldiers themselves had faired far worse. The bodily impact of the GTSC *Achilles* into the ground would have caused less overall damage.

Teresa's wing was quickly forming up into their respective squadrons and going on the offensive, taking advantage of the confusion they had just caused. It wouldn't be long before the enemy forces retaliated with a hailstorm of withering fire targeting the towering bulk of the *Achilles* as it manoeuvred out of its position towards the relative safety of friendly lines.

Four lonely marauder fighters came streaking out of the ring of defensive warships, the towering fortifications standing tall and blackened against the darker backdrop. Only four fighters out of so many that had once been carried by these proud warships. These were all that remained of the aerial defences that this besieged outpost had left after just over a week and a half of combat.

What savage battle had these pilots seen?

As the *Achilles* manoeuvred towards the defensive position, the other two wings began launching; they would dominate the skies for today at least, but their presence would also unleash hell from the enemy forces. Every available fighter and bomber within a hundred-mile radius was no doubt being scrambled and vectored their way.

A reign of fire was about to commence, marking the embattled position's first relief from the siege.

**Lieutenant Rebekah Le Sabre,
On board the GTSC *Nova*, Cruiser,
Two years, three months before Operation *Trident***

Fire burst from the adjoining corridor entrance, spewing from the gap in the wall as if from a dragon's mouth, filling the passageway ahead of her as another explosion rocked the ship, the deck lurching and dropping beneath Rebekah as she ran. She dropped to the deck mid-stride as she sprinted for the hangar, momentum sending her skidding along the floor as she passed under the belching flame that billowed across the ceiling and licked at the vents and equipment. Heat beat at her face and she could smell the burning of her own hair and the barbecue tang of searing flesh as she passed the hallway now ablaze with an inferno. For the briefest instant, she could see two shadowy figures writhe in the flames within the corridor, the vision lasting only a fraction of a second before it was gone. She shut her eyes as the flames engulfed her, fire lashed at her exposed skin as she slid out the far side. Rolling with the tilt of the deck as it wallowed in the aftermath of the explosion, she scrambled to her feet. Running along the hallway, pushing herself off the walls as she pinballed to and fro with the rise and fall of the deck, while the corridor pulsed with red light from the echoing alarms and she sprinted as though all the demons of hell were at her heels!

Two decks to go and the cruiser shook beneath her feet again. The punishment suffered by the GTSC *Nova* had been rapidly worsening — who knew how long it would survive on its own now that the *Adventure Sun* drifted, its dead hulk another relic for future generations to discover. The way things were going, it seemed like the GTSC *Nova* was not far away from joining it.

Sliding down the stair railings in the narrow passage that lead to the final open gangway that spanned the length of the hangar, Rebekah used her momentum to launch herself across the grating in one bound and leapt over the railings into the free fall drop to the hangar below, instead landing on top of the crates and boxes that the Chief Engineer kept piled next to the stanchions that separated each fighter bay from the next. Jumping down the pile in three fluid movements, she was on the flight deck and running for her fighter with all haste, her hair lifting from her shoulders in the wind of her passage. To her left she could see other pilots bursting from the archway openings as they streaked towards their fighters in a race of survival as part of the ship wide scramble. Their comrades of the 'ready fighters' whom had launched as soon as they had exited slip-space, were fighting for their lives against overwhelming odds.

Reaching her fighter, she jumped up onto the short wing, balancing on the curved surface, grabbing the side of the cockpit and pulled herself forward, she hurdled the side with the ease of a professional athlete, settling in the cockpit.

Clipping the harness around herself, Rebekah flicked on the switches along the lower length of the instrument panel with one finger as she pulled the straps tight across her body with the other.

Unfastening the top breast pocket, Rebekah removed the data pad that the Captain had given her before she left the bridge and stowed it in her hold-all that was stashed behind her seat as it was every time she launched.

Scanning the scene for any remaining mechanics in close proximity with her fighter, she engaged the engines and felt the fighter lift, caught in limbo amidst the gravity field that hovered the great metal bird above the solid deck. It had an effect similar to two poles with magnets repelling each other. There was no one immediately around her, so Rebekah lifted from where her fighter rested in its bay and turning it, the canopy closing as she entered the flight lane, accelerating along the dim hangar towards the pale gray, blue plasma shield at the far side.

Fire burst from another passageway, jetting across the hangar, the whole world around Rebekah revolving as the ship recoiled from another concussive blast.

Keeping the fighter steady, Rebekah worked hard to not let the world she knew so well distract her from flying straight and level. Her fighter was at an odd angle to the deck, but it was no different to when she had flown through the drifting hull of the great war destroyer when she had been with the *Ulysses*.

***

Bursting forth from the side of the aged Special Operations cruiser, GTSC *Nova*, Rebekah was appalled at the amount of destruction that greeted her. Two full wings of fighters and bombers amassed around the few remaining aircraft from both the *Adventure Sun* and the 'ready fighters' from the *Nova*, their battle was a hopeless endeavour without the support that was only now launching and even that was questionable in its ability to alter the outcome.

Two enemy cruisers were broadside, their weapons pounding out shot after shot that slammed into the side of the *Nova* with devastating accuracy.

Clearing her thoughts, she quietened herself, running through her routine, hearing the echoing voice of Sebastian and Tim giving her the advice in their calm voices that had accompanied her ever since she set foot on board the GTSC *Repulse* and joined the ranks of the Academy.

Flicking her HUD to a dimmer setting, she angled her shields to favour the front quadrant for her first pass. Guns selector off safe and cycled through the missiles.

Several other fighters were now streaming from the hangar bay, their blue plasma trails leaving bright white arcs marking where they had engaged afterburners and were now boosting towards the fight.

More heavy rounds flashed passed, humming with proximity, there was little she could do for the *Nova*, but her friends of the past year who were fighting for survival, those she could potentially help.

The heavy rounds smashed into the bulk of the Special Operations cruiser; she knew it was only a matter of time now.

"All hands! Jump drives are offline!"

There was a finality with that statement that surpassed everything else she had experienced.

In every engagement, she always had an inexplicable belief that she would make it through — something ingrained within her, no matter how bad the situation or how damaged her fighter. She had always got home, pulling the wrecked hull out of the fire as though through a magic trick, but those words weighed heavy on her.

A doomed ship with no jump capability, outnumbered by a superior force, it was a one-way ticket.

Was this what she had trained for? Eighteen years of age and destined to die in some backwater system picking up a message from a crippled pirate ship that had been used as bait?

If that was the case, she'd make her mark on the enemy forces, she'd make her death so costly they would regret the day they had crossed paths with her.

She had always been cold, calm and calculated in battle, but now she sank into a sub-world, a part of her conscious that she had never known existed. Clarity formed within and around her. Her heartbeat slowing down, her mind speeding up and the situation before her changed from a one-sided battle to a slow enactment of war, as though time had slowed down but forgotten about her. She took in critical details throughout the battle, noting the pulse of laser flashes from the turrets that lined the two cruisers; the fact that the enemy fighters had tighter turning circles than the

Typhoon fighters that they were flying. The pilots of the *Adventure Sun* were holding their own, managing to keep the enemy forces at bay temporarily while another GTN fighter exploded in a vivid flash of bright purple and white.

She watched as the cloud of enemy fighters approached, their engines glowing like a mass of fireflies while behind them the curved arcs of the fighters' engines scoring trails across the sky as though carved by the tips of razor-sharp scimitars dancing in an epic display of some macabre ballet.

Beautiful yet tragic, the finest hour was also the last.

Purple laser fire slashed passed Rebekah's canopy as the lead enemy aircraft opened fire still outside effective range. The wild shots scattered past, the occasional one misting over her shields as it struck home, but nothing to concern herself with just yet.

Rebekah grimaced. They must be fleet pilots, their lack of self control causing them to open fire far too early. In a Special Operation fighter pilot's world, that meant death, usually for that pilot and often their unit after they had just given away their position, allowing the enemy unit the luxury of forming up and closing their ranks in a defensive position and call for reinforcements.

Holding her fire until the lead fighter was dead centered within effective killing range, she zeroed in and fired. Chewing through the shields quickly and punched through the canopy and armoured hulls accounting for her first victory of the engagement.

As in the Greek battles of old, the fighters engaged with the first pass, sweeping through the other formation, wheeling and diving as they turned to attack, falling into a chaotic, pell-mell world of a dogfight.

Rebekah dodged and multiple aircraft flashed passed in close proximity, their hulls close enough that she felt like she could reach out and touch them, instead, she fired at as many targets as she could, hoping that the near pointblank impact would sustain greater damage to her foe.

As she burst from the far side of the formation, she turned quickly and dived back into the fray. Ducking and diving, Rebekah chased after one fighter and then another, breaking off only when another fighter engaged her on a deflection shot. She made her presence count, quickly dispatching several fighters with a strange remoteness, feeling cut off as though it was a mere training exercise with no consequences instead of the impending ultimate price that faced them all.

She latched onto the tail of a passing fighter, sticking to him as though there was an invisible cord that connected them.

Even if they managed to secure a victory on the field, they were still dead, facing a slow and painful death as they crawled back to friendly lines at reduced sub-light speed, waiting to be found by any passing enemy vessel. Their distance from GTSC held territory would take them six years to cross without the ability to jump, plenty of time for the enemy forces to find them and finish the job.

Three diamond-bright twinkling lights flashed past Rebekah's canopy breaking her reverie. Holding the tight turn, she looked in the opposite direction, identifying the three bright lights scoring straight lines through the chaos of battle.

"Warheads locked on the *Nova*!" she continued her turn, shooting down the fighter she had been engaged with and continued turning towards the three warheads. She accelerated to full power and hit the afterburners as she chased down the warheads, but they had too much of a lead.

She watched helplessly as the trio struck home — three flashes as bright as the sun. The aged cruiser reeled in the wake of destruction, the previous damage proving too great. Cavernous stress fractures showed in the armour plating.

She twisted away, looking for the offending bombers who had shot the warheads, but she could not spot them.

As dogfight often were, this one was short lived, they had not been engaged for long, maybe only fifteen or twenty minutes, but Rebekah noticed that fewer fighters and bombers filled the open space.

Close on the tail of her next quarry, she doggedly clung to every twist and turn, nothing could shake her.

She was skeptical that their efforts had shot down so many, rather they seemed to be retreating back to their parent cruisers.

Why?

A frown furrowed her brow. Something didn't add up, the enemy had the GTN forces outnumbered and outgunned. One more hit like that last one and the Nova was done for, so why retreat?

Just then her fighter's systems picked up the distress beacon from the *Nova,* she also knew that it was routine to send the coded signal to High Command before firing off the SOS.

The fighter she was chasing peeled off towards the enemy cruisers, she followed instinctively, close on its tail and blasted through its shields. The fighter exploded with a vivid flash of purple and orange fire that vanished as she flew through the cloud of shrapnel from the disintegrating fighter.

The majority of allied fighters were closing formation just outside of the savage anti-aircraft barrage that the two cruisers were putting up. Only a few had followed their targets into the hellish world, and they were faring poorly. Their dashing bravery had won them a few extra victories, however Rebekah watched as two GTN fighters flashed diamond bright at the base of their engines before vanishing in a colourful fireball in quick succession. *Gone!* Their names removed from the order of battle as though they had never existed.

One of their number had fared better than the others, accounting for another five fighters before being winged badly.

Rebekah watched as the fighter turned, seeming to have a charmed life as it floated through the barrage of anti-aircraft fire, following another damaged fighter that made tracks for the hangar bay.

"That's the wrong hangar!" someone shouted over the radio, obviously engrossed in the scene, thinking that the pilot had gotten himself confused in the situation. Maybe he was injured or even dead and the aircraft had locked onto the automatic landing function that guided returning aircraft back to safety.

Rebekah was pretty certain that she knew what the pilot was doing, and surprised that the only feeling she had was one of respect.

They watched as the GTN fighter vanished from sight into the hangar, still streaming plasma fire from one engine.

It felt like an eternity, watching as the great bulk of the two cruisers turned to head away from a sure victory.

Then it happened.

Fire belched from the side of the cruiser, an inferno pluming out of the hangar bay. The great armoured doors slid closed to protect the integrity of the ship's hull.

The pilot had detonated all remaining ordinance deep within the unprotected belly of the enemy cruiser, mixed with the munitions stored ready to rearm the fighter and bomber wings, the devastation must have been extensive, but that didn't stop the two large enemy cruisers from accelerating away and jumping out of the system.

***

Following a slow circling patrol path around the floundering Special Operations cruiser, Rebekah examined the damage. It was exceedingly lucky that the *Nova* hadn't detonated with that last explosion, some would call it a miracle. But this absurd lull in such a savage battle where the enemy had quite literally spared them from destruction still baffled her.

"All GTN crews, standby to deploy life pods. Fighters, protect the crew of the *Nova* for as long as possible."

Between the remaining fighter wing and those fighters surviving from the *Adventure Sun* they still had a fighter force to be reckoned with, although without backup from a capital ship, they wouldn't survive long.

On one pass, as she was facing away, towards the engines of the *Nova*, Rebekah noticed an inflection in the stars far outside the range of her scanners, but she couldn't be sure.

As she circled, she kept watching and after a while she could make out the outline of a warship approaching at extreme range. She checked her scanners again, but nothing showed up. Was she about to make a fool of herself or was she about to ruin someone's day?

Locating the section leader, she broke formation and flew across his bows, swinging around to match his flight path, only backwards.

She knew she was about to get a roasting for performing such a manoeuvre without permission, but she acted quickly, triggering off her forward lights in a rapid series of Morse code, transmitting her observation to the senior pilot. She didn't want to use her radio, knowing that her transmission could be picked up by anyone who was listening.

The section leader watched until the message finished and brought his fighter around onto the new bearing. It took him a few seconds to be able to identify what Rebekah had seen, but in the end, he found the bulk of a warship running dark against the darkness of space. Rebekah could see the pilot initiating a scan on his instruments before returning to stare out of the forward canopy windscreen. Copying his actions, Rebekah initiated her own scan once again to see if the ship was within range now. *Nothing!* Before Rebekah could stop him, the senior pilot 's voice came clearly over the radio.

"*Nova* command, warship bearing zero, five, seven, seven, one, four, running dark!"

Captain Hamilton of the GTSC *Nova* was instantly on with a reply.

"Nothing on the scanners, are you sure."

"Yes, I'm sure, myself and Red Three have eyes on it now."

"Red section, Blue section, engage the warship. All other fighters standby for life pods."

Rebekah followed the section leader as what was left of red flight boosted power and sped away towards the incoming warship, their formation closing up in a tight Vic with Red One in the lead. As they grew closer, they could make out the impressive lines of the grand warship, but Rebekah wondered why no one was shooting yet, they were clearly within range of the guns, but the ship behaved as though they were not there.

Swinging wide, Red flight allowed the vessel to pass so they could scan the full length of the Heavy Cruiser. Noticing that all the guns along the length of the newcomer were alive, tracking their position and movement, Rebekah looked down the length of the vessel at the name that adorned the side, proudly announcing the ship to be the GTSC *Achilles.*

"Sir, it's the *Achilles!*" Red One practically yelled with excitement as he too had seen the name.

She could well imagine the stunned consternation coupled with excitement that would have broken out on the bridge. Some shouting for joy while others, looking around at their surroundings with mouths open. She could picture it as though she was there.

Despite their monumental good fortune, something felt off for Rebekah. Call it a gut feeling, a tingling at the base of her spine, something was out of place and she didn't like how things were shaping up. *They had been saved, so why couldn't she let go of this feeling? Was it simply hard for her to accept that she was going to live beyond this day that was throwing her?* And then it struck her; why the cruisers had retreated when the *Nova* had transmitted the distress beacon, leaving them there, a wounded beast in an open field. Just like the *Adventure Sun* had been waiting for them when the *Nova* had arrived, waiting with a warning message for them to run after transmitting a coded top-secret message across to the cruiser. The enemy cruisers hadn't retreated, they had simply re-baited the trap, and now awaited their next victim to wander blindly into helping a wounded vessel that had called for help. This way they didn't need to hunt, their prey would come waltzing up right into their killing zone.

The radio silence was broken at that point as the *Achilles* made contact with the *Nova*. Rebekah could picture the main screen coming alive in the control center across the front of the bridge. The commanding figure of Captain Qadir Vasilios, of whom she had only once seen a picture, would be dominating the bridge with that steely eyed stare he was famous for.

"Captain, prepare to evacuate! Thanks to your pilots, we don't have much time."

Captain Hamilton on board the *Nova* paused for a second. He knew that it was a thousand to one that they had won the previous engagement, but still found himself saying, "The cruisers have made off, dock alongside, we have many wounded that need to be lifted off."

"Your naivety makes me wonder about your command. The two ships haven't *made off*, they're waiting for their next victim to respond to your mayday."

The message went dead.

"Captain! Jump signatures!" Someone on the command bridge had evidently left a transmitter on.

"Do we have a bearing on the *Achilles*?"

"Yes."

"Launch life pods. Engage the enemy..." the microphone went dead as the unknown person clicked off.

Radar signatures lit Rebekah's screens as she turned towards the incoming fighters once again, this day was far from over.

Boosting power, she sent her fighter streaking towards the incoming fighters that had jumped in ahead of the two cruisers.

Like so many other battles, things were happening at high speed and yet in slow motion. Her mind recording every detail of the swarm of fighters coming towards her, the silver purple glint of their transparent shields, the huge blasts of cannon fire reflected in the canopies as heavy fire blazed overhead. Twin wheels of slip-space spiralled in the far distance as the two cruisers came charging in, fore cannons firing even before the full length of the ships had fully emerged through the reentry points of slip-space.

Coloured flames burst into savage patterns along the length of the closest enemy cruiser as the GTSC *Achilles* opened up, engaging the twin formation before they had chance to attack with that devastating first salvo that had caught the *Nova* broadside.

To Rebekah, it felt as though an exaggerated ballet was taking place in slow motion; both battles so entirely dependent on the other, and yet detached as if neither one had any bearing on what happened to the former.

Reading the scene before her, it was as if she could see the future, planning her first moves into the battle, seeing every action and reaction enacted in her mind before the first fighter came within range.

She ducked left, allowing the first stream of fire to tear harmlessly past her. Closing in on the fighter, Rebekah opened fire, ripping through its shields and gutting it from nose to tail, switching to the next fighter as the first blew up.

The first four fighters fell to her guns just as she had envisioned. The dogfight was as savage and as bloody as ever.

Turning her head, she was just in time to see the shape of Red One weave around a drifting dead bomber only to take a direct burst from an oncoming fighter and disintegrate in a fireball. The section leader as no more.

Rebekah fought as if it were the last battle she would ever fly in. Their numbers had fallen. The fighter squadrons on board the GTSC *Nova* were half as strong as when they had launched, backed up by the remaining pirates that had been protecting the *Adventure Sun*.

One squadron from the *Achilles* was launching, the bright glow of their engine cores burning intensely as they boosted power, making swift tracks to join the fray as quickly as possible.

The battle drew closer to the GTSC *Nova* where she struggled to maintain station on the *Achilles* as it accelerated past.

Bombers closed with the damaged bulk of the aged cruiser, as the allied fighters desperately tried to fend them off to give enough time for all to be evacuated from the dying warship.

Three bombers dived for the *Nova*, their tight formation making it seem like one giant bird was on an attack run, however Rebekah saw them while she was inverted with an enemy fighter close on her tail.

She rolled onto an intercept bearing and dived across the path of the incoming bombers, sending a torrent of fire on a perfect deflection shot. She watched as the lead bomber flew straight through it, causing the aircraft to disintegrate between the two that flanked it. Before she could account for the other two, warnings rang out on her instrument panel as the fighter on her tail deluged her fighter in plasma fire.

Peeling off, she saw the ruler straight lines of two warheads streaking straight for the damaged cruiser. There was nothing she could do to help them, simply evade her attacker and survive herself.

Two tremendous flashes of light lit the battle-scape as the warheads detonated against the badly damaged hull of the GTSC *Nova*.

As she relinquished her vigil over the floundering vessel Rebekah rolled to gain more distance to start the next attack run, five more bombers closing with the *Nova*. It felt as though she was the only one trying to protect the large ship, although she knew that not to be true.

Diving, going head-to-head with the next formation of bombers, she accounted for one and switched to another. However, she watched the as the warheads detach from the other bombers, scoring a straight line towards the helpless vessel as the twin engine aircraft in her sights blew up in a cascade of bright colours.

Knowing what was about to happen, she flew as fast as she could away from the cruiser she had called home for the past year.

"The *Nova* is going to explode!"

All life pods that had not ejected yet had only a score of seconds to do so and then pray hard that they would survive the blast.

The cruiser detonated behind her; her fighter being rocketed around in the blast as though passing through the inner wall of an intense storm.

Time had lost all semblance of meaning, only the count on her ordinance and capacity of her weapon cores meant anything to her. Her gun cameras would record her victories for her logbook, but it made little to no difference to her at this point whether she lived long enough to fill in the details.

"All crews of the GTSC, return to the Achilles; we're jumping away."

Hearing that, Rebekah finished off her chase with one last missile at the fighter she had been chasing and broke off.

Hitting the afterburners, Rebekah weaved between broken fighters and the maelstrom of enemy forces flying in the opposite direction, it had become a race of death. The prize: life.

A fighter tried to latch onto her tail but couldn't keep up with her manoeuvres through the decimated remains of the former GTSC *Nova*.

Two more slammed into each other in a mid-air collision as they gave chase.

The unlucky pilot barely had time to register his fortune as another enemy fighter crashed into him head on, the two disintegrating before they fire-balled.

Firing at anything that got in her way, Rebekah accounted for another two enemy fighters before she was in the safety of the *Achilles* anti-aircraft barrage. She flew close to the hull heading for the hangar, weaving through the continuously firing turrets as she went. If it was not so tragic, it would have been one of the most beautiful and awe-inspiring moments of her flying career.

As she swung wide onto the final vector for the approach into the hangar, Rebekah saw the commotion as the two cruisers manoeuvred in the distance. The last thing Rebekah saw of the battle was the damaged cruiser still streaming smoke from its damage in the hangar before it vanished behind the great bulk of the Special Ops Heavy Cruiser, GTSC *Achilles*.

Flying the length of the hangar deck in the new surroundings was a little surreal after the savagery of the recent battle. It was a stark reminder that the GTSC *Nova* with goodness knows how many crew members, was gone for good, the rest in an unknown state of disarray. Just then, she remembered the data she carried and realised that it could be the only surviving copy. Once landed, she would need to get it to the Captain as soon as possible. Pushing that to the back of her thoughts, she followed the signals of the deck crew that lined the sides of the busy hangar, Rebekah guided her fighter to the indicated landing area. Someone was guiding her through the final stages of touchdown. She watched as he held a marshalling wand out sideways, circling the glowing top to indicate that he wanted her to rotate the fighter around so others could fit in past her vertical stabiliser.

She relaxed on the controls as she felt the aircraft settle. Running through the post flight checks and final shutdown procedure, she finally flicked the last switch off and her fighter came to rest and simmered down, the plasma cores beginning to cool. She had asked a lot from her fighter during the battle. Casting her eye across the wings and nose, she could see that she had sustained a significant amount of damage as well.

Little did she know, it was to be her last flight in the *Typhoon* fighter for her career.

The last few hours caught up with her then, the tiredness in her limbs was a physical thing. Moving them felt like they were encased in lead.

She sat there for a time, just absorbing the events that had brought her to this new ship. So many familiar faces were gone; not that death was a new thing in her life, the first time she had seen so many people dead was when she had been almost ten. She pushed that memory out of her head quickly; that was a rabbit hole she did not want to go down.

Reaching behind her, Rebekah retrieved the data pad she had stowed in her hold-all, returning it to her breast pocket.

Heaving herself up out of the seat, her harness falling by her sides, she held the cockpit side as she swayed for a moment. Something had changed out there for her; she could feel it.

Swinging her legs over the side, she lowered herself down to the scarred wing. Casting her eyes over the rest of the fighter, she found herself somewhat shocked to see a tremendous scar that burned through the armoured hull, severing circuits and pipes just behind the cockpit. A few feet further forward and it would have struck the cockpit, and it looked like it would have gone through too. She unconsciously touched the little gold medallion that hung around her neck, the one that Samara had given her.

Climbing down to the deck, her legs shook with fatigue and adrenaline, but she took a deep breath, forcing her mind to take command of her body and surpass her tiredness. She touched the side of her fighter, thumbing the selector under the cover, the canopy closed on her fighter. That would keep her belongings safe until she had a room to move them into.

Rebekah looked between the fighters that littered the deck, there were a lot of people in the hangar. Pilots from both the *Nova* and the *Adventure Sun*, survivors from both ships and empty life pods in between all the new aircraft.

They had been lucky. A significant portion of the crew from the *Nova* seemed to have survived, but the aerial wing hadn't fared nearly so well.

Crew members of the GTSC *Achilles* mixed with the survivors, medical aid being offered where needed, or blankets and food being given.

The outlandish appearance of those from the *Adventure Sun* made some feel a little off guard. It was not common for pirates to be on board a powerful black ops warship such as the Heavy Cruiser. Rebekah could remember her first time on an Alliance hangar deck. She was thirteen, and every inch a privateer like those who had been saved with her. Knowing how it felt to be an alien on a ship whose crew were reluctant to have anything to do with them, she made her way across to where the pirates had grouped together. Only a few crew members offered their assistance as she crossed the invisible line that separated them. Offering her hand to the nearest of them who happened to be one of the few remaining fighter pilots. "Good hunting out there. It would have been a much messier business without your guys' help."

The other shook her hand. "Thanks for coming to our rescue. It would have been a totally different story if it had been some poor freighter."

Rebekah raised one eyebrow with a slight grin on the corner of her mouth.

"Corporal!" she called to a young man that looked lost in the commotion. "I need to see the Captain… NOW!" she added seeing his hesitation. His back straightened as the force of her order kicked in and overrode his uncertainty.

"Yes, ma'am." he gestured in one direction past her fighter that stood behind her. "Head that way to the door, take the third corridor on your right and find the transporter two bays down. Take it to the top deck and then follow the arterial forward to the nerve centre and take the concourse to the top."

"Thank you, Corporal. Can you organise food and water for these people and see what the plan is for them to be housed."

Nodding, he saluted before turning to his task.

The walk up to the bridge was surreal after the battle, both chaos and order reigned.

It was a very different experience to that onboard the *Nova*. Her first introduction to life onboard the Heavy Cruiser was when she had tried to go out of the hangar. Two soldiers backed a thin young officer, his hair neatly styled, slightly longer than regulation length. He had a data pad with him and was questioning everyone before they were allowed off the hangar deck.

"Name, rank, number?" he asked when Rebekah reached the front of the crowd.

"Le Sabre, Rebekah. Lieutenant. 716248977704."

"And where are you headed?" his voice languid after the influx of so many new faces.

"I need to see the Captain. It is highly important that I do not delay."

"You can't, not without proper authorisation, especially as you're from another ship."

Rebekah leveled her gaze at the young man. He was nothing special to look at, shorter than average height, reddish brown hair, and a glint in his eyes that expressed his distaste for a task that was beneath him, but also one that hinted that he was enjoying putting a roadblock in her path. She looked at the soldiers behind him, knowing instantly she would get no help from them.

"Return to your area and someone will get to you." his words touched with a malicious flavour.

Rebekah didn't feel like causing a scene that would ultimately delay her prospect of getting to the Captain.

She turned and headed back into the maze of people that filled the hangar. There was a way to get off the hangar deck, but she just needed to think of it.

Two pilots rounded one of the fighters before her and headed for the access way that she had just vacated.

Stepping into their path, she saw them both look at her. "Thanks for coming to our rescue."

"That was quite the party out there," said the first as he stopped in his path.

"Who was the idiot that gave us away?" the other asked with the displeasure of one subjected to someone else's danger.

"He's dead now, so it doesn't matter."

"I'm not surprised ..."

"What can we do to help you?" the other one cut his friend off.

"I need to see the Captain but the young officer on the door won't let me through."

They both laughed. "That's only Stan, insignificant most of the time and a pain in the neck the rest."

"Come with us, we'll show you the way."

Rebekah fell into step beside them as they weaved through the throng of people back to the doorway.

"She's not allowed off the hangar deck."

"She's needed on the bridge." the three kept going.

"But she ..."

"Attention!" the older of the two pilots snapped. Watching the automatic stiffening of the young man despite his face remaining defiant, "isn't it customary for lower ranks to salute their superior officers?" the older pilot asked his friend.

"I believe it is. Not doing so is akin to mutiny. And we throw mutineers out the airlock." the other pilot replied.

The two turned to go and Rebekah followed, no feeling of sympathy for the officer who was only so ready to abuse his power for his own personal satisfaction.

Reaching the command bridge, Rebekah surveyed the scene with a practised eye, her days onboard both the *Ulysses* and the *Nova* coming back to her. It was funny to think that she was one of the most junior members in her squadron yet had lived three lifetimes already.

The Captain stood by the large plotting table in the fore corner of the bridge close to the large windows from where they could see the elegant lines of the Heavy Cruiser.

It was an odd thought, that a ship could be described in the same way as an attractive woman, but the GTSC *Achilles* was such a ship. The design had been done by someone who knew how to combine both the concept and the practical, bringing the ship together without the clunky need for practicality in a warship. She was a new breed of warship, one not long commissioned and already a legend in the GTN, lead by another legend, the Captain having made his name in several campaigns before being given command of the *Achilles* only to further his exploits thereafter.

Rebekah walked across the bridge, weaving through the contingent that formed the defensive structure of the bridge. Her flight suit stood at odds amongst the uniforms and daily fatigues that adorned the bridge staff.

Stopping short of the plotting table, she took a deep breath to quell the nerves that churned in her stomach, this was Captain Qadir Vasilios, someone with an impressive service record, nearly as impressive as Antonio Wind-Hawk, the hero of Cal'Mar Gar in the War of Ascension.

Rebekah saluted when the Captain looked up at her.

"What is it, Lieutenant?" the Captain saluted her back.

"Sir," she produced the data pad from her pocket, "Captain Hamilton asked me to ensure this reached you if I survived."

Passing it across, she watched the expression on his face.

"It's the information that the Captain of the *Adventure Sun* transmitted to us before being destroyed. There may be other copies on their way here; I'm not sure who else made it."

The Captain looked at the data pad and then at her, reaching out to take it from her hand. "Thank you, Lieutenant, I shall review it shortly. I'm glad you made it."

Rebekah nodded and was about to leave when the Captain flipped a coin that she had not seen him holding.

"What happened out there?"

"We were close to the Jar'mine cluster when we picked up a distress signal close enough to jump to. The Captain decided to go check it out as the beacon matched that registered to an old fleet transport that he said had been reported destroyed with all hands at the end of the War of Ascension…"

Captain Trevor Hamilton walked across the open bridge to the communications officer. "Have you sent off that message to High Command?"

"Yes, sir."

"Let me know immediately when there's a reply."

He turned away back to the bridge at large. It had been fairly routine up to that point. They were set to sweep the Jar'mine cluster and then jump back towards the moon of Yatze where they would refit with a clandestine freighter and receive new orders.

"Sir, we have a reply."

"That was fast," the Captain whispered under his breath. This must be important.

Scanning the classified message that the officer handed to him, the Captain had to read it twice to appreciate the significance of the message.

"Everything OK, sir?" the XO asked, coming around the nearby holo table.

Wordlessly, the Captain handed the data pad across to the XO, the Captain leaned on the side of the holo table lost in thought.

"Ordered to play dead?" the XO questioned as he handed the pad back to the Captain. "What on earth?"

"Yes, but look at who the message was sent from."

"Section four?"

"It's colloquial name is 'the hill'."

The XO turned a blank expression to the Captain.

"Mount Olympus." The XO's eyes widened. "This has come from beyond High Command. I imagine that they are pretty keen for us to intercept that ship before anyone else does."

"What were they doing out here?"

"I don't know. All the message says it that their last report was over a year ago."

"I was on the bridge when we jumped in, we could see the drifting hull of the *Adventure Sun* on the main screen and I remember the Captain commenting that it looked more like a freighter that had been converted into a ship of war."

Rebekah looked down at the holographic image suspended above the plotting table.

"They had transformed it into a powerful medium cruiser using many different parts of other ships, not all of them Alliance."

"Was it a trap?" the first officer questioned from the other side of the plotting table.

"The Captain was pretty confident from the lack of activity on the scanners that it was not. He launched the ready fighters while he conversed with the Captain of the *Adventure Sun*. I could see the extensive damage to the armour plating; it did look like they had been through one heck of a fight."

The Captain and the XO exchanged glances. "Then what happened?"

"The closer we got, we could see the plasma scoring and fresh scarring in the armour plating. It looked like a bitter story of bravery, sacrifice and one hell of a fight." Rebekah smiled at the quizzical expression on the Captain's face, her creative and literary side getting the better of her.

"As soon as the GTSC *Nova* jumped in, *Adventure Sun*, launched all available fighters and bombers: their numbers too told of a hefty price that had been paid to for survival. When we got within range, the Captain of the *Adventure Sun* contacted us on the front screen. He looked more like a wild pirate rather than a former Naval officer ..."

"Captain, I'm going to transmit a secure file to you. You need to get it away from here, FAST! Do not try to save us!"

"Negative Captain, prepare your people for evacuation, we will lift you all off ..."

"Captain, secure transmission has begun." called the communications officer.

"Bridge, Nav. Two slip-space ruptures detected. Range fourteen thousand. IFF is … KANE CLASS CRUISERS!" the officer shouted the last part as he turned back to the command screen, punching the red button beside him. Alarms rang throughout the cruiser.

On screen, twin sisters slid out of slip-space in perfect firing position. Their opening salvo, lethal and accurate, struck the hull of the Adventure Sun. *The old ship wallowed in the concussive blast. Its hull breaking up almost instantaneously.*

A stream of fighters and bombers had launched from both enemy vessels, like bats pouring from a cave, they had flocked together into a swarm that charged down the fighters that had launched from the Adventure Sun *and the ready fighters from the GTSC* Nova.

"Nav, plot a jump to safe coordinates. Weapons, target those two cruisers. SAR, begin recovery of those life pods."

He looked at the status of the transmission. The board was green, file transfer was complete. It must have been within the last seconds before the Adventure Sun *went offline.*

Instead of heeding the Adventure Sun's *warning to jump away, he ordered them in closer towards the drifting pirate ship's hull, attempting to use it as cover as the two cruisers shifted targets to the GTSC* Nova.

It was not long before the first of the Adventure Sun's *life pods were within range of the* Nova, *their recovery function beginning a retrieval operation. Saving as many as they could before the life pods were blasted from the sky.*

The first salvo that struck the GTSC Nova *was devastating, damage reports from all over the ship started coming into the command centre, lights flashing on all the control stations; bridge staff calling out, their voices mixing together in a rising clamour.*

As an outsider of to this world, Rebekah found she could watch the scene with total detachment. Her first instinct was to run for her fighter which she had prepped for launch before coming to the bridge despite not being on duty. It was just something that she had always done since before joining the Nova. *The crew had gotten used to it and didn't even ask any more, simply had her fighter ready whenever there was an operation at hand. It had paid off too on several occasions when she had launched without permission during an operation and saved the day because of it.*

Predicting the scene was a large part of being a successful fighter pilot. She knew when the Captain was about to launch a full ship wide scramble; yet she lingered a moment longer before leaving the bridge.

Grabbing a data pad, the Captain hit the alert button, the tannoy blaring out in the background behind the bustle of noise, calling for all flight crews to man their aircraft.

Still, Rebekah stayed, knowing.

The captain came across to where she stood. "Sabre, take this just in case." he handed her the data pad.

"At least one copy of the message must make it to safety." he had grown up a lot in the last thirty seconds, she could feel the difference within him.

Grasping the data pad, she nodded once and he was gone. She performed a similar disappearing act and left the bridge with all haste for the hangar.

***

Nodding at the conclusion of her story, Qadir Vasilios looked at the fighter pilot from the Nova as she stood before him.

"How old are you Lieutenant?"

"Nineteen," she lied, being a full year younger.

"And which flight training school did you go to?"

"Moctezuma Academy. I became a Kwāwo'sēlōtl."

Qadir Vasilios' eyes narrowed a fraction. "You served as a flight instructor?"

"Yes, before I graduated."

"So, you're the one. Loyal to the end."

Rebekah shifted her head right by a millimeter, not sure what the Captain meant by that, but he didn't elaborate on the subject.

"Welcome aboard the GTSC *Achilles*. Go get yourself sorted and cleaned up. There will be time for a debrief later."

She read the look in his eyes, he wanted to tend to his ship. Saluting, she retreated off the bridge, leaving the command centre heading back towards the hangar. She wondered about his questions. *What had he meant?*

While there had been no mention about the Nova, nor her former Captain, she had a pretty good idea what that meant. Rebekah felt drained. Trevor Hamilton hadn't made it. His first Black Ops command, his only command, the GTSC *Nova*. He had gone down with his ship, making sure that their sacrifice wasn't in vain, the only surviving copy of the secure transmission having reached the Captain of the *Achilles*, she had accomplished the last order he had ever given her.

Back down on the hangar deck, Rebekah once again weaved through the throng of people, lost in thought. Reaching her fighter, she climbed up, opening her canopy and grabbed her bag from behind the seat and pulled the leather flying jacket out too. Dropping down to the deck once more, she lay the jacket across the top of her bag and thumbed the selector, hearing the familiar hum of the canopy sliding shut.

Figuring her next move was to get assigned to her new quarters and find out what squadron she was likely to get assigned to, she set off for one of the groups of officers that she had seen at various points along the side of the hangar, she hoped that one of them might be able to point her towards the Quarter Master, there she would be drafted into the ranks of the GTSC *Achilles*, Black Ops Heavy Cruiser.

***

Entering the dormitory lined with bunks which would now be her new home for the foreseeable future, Rebekah slung her bag and jacket onto the bed and looked around. The room smelled of recycled air, sweat and perfume. It was empty besides herself. That suited her just fine, allowing her the chance to adjust to her new surroundings.

Life on board a Black Ops Heavy Cruiser was far from luxurious, the walls sparsely decorated with pictures that some of the girls had hung up, but mostly bare military order reigned. Navy blue and khaki green dominated the décor, interspersed with grays, blacks and browns.

From her earliest memories, the importance of 'things' and a sense of belonging had evaded her. People, the few key specific people, stood out in her life, much more prominently, but otherwise, she had gotten used to the 'temporary' reigning strong. She opened her bag and took out the few daily items she would need and arranged them on her shelf by the bed, the rest she hung or stacked in the locker. The only three photos that still held any real meaning or value to her lay in a secure frame, back-to-back. She made copies from the frame before replacing the originals back into her bag, she hung the copies on the inside of her new locker door so that she'd see them every time she opened the door.

The smiling face, yet hard expression of Sebastian looked out at her, his leather jacket clearly visible in the photograph; in the other, Samara, her eyes bright with emotion against the tranquil background; the last, Tim, his casual pose as he leaned against the training fighter.

Rebekah had just finished hanging her belongings in the locker. That would do for now until she was issued with new uniform and kit upon which, once again, her bag would be filled and ready for the next scramble. Folding the bag away she shut the locker door when another young woman came in.

"Hi..." the woman greeted with an open friendly tone.

"Hi," Rebekah returned her greeting turning to see whom she was addressing.

"You're one of the new pilots that came from the *Nova*?"

"That's right."

"Welcome aboard. I'm Abby."

"Rebekah." The two of them shook hands.

"I'm also still relatively new on board. The *Achilles* picked us up a few months ago from the GTSC *Aleggra* when we got heavily attacked. I was a shuttle pilot until I was forced to become a fighter pilot in the last battle we fought before being rescued."

Rebekah raised her eyebrows to acknowledge the story.

Abby kept talking and Rebekah just listened, it seemed like Abby needed to express how she was feeling, perhaps she hadn't had chance for that form of outlet before now.

"It's weird starting again. No personal stuff with you. There are definitely things I wish I could have brought with me, but that's war I guess."

Of course, Rebekah would have to replace her wardrobe as she had figured before, but everything that was precious to her accompanied her on every mission in her hold-all.

Someone had once pointed out that if she ejected then all her special things would be lost.

Rebekah smiled at the memory of the men opposite, their expression's shocked as she had replied: "I've had my ejection mechanism removed, waste of weight, I can fit an extra two hundred kilos of ordinance in there, it gives me two hours more flying time and four thousand more rounds. I don't eject! I fight until there is nothing left."

She could hear Rick's rough voice backing her up, "She means it too, I damn well had to collide with her to stop her from ramming an enemy destroyer after she'd run out of ordinance."

The pilots had looked at her with a quizzical look, in hybrid shock and awe. That had been after their first refit, taking on more new pilots before heading out on the next patrol.

Sitting on her bed, she looked at the floor. It did not pay to make close friendships in this life. Rick hadn't made it on board the Achilles. His remains drifted with so many others near the dead hulks of the *Adventure Sun* and the GTSC *Nova*. Rebekah looked up to see another pilot come into the room. She had short, cropped hair, no longer than her collar, but it was chestnut brown with darker streaks. She had green eyes and stood slightly taller than Rebekah.

She did not seem old, but she carried a maturity far beyond her years; an old soul.

"You're the one who brought that data pad from the *Nova*?" She spoke with the authority of one in leadership.

"Yes," Rebekah nodded, a barely perceptible movement.

"That was fortunate that it survived. Have you been drafted?"

"No not yet, I didn't manage to see the quarter master in the hangar. I was just told to come here until further notice."

"So, you haven't been assigned to a squadron yet?"

"No, the Petty Officer in the hangar said he'd have to wait for everyone to be accounted for before a decision could be made and that I'd hear shortly."

"Ok, I could do with someone like you in my squadron, I'll see what can be done."

"Your squadron?"

"The Black Griffins! Squadron Leader Teresa Palmer. My role is to assist Squadron Leader Blythe with the squadron and special assistant and tactician to the Captain."

Rebekah nodded and smiled for the first time.

"Welcome to the *Achilles*, Lieutenant."

VALKYRIE CHRONICLES

VALKYRIE DAWN

Chapter 1

Year 3129,
First Week,
Seventh Month,
Standard calendar, Alliance Navy
On board GTSC *Krasev*, Destroyer,
One week before Operation *Trident*.

Sighing with a soft, succulent whisper, the release of pressure hissed as the door to the cryo chamber opened and equalised with the ambient pressure of the main chamber that held the troop's cryo pods. Light blue iridescent cryo liquid poured out of the hatchway and cascaded down to the grating below. It had been two months of cryo sleep during the trip from their patrol out in the Mur'gon sector to this godforsaken part of the universe. Lieutenant Commander Douglas Manning rolled over, his body flexing, stretching from the first real movement after the length of relative inactivity.

His was a reality that few experienced in their lives. Only those who went from theatre to theatre as the war progressed, were subjected to constant lengths of cryo sleep. In an ironic twist to his fate, cryo sleep slowed down the body's function and therefore the ageing process, effectively lengthening his life expectancy. It was ironic because in his profession, it was not normally old age that claimed warriors such as himself.

His mind went back to his first trip and the unpleasant experience he had woken up to. Cryo sleep had evolved marvellously over the duration of his service.

He levered himself up, his muscles bunching as he lifted his powerful form from the supine position he had been in for two months onto his elbows and knees.

'Mars', as he was known to his friends and teammates, crawled to the hatch, pulling the breathing apparatus off. It was not a pleasant task, with the pipe stuck down his throat and nose covered by the small, fitted mask. It had been hard not to gag the first few times he had been through this process, but now it was fairly easy to quell the reflex. He looked out from the chamber and down to the gratings; he disconnected the neural transmitters, returning the six silver disks to the transmitter pad by the access way before rolling over onto his back once again and heaved himself headlong from the chamber, lifting himself bodily out to hang from the metal rod that spanned the length of his row of pods. He allowed himself to extend to its full length, arms stretched out before he dropped himself the four meters to the grating below. There was a ladder to his left, next to the array that led from the grating up to higher chambers, however it was unnecessary for his exit. Moving around the cryo bay was easy in space during transit when the artificial gravity was not engaged, but now, with the ship nearing departure, procedure required all personnel to be moving around normally to become accustomed to it again.

His muscles were a little stiff as he stretched, but nowhere near as bad as it used to be. The stretch always helped to boost his adaptation faster, it was something he had learned over his multiple trips throughout his service.

Previously, before High Command had commissioned the research, cryo sleep was a long time on one's back, then it would take a few days to a week or two before full movement came back. It always felt as though he had done a strenuous workout before laying inactive for a few days, then trying to move afterwards. The liquid of the old chambers cushioned the body and allowed for a little movement, but any more than that was suppressed, especially with the compartment in zero gravity. Now, it was like an active training ground that regulated their cryo existence.

The new pods were also filled with a gel like liquid that stabilised their bodies during transit, but also had enhanced properties that formed resistance training. Their neural link-up gave them access to a developed training regime, for the entire duration of their incapacitation during cryo sleep, their minds were suspended in a dreamlike state with combat scenarios and missions that they would go through while still in a state of sleep. Their minds controlled their bodies and the cryo liquid would restrain them with sufficient force to imitate the movement in their minds, as though in reality. It also allowed them to stay physically fit and nourished; their bodies absorbing the vitamins, minerals and proteins they needed through the liquid concoction.

He needed a shower and a change of clothes as he was still covered in the liquid gel, although it had already partially been absorbed leaving his skin sticky and damp. The temperature in the cryo chamber was warm enough though and his wet clothing was not uncomfortable to exist in for the time being.

There were others waking up at the same time. The troops were never woken up all in one go: partly because it would be too crowded in the cryo chamber, and partly because the sudden power draw could spike the reactor core.

Lieutenant Commander Douglas Manning looked up at the rows upon rows of chambers lit by blue and white panels marking the state of activity and vital signs of the occupant inside. Higher ranks were awoken first, in descending order of priority down to the rank and file. In a day or two, this part of the ship would be filled with troops waking up, but for now it was just the higher ranks and Special Forces—his Special Forces Unit would be awoken later that day.

There was a junior officer walking down the aisle towards him, her long hair bouncing with every step. The Lieutenant Commander nodded to the officer before pulling his t-shirt off over his head.

The young woman watched him as he turned ringing out the material from the liquid gel and dropped his wet t-shirt on the grating at his feet. He had his back to her and she could see scars that marred his torso and a large deep red curving indented valley scoring down the right side of his back, bluey purple laser scarring along the edges from where it was still healing. She stopped behind him, awaiting attention: she wondered what had caused a scar like that as she had seen these Special Forces in full combat armour and they looked like they could sustain a Heavy Cruiser crashing on top of them and still walk away with minor damage to their suits.

While she waited, she noticed more scars that lined his arms, one cutting through the tattoo of some unit insignia on his left upper arm and yet another that vanished below the waistline of his trousers.

Running one hand through his short hair, the Lieutenant Commander turned back to where the young officer stood, holding out the six neural transmitters that had been attached to his chest and abdomen under his shirt.

Taking them, she waited for him to turn around again before delicately detaching the other six that lined his spine. Each soldier had a very different personality, and she could feel the gentle power that emanated from the Special Forces team leader before her. Some made her feel scared, the sheer brutality that surrounded them, but not this one, he seemed more like a warrior of old: a sage whose path is war.

Weighing the twelve metal transmitters in her hand, she continued along the grating towards the terminal at the far end where she would load the biometrics into the computer from the Wraith team leader.

She looked back at him over her shoulder once. Lieutenant Commander Douglas Manning stood where he was stretching now that he was standing up, free of the wet t-shirt, feeling the wonderful release in his muscles as he twisted this way and that. The best part about the new cryo chambers was that the body was not weak and feeble after a journey. It had never been advised to sleep for more than a month at a time with the old system because after that the body matter would start wasting away and it would take months to build up full strength and fitness again, but the new system allowed the soldiers to keep peak fitness throughout the cryo sleep.

Another cryo chamber opened up somewhere above him and the blue cyro liquid poured out, splashing down to the grating a few pods further along from where he stood. Lieutenant Commander David Manning stooped and picked up his shirt and moved off barefoot down the aisle to the operations dock where the young woman still stood.

He punched in his ID into the control panel at the far end and the holographic figure of a young female officer appeared. "Welcome back, Commander."

"Good to see you, old friend. You really out did yourself with those simulations this time."

"Thank you. I thought you would like them."

"I have a suggestion though, next time can you put us on a wide beach by a peaceful sea?"

"That wouldn't prepare you for much, Commander, but maybe one day, I might surprise you."

It was nearly time. He looked down at his hands, bunching them into fists and watching the white patches appear and tendons showing in his wrists.

The anteroom, by comparison to the cavernous bay with all the individual cryo pods suspended in rows, was small and dark, a single room where the attending officer would notify the soldier of where his quarters awaited before directing them to the showers.

He looked around the room, the same familiar setting that he was used to over the last several tours he had completed in the GTSC *Krasev*. At first, when he had been posted to the GTN destroyer, he had been privately annoyed; it had seemed like a demotion after serving in a Heavy Cruiser that had been on the front line for his first two tours, but after joining the compliment of troops and Special Forces that were on board, he changed his tune.

They had been in the thick of it ever since returning to the front line, pulling out on only two occasions. The first time was to refit; the second was for reinforcements and repairs after one particularly brutal campaign. He had seen more combat in one single tour on board the *Krasev* than he ever had across his entire posting to the Heavy Cruiser, rising to his current rank, being awarded more black campaign medals than he knew existed, not that they meant much to him, but each one a reminder of the hell he and his team had lived through.

Their Captain was an older officer, but he fought more like a progressive officer who had a wild imagination: and it had worked too. The destroyer had seen some of the most savage battles in their sector, the Captain always seemed to be heavily involved; committing the destroyer to seemingly impossible situations and always managing to take victory from the field.

The shower had been refreshing, the feeling of cleanliness after the syrupy gel stickiness of the cryo liquid was a welcome condition. Now in his combat fatigues, Douglas Manning retrieved his shirt and trousers, dropping them into the chute for washing. These would make it back to his cabin, likely, before he did.

Once again, he coded in his ID into the control panel and he was presented with his personal effects, including his dog tags, even though his information was etched into his biometrics.

Pulling them over his head, he tucked them into his shirt, picking up the other items; he headed out into the rabbit warren of the ship and toward his cabin.

As soldiers go, Lieutenant Commander David Manning was tall, six feet nine inches and lean, but still built like a tank. He had forged his body into the toughest fighting machine he could manage, with a great deal of power in his muscles. He could lift some of the heaviest weapons on his own and use the powerful turrets even without the aid of his combat armour suit.

A week of briefings, mission layouts and weapons checks lay ahead of him before seeing active service again, it was always the same. Each day would be vitally important and yet monotonous with regularity: weapons checks, drills, briefings, PT, war games, briefings, sleep, repeat.

How much could a man take before his system demanded a change in lifestyle? he wondered. The question hadn't really been of any interest to him before now, but there is a time when the soul craves peace, that is the time to break away from a life filled with war. And now, with the combat training simulations during cryo sleep, they were all engaged in warfare and training almost continuously.

Dropping his gear on his bunk upon reaching his cabin, he looked around the sparse room that would be the last bit of luxury for the foreseeable future. Manning checked on the wall mounted data pad that his armour was scheduled to be delivered to his cabin later that day. Unzipping his hold-all, he took out the item that lay on the top, his combat knife, something he never existed without these days, not even in the relative safety on board the destroyer; not since that last time, the consequences of which didn't bear thinking about. Casting his gaze up, he surveyed the weapon security against the adjacent wall. The racks were bare and lockers empty, likewise his recessed wardrobe and shelves lay bare, all to be filled later that day except for the one full uniform that hung on the wall mount next to his bed.

Crossing to the control panel on the wall again, he checked the requisition order was present. His weapons would be delivered later that day. Hefting the knife in his hand he chucked it onto the bed to put on once he had changed into his preferred clothing.

Turning back to his bag, he pulled out his form-fitting combat suit that was part of the armour he would wear. It formed the under layer that all Wraiths wore before he would put on his environmental suit which would regulate his existence to be completely self sustainable for the duration of being in his armour and then the exo-suit that formed the majority of his protection and that the armour would be fitted onto.

Time enough for that later. While he still didn't need to have the full armour on, he would make use of the freedom that was a luxury for now, although an unfamiliar one, having spent more time in his armour than not over the last several years.

The under layer was extremely comfortable, so a lot of the Special Forces teams wore it as daily functional fatigues. Next Manning took his uniform from where it hung and pulled it on over his combat suit, attaching his knife to his leg and pulling his trouser legs down over it and his boots. Retrieving his spare sidearm from his hold-all he clipped it onto his belt at the small of his back and picked up a second knife from the bag. This he attached to the inside of his left forearm with the handle pointing to his wrist; finally pulling on his uniform jacket over the top, ensuring that his tie was perfectly central. Opening the reflective screen on the wall, he checked to make sure that he was presentable for when he would go to the bridge to see the Captain. It took him by surprise to see himself again, especially dressed like this. New ribbons had been added to his left breast with the latest citations he had apparently been awarded from the last campaign. He was running out of room there, but ultimately, *what did it matter?* His real honour was life and the lives of his team, each time they got back safe and sound, that was the real badge of honour, the fact they had all survived.

Ordinarily the troops wouldn't get armed until the order for launch was given, unless they were in the training range. However, being one of the top Special Forces Commanders on board the ship afforded him certain liberties not extended to many others.

Leaving his quarters, he went to check on his team and their equipment, making sure it would be ready for when it was time for them to awaken from cryo sleep.

It was a task that kept him busy for the next few hours. Organising their combat equipment and training regime until he was satisfied that they would be ready to start once they had awoken.

It was always slightly surreal walking the hallways of the destroyer while the majority of personnel on board were stored away in cryo-pods. Imagine doing that for weeks at a time as the destroyer was in transit. There were times when the whole ship went into cryo sleep leaving the ship's AI to safeguard the destroyer and guide it on the chosen path, but that didn't happen very often.

"Sir, Captain's compliments, would you report to the bridge." A young officer saluted him while talking.

Returning the salute, Lieutenant Commander Manning looked at the young man, his eyes bright with the excitement that greeted all of the Special Forces when junior ranks had to interact with them for the first time, but not everyone had spoken to a Wraith before, their military status legendary amongst the regular soldiers made most junior ranks and soldiers treat them like they were Titans that had just stepped down from the Upper Kingdom.

***

The bridge was busy, with people everywhere, clustered by the computer banks and holo tables that filled the open expanse of the nerve centre. The Captain and the first officer stood by one of the great bay windows that wrapped around the front of the bridge.

The fuller features of Captain Owen Hendrix, his silver-grey hair and intense brown eyes commanded attention. He had risen to his current position and stayed there, having turned down a promotion which sealed his growth in the military but ultimately put him in charge of the GTSC *Krasev*, which was the greatest posting of his career, such that he and the ship had become legendary.

Executive Officer David Marz was saying something, his hand gesturing his explanation in silent motion from across the bridge.

Feeling uncomfortable in his 'class A' uniform, Douglas Manning walked through the bustle of people, their world was one that held nothing for him, the ordered life on board the destroyer was not his scene, although he had a lot of respect for the crew members, the existence that he understood was the uncertain world of combat. A small unit operated deep within enemy territory where every moment is threatened by death — that was the world he felt at home in.

He was aware of their attention, his presence on the bridge was causing quite a stir. He frequented it only occasionally, when operationally necessary. For most junior officers and lower ranks, it was not very common to see a Wraith, no matter their rank. Mount Olympus still had a lot of influence keeping their shadow soldiers from direct public attention, none the less, their legend had spread throughout the GTSC and civilian worlds.

Whispered comments spread like wildfire between the junior bridge staff, for some of them, this was their first encounter with a Wraith; several pointing out the tapestry of decorations emblazoning his chest, each bright ribbon marking yet another victorious campaign and daring feats of bravery. The one that caught a lot of attention was the small red ribbon with the miniature cross in the centre. That one was the hardest to earn and even harder to wear.

"Lieutenant Commander..." the Captain and XO turned and saluted him, as Manning approached them, saying, "you and your troops will be dropped as soon as we arrive, the rest of the ground forces will be deployed when we descend to the surface. It will be a fight as hard as any we've faced, according to the intel."

"Yes, sir. We'll go into the last simulations as soon as my team has awoken. We will be ready," Manning saluted back. It was awkward for him to receive the salute from his senior officer first, mostly he preferred the informal routine where no one saluted anyone, as part of the accepted nature of the day-to-day, but tradition dictated it. Anyone holding a Victoria Cross surpassed the military rank structure.

"I know you will be, Commander."

The Captain turned to the closest hologram displayed on the table. It held the formation of ships in orbital formation.

"This is the situation that we are launching for..." he gestured with one hand. "Anteiha, can you bring up the coordinates of the city." The image changed to that of the ground scan. "From what we know, there is a fortified base here..." he observed as he motioned with his hand, pointing to a spot on the planet.

"Your job will be to drop and secure a landing zone for our troops to form a base of operations, this will be no easy task as you well know."

Anteiha's glowing form appeared from the corner of the holo table. "Our recon is limited, but what we have been able to pick up is that there is a great concentration of troops here." the image changed to that of the base that the Captain had mentioned. "Your drop zone will be here at the head of this valley, which some clever spark had named 'The Valley of Death'." again the image changed but linked the two together with distance and terrain information. "All the Black Ops teams will be dropped there to have a staging ground. The rest of the troops will be deployed here on this hilltop dubbed Megiddo." the image shifted to a small hill that rose, backed into a cliff that circled two thirds of the elevated ground. "High Command anticipates this will become a staging ground for a Forward Operating Base, with the next wave of troops landing here before pushing to link up with all Wraith teams."

"You sound skeptical." Manning asked the AI hologram.

"I think the High Command will find things aren't as they expect on the planet."

"Thank you, Anteiha." the Captain cut in. "Bring up the schematics for the GTSC *Krasev*," he asked as he began walking the Special Forces Lieutenant Commander through the plan in detail, giving him a greater understanding of the importance of their role, once on the ground.

The Executive Officer, Commander David Marz turned to a young junior officer who was standing close by, a data pad in hand. His face was a whiter shade than normal; it was a common state for most of the crew after the order had been given for the fleet to rendezvous in orbit for the final approach to a major campaign.

Their war had predominantly been skirmishes, the duration of their battles long enough to gain the upper hand. The campaign they were in final preparation before making the jump for, was going to be a monumental battle! They all felt it.

"What is it, Mid?" Commander David Marz gave the Midshipman his opening.

"The coded signal that the Captain was waiting for, has just now come in." The young officer held out the data pad to him.

"Thanks," Marz nodded and took the offering. "I'll give it to him."

The junior officer turned to go, but David Marz stopped him.

"How are you holding up?"

"We're all doing OK," the young officer's voice was a little unsteady.

"No, Mid. How are *you*, doing?"

"I don't know, sir. I know we have a good chance, but all the information coming in indicates that this campaign will be very different to the last one."

"You did well in the last one, J'kar. For your first combat experience, it was a hard one. You're correct that this one will be a much bigger affair, but remember your training, trust the Captain and we will get through this one together too."

"Yes, sir."

"If you need to talk, remember you can always come and get either myself or the Captain."

"Thank you, sir" J'kar returned to his station.

Commander David Marz saw the Captain still engaged in discussion with Manning, leaning on his elbow over the hologram table indicating something just out of reach with the other hand; he approached them.

"Sir!"

The Captain looked up at Commander David Marz.

"The signal you've been waiting for. J'kar just handed it to me."

"Good lad. Thank you, Commander. Take over for me."

Nodding, David Marz swapped places with the Captain who took the data pad with him off to his command station.

"What do you think, Lucky?" Manning used the shortened form of the Commander's nickname.

David Marz looked at Douglas Manning, and said after a weighty pause, "I think it is going to be a bloody affair. The resources the GTN is putting into this campaign indicate that this might be the big showdown that we've all been expecting." his face grave.

Manning blinked once, his strong expression never wavering so as to not betray his professional exterior.

The two of them were friends and had a great respect for each other that was born out of professional understanding and mutual admiration for their respective tradecrafts. They had both seen each other in action and been saved by it on multiple counts. Marz had directly been involved with many of the extractions that lifted Manning's unit out of the war zone, many of them being very hot

Landing Zones and often costly. Marz had also been the attending officer to handle the majority of post mission debriefings of the Special Forces teams and had grown very popular with all the Wraith teams on board the *Krasev*.

Manning looked at the hologram table for a long while in silence. Both seeing the holographic projection from different points of view, their wars being at opposite ends of the scale and likewise their responsibilities requiring a different preparation from each. Marz ran through the remaining details that the Captain hadn't covered before they just stood, allowing things to sink in.

"I'm going to check on my team," Manning said abruptly.

Marz nodded. His job was far from over, and once the Wraith Commander had gone, he would have to go back to planning the future of the ship and all its crew alongside the Captain.

He knew from hard experience that even the best laid plans were futile as the first casualty of war was always 'the plan', but without which was a virtual death sentence for them all. He remembered one officer lecturing him while he was a junior officer remarking about the seven 'Ps' of planning.

How many times had he witnessed that in combat? Even a bad plan was better than no plan at all.

***

Commander David Marz moved across the bridge, that unhelpful knot in his stomach still persisted no matter how much he tried to get rid of it. After all the campaigns he had gone through with Captain Owen Hendrix and everything he had learned from the wise old Captain, he could not get rid of the apprehension he felt each time before they deployed.

Maybe that was a good thing? He didn't know, but it was not a comfortable feeling to live with. How did people like the Lieutenant

Commander survive with it? After all, theirs was a much more dangerous existence on the ground behind enemy lines.

Looking back at the Captain who stood at the plotting table with one of the junior navigation officers, Marz watched as the Captain was teaching the young man something. Commanding under the Captain had been a true honour and privilege and the highlight of his military career so far.

Throughout his training and junior years in the Navy, David Marz had often disagreed with a lot of the strategies and procedures employed by the GTN, but Captain Owen Hendrix had changed all of that for him, teaching him so many new ways of being an officer and a leader, his strategies and plans. For the first time in his career, David Marz had truly learned how to think outside of the box when it came to planning.

"You look thoughtful Commander." Anteiha had arisen from one of the AI stands.

"Just thinking about the operation and the crew."

"He is a good Captain, isn't he?" she asked with that incredible way of reading his thoughts.

He looked at her, her colours changing from the amber glow to a regal blue as she stood with her arms crossed low across her rib cage and ankles crossed. Her favourite pose.

"You will be a great Captain when your time comes. Trust in what he has taught you over the years."

David Marz looked at her. "Thanks. I thought I felt ready for it when I was put forward for promotion, but at times like this, I don't know if I am."

"Remember, David. You're not called 'Lucky Bradshaw' for nothing. Like your namesake said: 'I remember the lion and the bear that you delivered into my hands'. So, too, Commander, you must remember the path that brought you here to this moment."

Marz looked at her, she was right of course. But even the mighty need a reminder every now and then. Nodding, he smiled. Anteiha's colour turning from blue to purple, a sign that she was happy once again. "The crew trust you both to do the right thing, Commander. And if I do and they do, you should too."

***

Down on the cryo deck, Lieutenant Commander Douglass Manning entered the grilled walkway that spanned the length of the cryo chamber. Looking up at the line of pods that held his team three rows up he pondered the coming events of the campaign. His team would once again be in the thick of it from the moment they dropped. They needed to prepare: it was time.

Walking to the control panel at the far end of the chamber, Manning entered the serial codes of all nine members of his unit.

"What are you doing?" an angry voice behind him demanded.

"Waking up my team."

"Under who's authority?" the newcomer's tone hadn't changed.

"The Captain's," Manning finished, turning to face the person in question.

This was a new officer, evidently one of those whom they'd taken on board after their last mission during the brief refit.

Manning's height towered over the officer, his citations and ribbons eye level with the newcomer. He saw the junior officer's eyes widen as he realised just who he was talking to.

"Apologies, sir. But protocol dictates that they shouldn't be woken up for another day."

"Not my team. I need them awake *now*. The Captain needs them to get ready, part of the operational requirement."

"Yes, sir. If you've got the Captain's blessing, go right ahead."

Without even looking, Manning pressed the green button and simultaneously nine cryo chambers beeped with the new command, their systems hissing softly as they pressurised, readying for opening.

As he watched, the doors swung open and the luminous, translucent blue liquid poured out, down through the metal grating.

Patiently he waited as the team woke up from their transit. Anya was the first to emerge, her lithe body swinging out of the chamber, she dropped into a crouching position, her tight clothing revealing the muscular body beneath, her hair sticking to her neck and shoulders. Like him, scars adorned her exposed skin as memorials of previous battles and campaigns.

As she stretched, wringing out her hair, Dan hauled himself out of the chamber further down the line. His frame well sculpted, his short dark hair brushed back. A tattoo ran the length of his left forearm, reaching up the back of his triceps.

Switching from one hand to the other while he hung from the bar above his cryo pod he looked down at the metal grating, one arm dangling by his side before he let go and dropped the few meters to the floor.

One by one, the team emerged until they stood in a ragged line, their various items of clothing still covered in the liquid, sticking to them. Only the two women hadn't stripped anything off to wring out the syrupy goo.

Orion was solid in build, the scarring around his artificial arm webbed his chest from where they had reattached his new limb. He had been lucky, double lucky, as he had taken such a hit when they had made their escape before being transferred back to the cruiser who had the facilities to conduct the extensive surgery upon their return. Otherwise, he'd have been shipped off as a mangled result to be put back together on some home-world, his front-line days well over.

Mirage was lean, his athletic body built for speed and stealth; Meyer and Rayn stood next to each other, both about the same height, they could have been brothers if no one knew their backgrounds. Jasper was at the end. His close-cut hair hadn't grown much over their transit time, hardly surprising with the cryo sleep function.

Cailyn was next, her wet, short, blonde hair turned sandy with the goo. She brushed it back away from her face, tattoos on her neck stood out against her pale olive skin. Jesse was of average height and build, but no less powerful than his other comrades. Manning had seen him carrying a fellow Wraith over his shoulder, while still firing at the enemy position and running over a rocky outcrop towards the evac bird.

"Slept well?"

They all looked at him.

Anya said dryly, "Sure, but room service could be improved."

"You know the drill, clean up. We'll need to brief and start preparing for this next engagement as soon as you're ready. Your armour and equipment should already be in your rooms by now. Get yourselves sorted and I will see you all on the training deck, our usual spot in two hours. This show is going to be big, so we need to make sure we are on top line."

"Yes, sir!" they all chorused.

***

An hour later, Douglas Manning was back in his cabin. His armour was there, waiting for him, just as he had organised for his team, theirs in their respective cabins.

He looked at the armour, the latest upgrades to it had been finished and it looked good. The colour shimmered with mat chameleon like properties. Its outer layer had semi-cloaking abilities; not perfect, but often enough to blend into the background foliage during combat. It made them harder to find and hit, and that was the main objective.

They still had to rely on their own skill for the rest.

The suit hung, suspended in a gravity field until he was ready to put it on, the 'technician', as it was referred to, stood behind. The semi-robotic device both provided the gravity field and assisted the Wraith to adorn the armour when the time came, locking it around their body, coding in the biometrics to the suit and enabling the environmental controls. From then on, it formed a symbiotic harmony, suit and Wraith forming a bond that surpassed the basic requirements of life.

It was going to be heavy, at least until he got used to wearing it again. That process was now a quick one. After that the capabilities of the suit would enhance his own abilities, creating a deadly weapon: himself.

As he reviewed the last details he wanted to cover before suiting up, he noticed the shimmering amber, gold figurine standing, patiently waiting on the pedestal in the corner of the room close to where the armour stood.

"Anteiha, welcome," Manning greeted the ship's Artificial Intelligence. He was one of three onboard the ship that knew the truth about Anteiha and it was a privilege he did not take lightly. *She was no ordinary AI!*

"Good afternoon, Commander," Anteiha nodded her head in greeting, rather formally considering their relationship. She had her hands clasped below her waist and her ankles crossed and she waited with reverent patientce.

"Good afternoon," he offered a rare smile. "What do you have for me?"

"Further intel, I have been scanning for anything that the GTSC has on record about the new system."

"What did you find?"

"Only two documents, both from Mount Olympus."

"You know you're not supposed to go digging in top secret files."

"Then how will I keep my people safe, Commander?"

Manning looked down at the floor, it was a problem he understood well, he had crossed many lines, breaching many security protocols in order to ensure his team had the most information possible, to keep them safe. It was something he had promised himself after one mission — one bloody mission! He had lost over half his team because of incorrect intel from intelligence.

"Do you mind?" he gestured at the suit of armour.

"Not at all, Commander." Anteiha replied as she started briefing the Lieutenant Commander on the information. She watched as he stripped off his uniform down to his combat suit, removing his knives and sidearm as he did. Locating his environmental suit, he pulled it on over the form-fitting primary layer that would help boost his muscular abilities. Once this second layer was on, he went over to the technician, presenting his biometric coder to the reader. Once he heard the three beeps indicating that his information was uploaded, he pulled out the much heavier exo-suit. And pulled on the lower half. It covered everything, built in feet coverings which would in part make up his boots; gloves were on the end of the sleeves, and the neck covering. Only his environmental suit would extend up over his head before he put his helmet on. Then, he positioned himself for the 'technician' to help assemble and secure the armour around him.

***

Once dressed in his armour, Douglass Manning had donned his robes that would cover the armour while he was onboard the GTSC *Krasev*. It was similar in the design to both the musketeer tabard and the samurai kimono. Each one was slightly different, designed to represent the character of the Wraith, with colours to match. Long flowing lengths of a silky material mostly covered the armour like the tabard but was also worn as a kimono-style robe. Often the robes were split into two parts: upper and lower. The lower was secured around the waist and forming the flowing trouser robes, segmented into four. The upper had a tighter piece that covered the back down to the belt, but then also had the loose flowing sleeves like the tabard and kimono style front, however some preferred to have theirs open, their armour showing through.

Without his helmet, each Wraith looked dis-proportional, but he was well aware of the affect that the presence of a fully dressed Wraith, robes and all, had on the crews on the hangar decks.

Pulling his environmental suit head cover up over his head, he adjusted it to cover all but his face and his ears. Picking up his helmet, Douglas Manning turned for the technician, leaning forward for it to complete the next component of preparation before he secured the helmet in place.

Once he was completely suited up, he stretched and flexed, letting the suit settle around him. Turning to the racks that held his weapons, he selected his side arms and placed them in his thigh holsters, adding the combat knife that he always wore and the much bigger knife that clipped into his chest rig.

Heading for the door, he picked up his assault rifle and clipped it to his back. From this moment on until the end of the mission, the only time he would put any of his weapons down was when he was changing to a new one or in hand-to-hand combat.

"Good hunting, Commander!" Anteiha voiced, knowing the commander had heard, but he made no reply, the door sliding shut behind him.

Anteiha's figurine shimmered in the cabin's lights, dimming them down to that of a late dusk. Her glow filling the room until… she vanished!

There was still a significant number of things that she needed to prepare for before the destroyer launched for the rendezvous co-ordinates laid out by the Admiral.

ACKNOWLEDGMENTS

The first person I would like to acknowledge and thank for her endless patience and encouragement to keep writing is my loving, strong mother, Anne Marie Pauw. Her words 'write from the heart, not the head' have helped me throughout my many years of writing. She inspired and challenged me, to write many female characters the way they are.

I would like to thank the team at Ultimate 48 Hour Author for their support, encouragement and opportunity for starting out authors to take this first step.

I would also like to thank my editor for the guidance with developing the story and flexibility with my changes mid-edit.

About the Author

David Pauw has lived in both hemispheres across islands and continents and currently resides in Australia. A pilot and flight instructor, he has combined his passion of aviation, history, science fiction and writing with his vast imagination — what started out as a single idea has grown into a forthcoming series of books. David has drawn inspiration for his characters from people he has crossed paths with throughout his life, be they strong, passionate and determined or otherwise.